NO TEARS

"Preston is dead."

There was a flicker of something in her eyes. "What happened?" she asked; then without missing a beat, added, "Did he choke to death on his ego?"

"They don't know yet. Some kind of poison. Probably slipped into his vitamins."

For several seconds there was dead silence. Then she started to giggle. The giggles escalated into laughter . . .

Diamond books by D.C. Brod

ERROR IN JUDGMENT
MURDER IN STORE

MURDER IN STORE

D.C. BROD

DIAMOND BOOKS, NEW YORK

All the characters and events portrayed in this story are fictitious.

MURDER IN STORE

A Diamond Book / published by arrangement with
Walker and Company

PRINTING HISTORY
Walker Publishing Company, Inc. edition published 1989
Published simultaneously in Canada by Thomas Allen & Son
Canada, Limited, Markham, Ontario.
Diamond edition / December 1991

ISBN: 1-55773-630-8

Diamond Books are published by The Berkley Publishing Group,
200 Madison Avenue, New York, New York 10016.
The name "DIAMOND" and its logo
are trademarks belonging to Charter Communications, Inc.

PRINTED IN THE UNITED STATES OF AMERICA

10 9 8 7 6 5 4 3 2 1

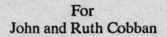

For
John and Ruth Cobban

MURDER IN STORE

1

THE WOMAN SEATED across the desk from me was the image of grace under pressure. From her style of dress to the way she held her head, she registered icy elegance and poise. The fur coat tossed over the back of her chair could have come from the salon in the upscale store her husband owned. She wore a cream-colored dress that looked like cashmere and a blue silk scarf draped around her neck, secured at her right shoulder with a silver brooch. Her hair was so blond it was almost white, and she wore it full and swept back from her face. You really had to be sure of your looks to pull that off. She was, and she did. She sat there, hands neatly folded over an alligator clutch, looking like a monarch reviewing her court, instead of a shoplifter staring down the head of security.

She crossed one slender leg over the other and glanced at the nameplate on my desk. Then she smiled a little and broke the silence. "What does the *C* stand for?"

Thanks to this woman, I was doing a mental calculation of what my unemployment check would be, and she was playing games.

I didn't respond. Still smiling, she said, "What happens now?"

The evidence lay on my desk. A conscientious floor detective had stopped the lady as she tried to leave Hauser's with a pair of fifteen-dollar panties stuffed in the pocket of her silver-fox coat. I looked at the white silk Christian Diors and felt vaguely embarrassed, wishing she had lifted

1

a necklace or a scarf. I also felt more than a little irritated. I had better things to do than waste my time with a wealthy neurotic who might wind up costing me my job. The detective who picked her up was new and hadn't recognized the infamous Mrs. Hauser.

She had introduced herself and he responded by saying, "Right. And I'm Dirty Harry." It started to get ugly then and they were drawing a crowd when another store detective sized up the situation and hustled her up to my office.

I made a mental note to brief new employees on this woman whose idea of great sport was lifting items out of her husband's store.

I lit a cigarette and pushed the pack across my desk, offering her one.

She hesitated, then shook her head. "Well?" she said, a bit impatient.

I felt like a chess player with his king exposed while she waited for me to play it safe and protect him by castling. I'm so predictable. I moved my king back and played my strongest piece.

"We called your husband. He's coming to get you," I said. "I guess that'll be it." I figured that would be it for me too, but I kept that observation to myself.

Watching her silently calculate, feeling for solid ground, I realized that part of the irritation I was feeling centered on the realization that my first encounter with Preston Hauser would be over this embarrassing situation. And history can attest that powerful men don't handle embarrassment well. They have been known to react by hacking off the head of the closest dispensable person.

In fact, it was beginning to look as though the only one who wouldn't be embarrassed over this incident was Diana Hauser. For a woman who had to be less than twenty-five, she had an uncommon amount of poise and composure. I wondered if her thoughts were as cool and collected as her demeanor. She began to drum her sculptured nails on her alligator purse. Probably not.

"I wish you hadn't called him," she said, turning to look at the gray sky outside the window. I would have given a lot to know what was going on inside her head at that moment, but before I had much time to speculate, she turned back to me, composure regained. "May I call you Quintus?"

"Quint," I said, adding, "It's hard to keep something like this from the guy who owns the place."

She hesitated, mouth poised in a retort, then said, "Quint, can't I just pay for them?" She gestured toward the panties.

I shook my head. "It's not that simple," I said, stubbing out the half-finished cigarette.

"I'm not a common shoplifter, you know."

I had to agree with that. "Does that make you an uncommon shoplifter then? Of the species kleptomaniac?"

"You don't know what it's like. If you did you wouldn't be making jokes." She paused and then continued, "We all have our dark tendencies. Most people are pretty adept at hiding them. I guess I'm not." It was as if she were speaking to herself or at least to no one in particular.

I nodded, leaning forward in my chair, about to ask her to tell me what it *was* like when she said, "I'll take that cigarette now."

I lit it for her. "You know there are people you can talk to about your problem, Mrs. Hauser," I prodded.

"Diana," she instructed me. "I've got the best analyst money can buy. She thinks I'm crying out for attention." A small laugh. "Can you believe that?" She sighed and looked out the window.

We both heard Preston Hauser's booming voice outside the door, ordering someone to have his car brought around. Diana immediately dropped her cigarette in the ashtray on my desk.

When Hauser entered a room you felt as much as you

3

saw him. He was several inches taller than my six feet and much more massive. The rumors I had heard about his glory days as a college gridiron star were probably true. I knew the man was close to sixty, but he looked ten or fifteen years younger. His gray hair was thinning only slightly, and if he suffered from middle-aged spread, he did a good job of hiding it.

"Let's go home," he said, taking her arm.

As he turned to lead her toward the door, he saw the glowing cigarette in the ashtray. He looked at Diana, but before she could speak, I picked up the butt and inhaled on it deeply, wondering if Hauser had noticed the faint blush of lipstick on the filter.

Hauser studied the woman at his side. Her expression remained unchanged. Then, for the first time since entering the room, he acknowledged my presence. "Thank you, ah, McCauley, I appreciate your discretion," and led his wife from the room, gripping her arm like he was showing her the way to her cell. She didn't look back.

I forced myself to relax. The ax hadn't fallen yet, but that shouldn't have surprised me, given the hierarchy in an organization such as this one. People like Preston Hauser pay other people the big bucks to bother with employee matters, especially the unpleasant ones. His words of appreciation didn't mean much. News of Diana Hauser's afternoon crime spree was, no doubt, already the leading coffee-break topic. My discretion or lack of it wouldn't make any difference.

I was speculating on how the story might be embellished by closing time when Frank Griffin marched purposefully into my office. Frank did everything purposefully. I think he believed that if you act with enough assurance and with the right amount of bravado, it doesn't matter whether or not you know what you're doing. People will think that you do. Actually, with Frank, I suspected that about eighty

4

percent of the time he did know what he was doing. That estimate combined with his no-holds-barred approach made him pretty formidable. And he needed to be. Griffin was store manager and, more than Preston Hauser, he ran the place.

Griffin shook his head slowly and sat down across from me. "Well, Quint, what are we going to do here? Issue a picture of Diana Hauser to new floor detectives with instructions not to apprehend her even if she saunters out the door sporting a diamond tiara?"

"I'm hoping that Mr. Hauser can appeal to her sense of fair play. Where's the challenge in shoplifting in your own store?"

Griffin allowed himself a brief smile. "Can you keep this thing quiet, Quint?"

"I trust my people, but there were others who saw her being escorted to security." I shrugged. "I can't account for them."

"I know," he said. "Do what you can, though." He stood. "I don't want to read this in the newspaper tomorrow. Art has a statement prepared," he said, referring to Hauser's publicity man. "If asked, we're calling this an unfortunate misunderstanding on the part of the detective."

I nodded. "Those silk underwear have a way of sliding off their displays and into the pockets of fur coats. Like metal to magnets."

Griffin ignored me. "I don't want word of this getting out, and if there is a slip, I want to know where it came from." He gave me what I would classify as a meaningful look and added, "With any luck, nobody will lose his job over this."

He got up and before he turned to leave said, "I think Preston's father was negligent in teaching his son one of the fundamental concepts of life." He shook his head. "Flashy, crazy women. You're supposed to fool around with them. You're not supposed to marry them."

Diana Hauser certainly was flashy and was probably a little bit crazy, but she was also something of an intriguing puzzle. So even though I was worried about the job, I had trouble pushing her from my mind. Did she think these thefts of hers through or did she act impulsively? It was hard to tell whether Hauser was more irritated with me or with his wife. What kind of relationship did I catch a glimpse of this afternoon? And what kind of work could a washed-up security man find?

I'd been head of security at Hauser's for almost a year now, and although it wasn't the most exciting, glamorous job in the world, it was all right. I'd begun to realize that hopping from job to job, never letting myself get settled didn't mean I could put off getting older. You wind up just as old, but with nothing to show for it. I don't remember telling anyone as a kid that when I grew up I wanted to make the world safe for gourmet pepper mills and Calvin Klein underwear, but the job at Hauser's wasn't bad. I had my share of life in the fast lane when I was on the police force. I sort of welcomed the slower pace and the occasional monotony at the store. I'd prefer to stick around awhile.

Consequently, it wasn't until I was driving to the apartment on Chicago's near north side that I managed to push Hauser thoughts from my mind. And it was the going home that did it.

I liked going home. Since I had moved in with Maggie six months ago, life was better. A lot better. I'd finally realized that being alone was a high price to pay for total freedom, which only meant that if you choked to death eating a burrito on Friday night, your passing wouldn't be noticed until Monday morning. Maggie had changed that for me. Life was better and easier and I had gladly traded freedom for commitment.

"Dammit." I banged the steering wheel with a clenched fist. Parking spaces on the near north side were almost as hard to come by as World Series tickets, and the space that was invariably empty because it only *looked* like reserved parking was occupied by a red sports car. I cursed again and drove around for fifteen minutes before finding a space and then had to walk four blocks to the apartment.

Maggie was pouring two glasses of wine when I walked into the kitchen through the rear entrance. She had read my mind. "Just what I needed," I said, reaching for one of them. She pulled the glass back from my reach. "Sorry. Not for you." She looked into the dining room. I followed her gaze. The table was piled high with textbooks, law journals, and law reviews. A young man, polished and scrubbed, was feigning immersion in one of the tomes.

"Third year?" I asked.

Maggie nodded. "He was brilliant in moot court today."

"Can't ask for more than that."

"We've got to talk, McCauley."

I felt a vague apprehension at her use of my last name.

"Bedroom?" I asked, indicating our usual conference room.

"Yeah, I'll be there in a second," Maggie said and went off to give one of the wineglasses to the young Perry Mason.

Once in the bedroom I couldn't help but notice the suitcase in the middle of the bed. It was mine, and it contained my clothes and my camera. Maggie stood in the doorway, waiting for my response. She looked, as always, relaxed and comfortable. She fit into any situation with little effort. Whether competing with fellow law students for the best grades or making love, Maggie was at home. If you were lucky, she pulled a little bit of you into that universe, and you felt like you belonged even if you never had before. She walked over and placed a hand on either side of my face. I felt like someone had just knocked the wind out of me and I prayed to whomever might be listening that this was the point where she giggled and said she was only teasing. But it wasn't.

She locked her eyes onto mine and said, "We knew this wasn't a permanent thing. Neither of us wanted that."

She was so bright and beautiful and alive that I couldn't imagine not wanting her, or her thinking I didn't. "Speak for yourself." I shook my head and pulled away. Too late to pour my heart out now. "Forget I said that. Yeah, I guess it was coming to this." Is this, I wondered, the same instinct that makes people want to die with dignity? "Let me just make sure I've got everything, and then I'll be out of here."

"Sure," Maggie said. She closed the door as she left the room.

I sat on the bed, sinking into the thick, down comforter. I knew Maggie well enough to understand there was no discussing this. When she made up her mind about something, she was immovable. I had to admit things weren't quite as good lately as they had been at first. You settle in a little and maybe some of the mystery and newness wears off, but what's left is good too. At least I thought it was.

I looked at myself in the full-length mirror on the door. I was in pretty good shape for a man pushing middle age. Maybe there was a little more gray in the brown. And maybe my laugh lines were starting to look like squint lines. And the mustache—maybe its time had come and gone. Hell. I'd had it for twenty years. Then again, maybe I just wasn't enough for an attractive, intelligent woman of twenty-three who had handsome pre-lawyer types bounding after her like the puppies they were. Maybe she liked puppies. What did I know?

Maggie's cat, Brandeis, watched me from the windowsill, eyes half-closed, wearing an expression that could only be described as smug.

"You won, asshole," I said, taking little comfort in the

knowledge that the object of his disdain—the competition—would not be removed, only replaced.

I paused in the dining room doorway on my way out. Maggie and her friend looked up. "Maybe I'll see you around," I said to Maggie. I turned to leave, then looked back at the young man. "Do you own that red Mazda parked next to the dumpster?"

The kid nodded.

"I thought so."

Maggie walked me to the door. "Where will you go?"

I shrugged. "Oh, I don't know. Someplace where the sky is blue, the air is clean, and the streets are lined with empty parking spaces."

"You'll take care of yourself, won't you?"

I wanted to tell her that I hoped she approached her cases with more commitment than her relationships, but I left without answering.

I stopped at a liquor store, then checked into a room at the Lincoln Inn. It took more than half the bottle of Teacher's before I felt a warm, comforting numbness setting in. I lay on the bed, the water glass of scotch resting on my chest, and caught blurred snatches of an old Gregory Peck movie. I remember thinking that if I had his voice I'd be holding Maggie right now.

2

I HURT. MY tongue felt like cotton and my mouth tasted like the pack and a half of cigarettes snuffed out and overflowing in the ashtray. My head ached and blood pounded in my ears. I popped six aspirin in my mouth and washed them down under a cold shower.

As I forced myself to stand under the water for several minutes, I considered the curative powers of a good bottle of scotch. It didn't exactly purge the melancholy, but it gave me another kind of suffering I could dwell on. I could deal with a hangover, but I wasn't sure how to handle losing Maggie.

Facing myself in the mirror wasn't easy either. The bloodshot eyes didn't make me look any younger. Gray had been creeping into my hair for some time, and now I noticed that my mustache was starting to turn on me as well. I couldn't do anything with the hair on my head, but I could show the mustache that I wasn't going to stand for it. Before I could change my mind, I slapped on some shaving cream and got rid of the thing.

I was immediately sorry. Not only did my face look funny now, but that mustache had been with me a hell of a lot longer than Maggie. Shaving off a twenty-year companion deserves more thought than you give to clipping your nails. My melancholy and sense of loss merged with irritation when I realized that Maggie hadn't packed my ties and I was reduced to wearing the brown striped one I'd worn the day before with a blue tattersall shirt. Now I looked like I felt.

Nonetheless, on the way to work, I stopped for breakfast at a fast-food place and, by the time I walked out of the cold, crisp January morning and into Hauser's I felt almost human. Early morning at the store was always a good time of the day for me, like standing on the stage in a theater, before the curtain goes up. The crew rushes to get the furniture and props in place as the cast comes on stage, adjusting a costume or giving a final bit of polish to that troublesome line, and I was in on the magic that makes it all work.

Jefferson Potts, the senior security guard, held the door for me. That was his function prior to store opening: he made sure that no customers happened to stroll in with the employees. He wore the Hauser green uniform as if it ranked him a rear admiral, politely joked with the clerks, and didn't miss a thing.

"Rough night last night, Mr. McCauley?" He winked. "Looks like you slipped shavin' too."

I shook my head and said, "Self-inflicted pain is the worst kind."

"Yea, well just think how good you'll feel tomorrow."

"If I survive."

When you first walk into Hauser's, your senses are attacked from all angles, struck by the apparent enormity of the place—apparent because what you see is partly illusion. The main floor is one huge room with dark, polished hardwood floors, massive pillars, and glass display cases grouped to give an uncluttered appearance. If you stand in the middle of this room and look up, you can see straight to the ceiling five stories above. Each floor is a balcony surrounding and overlooking the main floor, enclosed in dark wood banisters and railings. A combination of the old and new pulls it all together.

The store was built in 1883 to the specifications of Fritz Hauser, Preston's grandfather. And about all that had changed since then was the merchandise and the plumbing. The smell of polish and hardwood still mingled with the scents of women's perfumes.

The clerks were carefully screened and selected—no gum snapping, bored-to-tears high school students languishing behind the counters here. One needed experience, poise, and a whole lot of tact to get and keep a sales job at Hauser's.

After slapping on a little of the men's after-shave from a display, I headed for the elevators and my office on the third floor. Halfway there I changed my mind and turned toward the accessories section. Pam Richards was folding cashmere scarves and arranging them in an antique glass display case. She didn't see me approach and I nearly took that opportunity to retreat. We hadn't talked very much in the last few months, but we shared some nice memories and I didn't think there were any hard feelings. Pam wasn't the kind of woman to keep herself out of circulation for long. For all I knew, she was involved with someone now. One thing I did know was that I needed the company of another human being or this evening was going to be a repeat of the previous one. One night of a bottomless glass of scotch could be cathartic. More than that began to qualify you for a lost weekend.

"Hi," I said, approaching the counter. "Preparing for the big after-Christmas giveaways?"

If I surprised her, she didn't let on. She looked at me as though I had disturbed her reverie, then caught herself and laughed. "Yeah, some deal. Sixty dollars marked down from eighty-five."

"I'll take two," I countered. When she didn't respond I said, "How've you been?"

I noticed she wasn't wearing her glasses anymore. She must have won the battle with her contact lenses. And there was something different about her hair. It was the same style she always wore, but seemed softer, fuller. The vivid blues and greens in her dress did nice things for the color of her eyes.

"I've been okay." She shrugged. "I hear you've been keeping busy." She continued to move the scarves around as if there were only one perfect arrangement and she hadn't quite found it yet.

"Yeah, well, you know how those things go."

"Yes. I do." Chilly?

"How about lunch?"

After a long pause she shook her head, then asked, "Where are you living?"

"At the Lincoln. Nothing but the best."

"It beats a cardboard box on lower Wacker."

I nodded and turned to leave. This had been a bad idea. "Maybe some other time."

"Quint. When did you move to the Lincoln?"

"Last night."

She nodded her understanding. "Ask me again in a couple weeks. Maybe then."

"Sure," I said.

I understood her reluctance and had, in fact, practiced my own style of self-preservation on occasion. Still, I sure wasn't looking forward to another night with my silent partner.

I met Fred Morison, one of my floor detectives, in the elevator. I've never been much of a stickler as far as a dress code for the floor detectives goes. I just tell them to dress so they blend in with the crowd at Hauser's. I'm pretty lenient because I also understand that a floor detective at Hauser's doesn't have that much money to spend on clothes. Seeing Morison made me wonder if maybe it was time either to issue a memo or give everyone a raise.

Left to his own devices Morison would undoubtedly wear something along the line of a green polyester suit and a canary yellow shirt. As it was, his suit was rumpled and overdue for a trip to the cleaners, and his belly strained at the buttons on his shirt. Whenever it occurred to him he would hoist his vanishing waistband up over his stomach, suck it all in, then thrust his hands in his pants pockets so that within a minute he was back to where he started. He had a nervous way of addressing people, avoiding eye contact, that used to make me wonder if I'd forgotten to put my pants on or my tie had a gaping hole in it. Morison had been at the store for seven years—a lot longer than I—and I had sensed some resentment ever since our first introduction. When I was introduced to Morison, the first thing he said to me was, "So, you're the guy they gave my job to. Well, at least you're not a woman."

This morning he glanced past me and said, "I hear you nabbed the Silver Fox last night."

There was something I didn't like about his attitude. "Is that the title you've given her?"

"Oh no, not me," Morison was quick to point out. "That's what's going around though. Hard to figure. Woman with looks like that and money coming out the kazoo. She must get hot walking around with silk pants in her pockets."

The elevator doors opened at that moment and I was able to ignore his remark. Morison was either incredibly ignorant or a troublemaker. Either way I didn't trust him.

I was a few minutes later than usual getting to my office. There were already several phone messages waiting for me when I sat down with my mug of coffee. The first was from Millicent Wagner, the woman who was coordinating the gem show at Hauser's. She'd be out the rest of the morning and would call me in the afternoon. Another was from a security-system company, probably selling the foolproof, burglar-proof alarm.

And the third message. Ah yes, I thought. This one I half expected. I studied the two words. "Call Maggie." I knew what she wanted and it wasn't to have my suits returned to

14

my foot-and-a-half of her tiny closet. Maggie hated to hurt things, but not enough to change her abrupt and straightforward manner. She probably realized that she had played fast and loose with my feelings.

I recalled one Saturday afternoon a month or so ago when Maggie and I stopped at O'Banyon's Pub with a small group of friends for a few beers and some salted peanuts in the shell. Maggie and a third-year student got into a heated debate over some legal point, and she verbally ground her opponent to mincemeat. Maggie was unflinching and irrepressible in her arguments. The other woman was totally outclassed. Later, Maggie felt so lousy about the trouncing that she couldn't sleep. Finally she called the woman at three A.M., apologizing and extracting forgiveness from her.

Maggie's friends are used to this and put up with it the same way you put up with the eccentricities of a favorite aunt. It's almost part of her charm. I was used to her ways too, but I wasn't ready to absolve her, not while still nursing a hangover. I tossed the message, crumpled, into the wastebasket.

I leaned back in my chair, propped my feet on the desk, and allowed myself a moment to bask in a glow of well-being. This must be how a junkie feels when he tosses the needle down the sewer grid. Then the sound of the telephone dragged me back to reality. Hauser's had one of those new phone systems—they don't ring, they warble. I answered it.

"Mr. McCauley, this is Irna Meyers. Mr. Hauser would like to meet with you today to discuss the security plans for the gem show. Is ten o'clock convenient?"

I pictured Hauser; I pictured Diana; I hesitated for a moment, digesting the message. I said, "Ah, let's see," and hoped she would interpret the hesitation as the sound of a man trying to squeeze the boss into his already crowded

15

schedule. "Ten o'clock? Yes, that will be all right."

"Would another time be more convenient?" She worded it as a question, but the tone of her voice said there was only one answer.

"No. No. Ten o'clock is fine. I'll be there." I hung up the phone and loosened my tie.

Well, I allowed myself, she did catch me off guard. Panic was not an abnormal reaction, given the situation. Preston Hauser had never consulted with me about security plans or for any other reason. Hauser made little pretense about the fact that he was a figurehead for his store, preferring to let Griffin run the operation. Hauser was there for ribbon-cutting ceremonies and to lend his famous and respected name to various foundations and benefits. He made perfunctory appearances and staffed a secretary, but that was the extent of his involvement in the store his grandfather and father had established. Prior to the incident involving Diana Hauser, I had not received more than a nod of recognition from the man. And now he wanted to consult with me on security. "Fat chance," I said.

Hauser's secretary stood guard over the door to his office like a dragon protects its cave filled with bones and treasure. Irna Meyers motioned me into a chair and finished typing a letter. Then she walked over to Hauser's office door. "Wait here," she said to me before entering.

Irna Meyers was the sort of secretary a jealous wife might choose for her husband. Mid sixties, tall, stout, and buxom, she could have passed as one of Wagner's Valkyries. Or maybe Mrs. Nagel, my sixth-grade principal.

Irna reappeared. "Mr. Hauser will see you now." She held the door open for me and watched my progress from the chair into her boss's office as if I might stray or toss a grenade in. I was relieved when she closed the door behind me, leaving me alone with Hauser.

He stood up as I entered the room and extended his

16

hand. I was, once again, struck by his appearance. This man would not slip out of character. His ramrod posture accentuated his massive build.

"Thank you for finding the time for this meeting." His tone was so sincere that I almost believed he meant it. As he sat down he motioned me to take the chair across from him.

He looked at me closely, as if trying to figure out what was different. "Don't you usually wear glasses?"

"No," I said. "I shaved off my mustache."

"Ah," he said, nodding.

I glanced around Hauser's spacious office. The walls were paneled in dark wood, and his desk was a massive piece of oak, undoubtedly an antique. The smell of old leather and furniture polish permeated the room. I wondered if the office had changed much at all in the three generations of Hausers. Oil paintings of Hauser's father and grandfather hung on the walls to the right and left. I noted that the family resemblance had been diluted through the generations, although each man had that same commanding presence. Behind Hauser's desk was an exceptional view of Michigan Avenue.

There were three framed photographs in front of him. Two were angled so I couldn't see the subjects, but the one on the far right was in my view and was very definitely Diana Hauser. It was taken by the lake and she had a windblown, relaxed look that might or might not have been posed. She seemed more casual and approachable in the tweed jacket than she had in cashmere and fur.

"Isn't she something?"

He said that like he was proud of his creation, which struck me as an attitude that even a man as powerful as Hauser shouldn't have. Then I realized that he wasn't looking at the same picture I was. He apparently assumed I had a partial view of the center picture and now he turned it to face me.

He was right. She *was* something. As far as horses went, that is.

"Do you know Arabians?" Hauser asked.

"Only what I picked up from the Black Stallion books."

He smiled like we now shared something important. Then he turned back to the picture. "I don't think God ever created a more perfect creature." Then he sighed and added, with a touch of irritation in his voice, "Diana hates her."

I decided that Hauser had some serious problems with his priorities but figured it was probably useless to argue with a man who places a horse's picture between one of his wife and whatever the other one might be—probably his mother.

Hauser dragged his attention from the animal and cleared his throat before speaking again. "Thank you for handling that matter with Mrs. Hauser."

"You're welcome."

"She has always been rather unpredictable." He sighed and nodded to himself. "But I suppose that is what you have to expect when you take a high-spirited young woman like that for your . . ." His voice trailed off.

It seemed to me that Hauser was describing a high-strung horse he had just added to his stable rather than his wife. I wondered if he always discussed his marital situation so casually, but decided I didn't want to get into it further. "You wanted to talk about the security plans for the gem show?"

Hauser stared at the leather-framed blotter on his desk for a moment before looking up at me. "Actually, no," he said.

I waited.

3

He placed his clasped hands on the blotter and leaned forward like the president does when he addresses the nation from his oval office. "I want to hire you to do some investigating for me. Personally."

He opened his mouth to speak, but a tinny beeping sound interrupted him. He pressed a button on a watch that resembled the instrument panel of a DC-10 and cut off the noise. "Excuse me. This is one of my oldest rituals." He smiled to himself. "There aren't many things you can count on anymore are there?"

From a desk drawer he produced five bottles filled with various kinds of pills. He removed a capsule from each bottle, set them in front of him on the blotter, and poured a glass of ice water from a pitcher on his desk. He took each pill, one at a time, knocking it back like a shot of scotch chased with precisely two swallows of water.

Almost as an afterthought, he offered me one. "Vitamin?" I shook my head and waved it off. The last vitamin I had taken I had to chew.

"I've been swearing by these little devils since my football days." He turned the picture that had been out of my line of vision. It was of Hauser, circa 1950, in full football regalia, poised on the verge of hurling the football, no doubt, into the end zone and the waiting arms of the receiver. The pose was both corny and impressive.

He replaced the photo. When he spoke again his manner and tone were, once again, formal and precise, almost as if he'd rehearsed. "As I was saying, I would like to hire you, but I also want you to understand that although you work for me at Hauser's, you are in no way obligated to take this assignment."

I hoped he wasn't about to ask me to follow Diana around to see if she was stepping out of line. I didn't think I had the stamina for that, and there was no way I bought the line about not being obligated.

Hauser continued. "I will explain generally what it is I want you to do, tell you what I will pay you to do this for me, and then, if you are interested, I will apprise you of the details. If you decide you would rather not, that will be it. I will not mention it again, and you, in turn, will forget what I have told you. You have already demonstrated that you are a man who can be trusted so I have no qualms about taking you into my confidence."

My common sense told me to thank the man, tell him I was flattered by his show of faith, and then get the hell out of there before I had to worry about talking in my sleep. But my curiosity made me say, "I'm listening."

"Let me explain everything before you ask any questions."

Hauser had an eloquence that matched his presence. His voice was deep and resonant and what he had to say was even more commanding than the way he said it. It was easier to listen than to interrupt or let your mind wander.

"For the past two months, I have been receiving subtle death threats. I say subtle because the threat is implied rather than overt. I do not want to involve the police at this point because, as I said, these threats are not blatant. I do not want to be perceived as a paranoid millionaire. And second, it is possible that these threats come from someone within this company. I will pay you ten thousand dollars to do the best job you can. I will give you that money when you accept the case.

"If, after conducting as thorough an investigation as you are capable of, you are unable to produce the person threatening me, you will be absolved of any responsibility in the matter. The money is still yours. What I do from there on is my business. I know you have some experience in police work, so I'm certain you aren't a total neophyte at this sort of thing. I believe you will give me my money's worth." Hauser nodded at me, indicating that I could respond now.

His stating that I wasn't a *total* neophyte seemed to indicate that the difference was only a matter of degree. But then, he was willing to invest ten grand in me. I wasn't sure, but I thought I had been insulted and flattered in the same speech. I didn't know whether to feel angry or elated. I settled for leery.

"Why not hire someone who does this sort of thing for a living? Discretion is included in the price of service."

"Two reasons. First of all, I did hire a private investigator initially. A fellow named Ray Keller. He did some work for me, the results of which I will show you if you accept the job. Unfortunately, he was killed by a hit-and-run driver two weeks ago." He frowned to himself and quickly added, "I'm certain his demise had nothing to do with the investigation. He was quite a drinker and, as I understand, was stumbling out of a bar at two A.M. when he was hit. Unfortunate, of course, but purely coincidental."

I'm not a great believer in coincidences, but I didn't argue.

"The other reason is that, as I said, it is possible that these threats come from within this company. An outside investigation would only create suspicion, and I believe the entire matter would best be handled by someone who knows the company and the people who work here." He paused a beat. "Are you interested?"

No. For a lot of reasons. The money would be nice, but I don't really need it. And even though I was a cop for a few years, I don't have much experience in this kind of investigative work. Hauser must know that. And what's more, investigating fellow employees can be awkward and uncomfortable.

I looked at Hauser. Despite his reassurances, refusing to accept a job offered by the owner of the company was tantamount to professional suicide. Not that I really cared anymore. Since yesterday, my vision of the future had undergone drastic changes. The image of Maggie beaming proudly as I accepted my gold watch at a retirement party thrown by Hauser's had been replaced with the image of an old and wizened Quint McCauley sitting in an old wizened rocking chair outside a little cottage somewhere in northern England, alone except for a Lassie-style dog and maybe a few sheep.

But this whole situation was intriguing. Yesterday I was sure the guy was going to fire me. Today he was handing me ten grand and taking me into his confidence. Not only that, he had aroused my curiosity. Death threats to *the* Preston Hauser, but that wasn't the reason I took the job on. What swayed me the most was all those Maggie-less hours I was going to have to fill.

I swallowed my common sense and said, "Yes, I am interested."

Hauser regarded me for a moment, then took a large brown envelope out of his middle desk drawer. From that he produced two smaller envelopes and handed one of them to me.

It was a plain white envelope addressed to Preston Hauser, in care of the store. The address was typed and, judging from the uneven shade of the letters, probably on a manual. The envelope was postmarked Chicago. Inside was a newspaper clipping folded once—a photo of Preston Hauser congratulating a recipient of a foundation grant. The attractive young woman was all smiles and so was Preston. It would have been one of those typical grin-and-grip poses but for one difference. Someone had severed Hauser's head with a knife or a pair of scissors and spattered the picture with blood. At least I assumed that the dried brown substance was blood. I looked up at Hauser, who was watching me for a reaction.

"When was this picture taken?" I asked.

"About two months ago. That photo appeared in the *Chicago Tribune*. I received that particular rendition approximately seven weeks ago." He handed me a second envelope. This one was larger, the kind an eight-by-ten photo could be mailed in. The address was the same and the lettering could have been from the same typewriter. "This one came four weeks ago."

As I pulled the picture out, Hauser explained, "The photo came shredded in that envelope. It had to be assembled like a jigsaw puzzle to get the full effect." Hauser had taped the pieces together on a piece of gray cardboard. The photo was a head-and-shoulders publicity shot of him and was probably the standard one his PR staff used to fill requests. And, except for the paraphrased nursery rhyme typed across his forehead, it was a good likeness.

I read his brow out loud. " 'All the king's horses and all the king's men couldn't put Preston together again.' Well, at least we know this person's literary leanings."

Hauser looked annoyed. "I shouldn't have wasted my time putting the damned thing together. Anyone who resorts to childish puzzles and Little Bo Peep threats probably isn't capable of committing a crime any more serious than jaywalking."

I almost smiled at the image of Hauser assembling this picture, searching for pieces that fit, matching and rematching. Somehow he didn't impress me as the sort of person who liked puzzles. I suspected he had a low frustration level.

"This one came last week," he said, pulling another photo out of the large envelope. This was a blowup of Hauser and apparently a candid one. He was climbing into the backseat of a stretch limo and had turned to acknowledge someone or something behind him. The photographer had captured Hauser, mouth open in reply, wearing a slightly startled expression. And then, as if to justify that expression, the cross hairs of a rifle sight were superimposed on his forehead.

"Unless I'm mistaken, that was taken a week and a half ago, after a meeting at the foundation," he said and added, almost as an afterthought, "I was not aware that I was being photographed."

I looked at the three pictures he had shown me. "Are there any others?"

"No. That's it. You can see what I mean by subtle. Frankly, I think this person is more interested in scaring me than killing me. Nevertheless, I don't like being threatened. I won't stand for it."

"Does anyone else know about these letters?"

"Irna. She often opens my mail for me."

Maybe that explained her dragon lady routine in the outer office.

"Anyone else?"

"My sister, Grace Hunnicutt. Actually, it was her idea to hire you. She'd been after me for some time to hire someone who knows the store and its people." He shrugged. "After yesterday's incident, with Diana, your name came up." He paused and grinned sheepishly. "Elder sisters have a real knack for bending your will."

I smiled and nodded in agreement. "I know what you mean. I've got one of them too. Suppose I do find out who is doing this. Will you turn him or her over to the police?"

"That depends entirely upon who it is. I won't lie. There are some people I would rather see in police custody than others."

"What about Keller? What was involved in his investigation?"

Hauser pulled a stack of manila folders from a drawer and placed them on the edge of the desk in front of me. "He was investigating a number of people in this organization who I thought might benefit from removing me from the picture. I looked over his files and nothing seems to indicate it was one of them. Maybe you'll see something I didn't."

I took the files. "This is fine," I said, "but I need to know what it was about each of these people that puts them on your list of people out to get you."

He glanced at his instrument panel. "I'm afraid I have to be somewhere in a few minutes. Look those files over, do whatever it is you do to analyze the photos, and we'll talk later."

Before I could respond, he pulled a bulky envelope with the Hauser logo on it from a drawer and handed it to me. The flap was folded in but not sealed so I was able to glance at the contents without making a show of ripping the envelope open. There was a crisp hundred-dollar bill on top of a large stack. I fanned a few of them, all hundreds. I didn't bother to count them. "You were pretty sure of yourself, weren't you."

He shrugged in a manner that was neither overly confident nor nonchalant. Instead, the gesture had a quality that was almost ingratiating. "I read people rather well."

If life was an open book to him, I wondered why he was hiring me to translate. I pocketed the envelope. "If you do, then you should know I have a thing about taking money. I won't unless I earn it, and like I said, I need some questions answered." When he didn't respond I added, "Am I conducting this investigation or am I just your ten-thousand-dollar legman hired to pacify your sister?"

Hauser studied me for a long moment, then consulted his appointment book. "I'll have Irna pencil you in at ten o'clock tomorrow morning. I'll tell you what I can then."

He looked relieved when the telephone interrupted.

I stood to leave. "You have a pretty good idea who did this, don't you?" I said, fishing.

He lifted the receiver to his ear and held it there without speaking as I turned to leave the room.

I had a nibble.

4

When I got back to my office, I found the day's mail stacked in a neat pile in the middle of my desk. As I shuffled through the ads and correspondence, it occurred to me that the worst thing I could find here would be a bill, maybe an overdue one, or some really offensive junk mail. But Preston Hauser didn't know if the next envelope he opened would be another sick threat or maybe the real thing. I made a mental note to make sure the mail room knew how to identify a letter bomb.

That was what didn't fit. Hauser didn't seem worried enough for a man who had received three letters from someone who apparently was not playing with a full deck. Regardless of whether or not the person who wrote the letters intended to kill Hauser, he or she certainly wasn't trying to improve his mental health. I think I would have discreetly called in the police after seeing the wit and wisdom of Mother Goose tapped out on my forehead. But Hauser wasn't sure he wanted the letter-writer exposed. To me, that's the sign of a man who is afraid to look under the rock. I guess that's where a man of discretion is useful.

I began flipping through the files Hauser had selected as possibilities. There were seven folders. I noticed that Fred Morison was not among them. I guess I wasn't surprised. Morison was a lowlife, but I'd be flattering him to think he would be devious enough or creative enough to concoct those letters.

I opened the top folder. This was interesting. In addition

to the surveillance log Keller had on each person, some-one had inserted a handwritten page of notes regarding the history and personal life of the employee. I checked the other folders. Each had one of these handwritten pro-files. If this was part of Keller's work, Hauser had certainly been getting his money's worth. This wasn't exactly the kind of information a person would volunteer about him-self. I'm sure I wouldn't respond to the Previous Employ-ment Experience part of an application with "Pressed uniforms at Joliet State while serving time for assault and battery." But Hauser's head of maintenance had spent two years in prison. As I read his file, I had trouble picturing this guy attacking someone, and I didn't see this information as damning. He'd done all right for himself since prison. In fact he'd done real well considering the odds, and the incident had happened fifteen years ago.

I was so engrossed in this guy's past, I wasn't aware that someone had come into the room until I saw, out of the corner of my eye, something pink flutter into my in-basket. I looked up, and Diana Hauser smiled down at me. It was a smile of triumph. She gestured toward the pink camisole draped over the basket like a carelessly tossed inventory report.

"Your people are slipping," she announced, settling into the same chair she had occupied the day before.

I closed the file and placed it face-down on my desk. Then, I leaned back and studied her for a moment. She wore a brilliant blue-and-purple sweater, black stretch pants, and black suede boots. Instead of the silver fox coat she had on a short fur jacket that probably hadn't cost the lives of quite so many small animals. Her hair was hidden under a beret except for one blond strand that fell against her cheek. If she was embarrassed about yesterday's incident, she wasn't showing it. Was it a facade, I wondered, or did she consider the matter insignificant?

I was betting on the former. "Care for a cigarette?" I said, drawing one out for myself and extending the pack toward her.

She faltered for a second, then took one from the pack. "I've been trying to quit for a while. I'm lousy when it comes to self-control." I lit the cigarette for her. "Preston asked me to quit as a birthday present for him this year."

"That's what you gave him for his birthday? A smokeout?"

She shrugged. "It was what he wanted."

I nodded. "Just out of curiosity, what did he give you for your birthday?"

"A coat." She smiled. "It was what I wanted."

I gestured toward her cigarette. "I suppose you gave him the coat back."

She chewed on her lower lip for moment before responding. "No. I just don't wear it on days I smoke."

I couldn't tell where this conversation was going and I wasn't sure I wanted to know. I plucked the camisole from my in-basket. "I'll see that this finds its way home."

She studied me for an uncomfortable length of time, then finally said, "How did you know I liked my men clean-shaven?"

"I didn't," I responded.

Undaunted, she continued, "Will you take me to lunch?"

"I've got plans already," I lied. "Sorry." That wasn't a lie.

She stood up and walked toward the window. It was starting to snow and the large, fat flakes whirled by the window. "Is this what they call lake-effect snow?"

"Probably."

"I hate winter," she said and turned to me. "I'm from California, you know." She looked back toward the snow. "My father owns a law firm out there. That's where I met Preston."

"How did that happen?"

She stood, silently watching the snow for so long that I was beginning to think she had forgotten I was there. Finally, ignoring my question, she said, "Preston is a wonderful man. He just never has time to take me to lunch." Then she turned toward me. "Thanks for the cigarette." She extinguished it in the ashtray and gathered up her purse and a Nikon camera from the floor.

"Pay a visit to the camera department on your way to lingerie?"

"Can't a person have a hobby?" She sounded more irritated than defensive, so I didn't pursue it. She raised the camera with her right hand. "I guess I'll play the photo-snapping tourist this afternoon."

It had a fisheye lens. The candid of Preston had been taken with a telephoto, but then it's easy to change a lens.

"Well, I'll see you around, Quint. Maybe next time I'll see what Hauser's carries in the way of black lace. What do you think?"

"Don't go to any trouble on my account," I said, beginning to understand how Maggie must have felt when her tomcat Brandeis would, in a feline gesture of warmth and appreciation, drop a dead bird at her feet.

After Diana left I held up the camisole to get a better look at the offering. Maggie would have hated it. It had a lot of ivory lace and the kind of straps you couldn't adjust. And it was pink.

"I never would have figured you for the frilly type."

Pam was standing in the doorway, arms folded across her chest, head cocked slightly, and a bemused look on her face.

"People change, Pam." I lowered the camisole, hoping she had reconsidered the lunch invitation. "What can I do for you?"

"Actually, it's more like what I can do for you. By the way, it's about time you shaved off that mustache."

30

"Why thank you, Pam. And what is it that you can do for me? Are you selling insurance?"

"Better," she said, sitting in the chair across from me. "I figure that unless you are working from unlimited funds, you are going to need your own apartment very soon."

She was wording this very carefully, so at no time would I get the idea that she wanted a roommate. That was fine with me. I wasn't in the market for a relationship that was going to last any longer than a two-drink lunch.

"I have a friend," she continued, "who has a condo on Lake Shore Drive, just south of Addison. Her name's Elaine Kluszewski."

"You mean as in Ted Kluszewski," I interrupted her, "first baseman for the Reds and the White Sox?"

Pam gave me a quizzical look, as if I had just lapsed into tongues. "Never mind," I said, recalling that Pam's idea of sports was walking the dog along the jogging path.

"Elaine works for one of these big computer companies. Does the training, I think. She's in Europe right now working with some of their overseas clients." She paused to digest what she had just said. "God, wouldn't it be great to get to travel like that with your company picking up the tab?"

"Join the army."

"That wasn't quite what I had in mind. Anyway, she left this week. Before she left she tried to rent the condo, but was having trouble because she couldn't be sure how long she would be gone. Three to six months, she thinks. So she told me if I found anyone who was interested in renting it, and I considered the person to be responsible enough"— her eyes laughed when she said that—"to go ahead and rent it. There would, of course, be a few dollars in it for me. Not to mention the fact that if you moved in, I wouldn't have to run over there once a week to water the plants. Do you think you'd be interested?"

"What's reasonable?"

"Six-fifty." When I didn't respond immediately she added, "It's pretty big. One bedroom and a small den."

"Then you consider me a responsible person, I take it." I couldn't resist.

"In terms of paying rent and not trashing a home, yes I do."

I probably deserved that. "So, I can stay there anywhere from three to six months. All I have to do is pay rent and water plants?"

I couldn't think of a reason not to take it. I probably could have found a place in a less desirable area that was cheaper, but I would spend some time looking and I'd have to pay a security deposit. If I wasn't convinced, Pam's next words put a cap on it.

"It comes with its very own underground parking space."

"Sold." I tossed the camisole in the air.

I was able to coerce Pam into lunch under the condition that we go dutch, keep lunch to an hour and the conversation light. I was developing the distinct impression that Pam had a new personal life that she intended to keep that way.

Later that afternoon Pam dropped the keys and the electronic garage door opener off in my office along with written instructions on the care and feeding of Ms. Kluszewski's plants.

Before driving to my temporary residence, I brought the letters Hauser had given me to a guy I used to work with when I was on the force. Harry didn't owe me any favors or anything. In fact, I am probably indebted to him for the rest of my natural life for a lot of reasons. The main one, I guess, is the way he and his wife, Carol, took care of me after Joan and I split up. I was pretty lost for a while there and they kept inviting me over for dinner. After a while, they started playing the matchmaker games. I think it was Carol's idea mostly. I never knew what to expect when I'd knock on the door of their apartment with a box of chocolates, or, if Carol was dieting, flowers. Then one week I brought chocolate-covered cherries, and Maggie was there. She loved chocolate-covered cherries—and me for a while.

Let's not get maudlin, Quintus, I mentally kicked myself.

Anyway, Harry was good when it came to pulling something out of nothing. He used to be a pathologist with the department and now he had his own research lab and contracted his work out. He also taught part-time at Loyola. The department was sorry to lose him. He was good. If there was anything to be told from these pictures, he would find it. Harry wasn't in the lab, and I debated whether to leave the pictures for him. I decided against it, leaving him a note instead. I'd call him later.

Driving over to the condo, I kept thinking how good it would feel to put my feet up, and I wanted to get started on the files Hauser had given me.

I slid the garage card into the machine and the door lifted like I had said Open Sesame. I pulled into the underground garage and followed the numbers labeling each tenant's space until I got to 1240. It wasn't possible. It was occupied by a yellow Mustang convertible. News of an empty parking space in this city spreads faster than a flash flood.

I had to park about three blocks from the building, and by the time I walked the distance, carrying a bag of groceries and a suitcase, my hands were freezing because I hadn't the foresight to put on my gloves and was too stubborn to put down my packages and dig into my pockets and get them. I decided that my first official act as temporary tenant in the building would be to call a towing company.

I had trouble getting the key to work in the apartment door, partly because my hands were freezing and partly because I was trying to juggle all the stuff I was carrying. When the lock finally stopped fighting me, I was so relieved to be in the apartment that it didn't immediately occur to me there was something wrong. Then, several things registered at once. An empty apartment shouldn't have this many lights on. It shouldn't smell like popcorn. And it should be empty.

I won't soon forget my first glimpse of Elaine Kluszewski. She stood in the middle of the kitchen, swaying slightly, stockinged feet firmly planted on the tile floor. Even without shoes she was tall. Her hair was reddish brown and pulled back behind her neck. She wore a dark green skirt that looked like it was part of a suit and one of those white, professional blouses with an ascot and a pin. In her left hand she held a whiskey collins glass filled with what appeared to be only slightly diluted scotch or bourbon. In her right hand, pointed in the general direction of my chest, she held a .38 automatic. It swayed, along with Elaine, from side to side a little. I froze, gripping the groceries with one hand and my suitcase with the other.

"Drop your luggage." Her words were slurred and as she spoke, she closed one eye and tilted her head back, as if trying to get me into better focus.

I let my suitcase fall and raised my hand, palm toward her, in a gesture of surrender.

"Don't move." She was still swaying and her words had that clipped, overly distinct quality that characterizes someone trying very hard to appear sober. "I don't want to kill you." She lowered the gun so that it was aimed about a foot lower. I swallowed hard. "I am not aiming at a vital organ."

"Look," I said, "there has been a misunderstanding."

"Don't interrupt me." She took three healthy swallows from her glass, teetered backward and caught herself.

Scrunching up her eyebrows, she said, "Explain that."

"Pam Richards gave me the keys. I'm a friend of hers."

Her posture relaxed a bit, but I still felt I was being judged and found wanting. Either she was waiting for me to continue or was on the verge of passing out.

"Are you Elaine Kluszewski?"

She nodded.

"Pam said you were leaving the country for a while and were looking for someone to rent the place while you were gone." A horrible thought smacked me upside the head. I laughed tentatively. "Either that or one of us has really irritated Pam and this is her idea of getting even."

"What's your name?"

"Quint McCauley."

Her mouth dropped. "*You're* Quint McCauley?"

I nodded, not sure whether I should dig my toe into the carpet or tell her I had identified myself incorrectly.

"You're"—she searched for the right word—"scum."

That was what I was afraid of.

"You dumped Pammy for some twenty-year-old legal-eagle, pseudointellectual nymphomaniac."

I didn't want to respond to that. It was easier to call her bluff. "Look," I said, dropping my hand to my side. "One of three things is going to happen now. A, you're going to shoot me. B, I'm going to place your keys on this table, pick up my suitcase, and leave this apartment, never to return. Or C, one of us is going to call Pam and verify my story. It's up to you. Personally, I would prefer B or C. But, please. If you're leaning toward A, I'd appreciate it if you would aim for a kneecap. I'd feel a lot better."

She didn't respond right away, just swayed back and forth. Her eyes were beginning to droop.

I smiled and played my trump card. "Your popcorn is burning."

Her eyes flew open. "Oh, shit."

35

She took the two steps to the stove and, without hesitating, put the gun on the stove and grabbed the smoking pot from the burner. The fact that the pot had a metal handle did not immediately register. When it did, she let out a yelp and dropped the pot, sending charred popcorn flying. She stood there, staring at her hand as if she were trying to figure out where it came from.

I put my groceries on the counter and, taking her by the arm, directed her to the sink. Her hand was already bright red when I pushed it under cold running water. She looked at me, nodded her thanks, and took a long drink from her glass.

5

ASIDE FROM THE scotch, Elaine didn't stock much in the way of first-aid remedies. I found some petroleum jelly in the back corner of a shelf in her linen closet. I spread some of that on her hand, wrapped it in gauze, and sat her down on the couch in the living room. She kept muttering something about her life going from bad to worse and I decided the time was ripe for my exit. But she looked so lost and miserable that I wanted to do something for her. "I'll make you some coffee before I go."

She looked up at me, startled. "You're going? Don't go."

I shrugged. "There obviously has been a major misunderstanding here. I think I've caused you enough grief for one night."

"No." She shook her head. Long wisps of hair, more red than brown, were escaping the elastic band that held them against the nape of her neck. "It's not you." She stood slowly as if balancing on a high wire. "You stay here tonight. We'll talk in the morning." Then she walked down the hallway, steadying herself against the wall with her good hand. When she reached the door at the end of the hall she said without turning toward me, "This may work out for both of us."

I considered my options. I could take my suitcase and groceries, leave this warm, comfortable apartment, walk the four blocks to my car, and spend the night in another hotel. Or I could unpack my groceries, spend the night on a reasonably inviting couch, and leave in the morning before Elaine regained consciousness.

Not one part of the first scenario appealed to me so I put the groceries away and poured myself some medicine. Then I made a sandwich and ate it in her dining room at a table that was old but probably not old enough to be an antique. It was dark wood with matching chairs. The seats of the chairs looked and felt like they were handsewn in a kind of crewel stitch. The background was lilac with large multicolored flowers at the center of each seat.

Compared to the dining room set, the living room was ultramodern. Teak and chrome dominated the large room, and the focal point was a large shelving unit along one wall. The titles on the shelves were as varied as her furniture. A set of *Encyclopaedia Britannica* looked like it had been given a lot of use. There was some popular fiction, self-help books, and business titles like *Marketing Strategies for the Executive* and *Dress for Success*, also several natural-science books with topics varying from animals to astronomy. I noted the telescope in front of the big picture window and wondered how much star gazing one can do from a high-rise in Chicago.

I wanted to look over the files Hauser had given me, but I decided to call Harry first. Carol answered and she reprimanded me for not doing a better job of keeping in touch. Then she invited me and Maggie over for dinner. I evaded a response by telling her I'd let her know. I was relieved when she finally put Harry on.

"Hey, Quint, how's it going?"

"Couldn't be better," I said, not in the least convinced.

Apparently Harry wasn't either. "Oh, yeah, you sound great. Everything okay?"

"Sure," I said and hurried into the purpose of the call. "I've got some pictures I'd like you to go over with your fine-tooth comb."

"Yeah. I saw your note, and I have to admit you've got my curiosity going."

I smiled. Harry was like an old coonhound on a scent when it came to cryptic notes. "How about I bring what I've got by the lab in the morning."

"I'll be there at seven," Harry said and added, "I hope you're not getting yourself mixed up in anything that's going to be trouble."

"Don't worry," I said. Harry could play the mother role better than his wife sometimes. "Is Carl Maddox still with Chicago PD?"

"Yeah. The Twenty-first Precinct, last I heard. Why?"

"I'll explain tomorrow. See you then." I hung up.

I didn't have a lot of contacts from the Chicago police department anymore and I had never known Maddox all that well. But, as I remembered, he was a decent guy and might not mind checking on Keller's death for me. If the guy did step out of a bar with so much to drink that he walked straight into a car that didn't bother to stop, that was one thing. But if it might have been more than an accident, I wanted to know. I understand what it's like to leave a bar with too many under the belt. Whatever god it is that protects small children usually sees that drunks don't go wading into oncoming traffic. Just a hunch.

I called the Twenty-first and lucked out. Not only was Maddox still assigned there, he was in and he remembered me.

"How ya been, Quint?"

"Not bad," I replied.

"How long is it since you left the force anyway?"

"About three years," I said.

"What's goin' on?"

I told him where I was working and about the Keller hit-and-run incident. When he asked me why I wanted to know more, I gave him as few of the particulars as possible and, fortunately, he didn't press. He promised to call back soon. He wasn't kidding. He returned my call before I was able to finish my drink.

"It went down as a hit-and-run, all right. But you never know. I guess the guy could barely walk when he left the bar. There was one witness, if you want to call him that. He said he thought it was a pretty big car, either green or blue. Really narrows it down, huh? Didn't see any of the license plate. And sobriety-wise the witness wasn't in much better shape than the victim."

"Not much to go on."

"Yeah. They followed up a couple leads, but nothing came of it. So, officially it's a hit-and-run. Unofficially, I'd be careful if I were you."

"I will. And thanks a lot, Carl."

As I freshened my drink, I couldn't help but wonder if Hauser was really convinced that Keller's death was an accident.

I grabbed Hauser's collection of undesirables and, kicking my shoes off, stretched out on the couch to go through them. I soon came to admire Hauser's or Keller's information-gathering techniques. The men in the six files had committed or been accused of crimes ranging from assault and battery and statutory rape to running a dogfighting ring. Some had committed no crime per se but had been involved in relationships they wouldn't be inclined to publicize.

Frank Griffin, Hauser's purposeful store manager, had made the lineup. His file didn't contain much except for a note of his periodic visits to an apartment building on Sheridan Road. Keller hadn't been able to get a lead on whom Griffin was visiting, but it didn't require a huge leap from credibility to picture Griffin with a mistress. Griffin was married, but he could very well be the sort of man who feels that limiting himself to one woman would place an undue hardship on the rest of the species.

I guess I don't shock easily, because only one of the files caused a momentary jaw drop. Arthur Judson, Hauser's

tacts.
more than
I guess I was
learn that he owe
unsavory characters
birds out of trees in flocks

But what surprised me eve   istence of
the file for Art Judson and the fa   ome reason,
Preston considered him a suspect a   was no secret
that Art Judson was Preston's golden boy. He'd hired Art
out of college and treated him more like family than an
employee. What had Art done to rate an investigation? Is
that any way to treat a protégé? Maybe it had something to
do with Art's penchant for beautiful women and his habit
of displaying them. Still, it didn't make sense for Judson to
send Hauser threatening letters unless he was planning to
extort him later. If you were trying to come by a large amount
of money illegally, there had to be easier ways to do it.

I wondered if Hauser might be blackmailing these people with this information. Then any one of them would
logically want him dead, but blackmail wasn't Hauser's
style. Even if it was, he sure as hell wasn't stupid enough to
dump the evidence in my lap.

I guess it was a combination of being tired from the

panic you get
...t into the places-I-
...iousness. There was a person
...at my eye level who did not immedi-
...e known part of my mind either.

...ke you," she murmured. "I thought maybe
...d you."

...makes two of us," I said. In the dim light from the
...could barely make out Elaine's shape. She switched
...the lamp next to the sofa. It must have had an automatic
timer because I didn't remember turning it off.

I rubbed my eyes and ran my hands through my hair.
"What time is it?" I yawned.

"Four A.M."

She was studying me as if for the first time. I did the
same. She wore a short robe, fastened at her waist. It was
blue terry cloth and slightly worn. Her hair fell loose
against her shoulders and her eyes were a serious shade of
brown. They matched her expression.

"What did we decide last night?" She took a cigarette
from the pack I had set on the coffee table and lit it with
my lighter. Then she sat back on the floor, legs crossed in
front of her.

"I believe we were going to discuss it in the morning. But
I assumed it would be when it looked more like day than
night." I hesitated then continued, realizing, to my conster-
nation, that there was an earnest quality about this woman
that would not allow me to lie. "I was planning to be out of
here before you got up."

Her mouth, set in a firm straight line, didn't give me a
clue. She might have been relieved or disappointed. "I was

42

going to leave my groceries," I added.

She smiled for the first time. It was unforced and warm, and I don't think I've ever seen a smile do so much for a person's looks.

"I guess I can't blame you." She picked at the gauze on her burned hand. "You must have thought you'd stepped into another dimension."

My mind replayed some of the highlights from last night. She must have been thinking the same thing because we both laughed a little. Then I decided it was time to get the whole mess straightened out. "Aren't you supposed to be in a foreign country?"

"I was," she said. "England." She sat cross-legged and picked at the carpet, making a pile of tiny lint balls. Finally she continued. "I was riffed."

"I'm sorry." What could I say? "You were what?"

She looked up at me. "Reduction in force." She pounded the pile of lint with her injured hand. "Damn."

She was bitter, and as she explained I could understand that emotion. She'd been with the company for ten years, starting out in data entry and working her way up to manager of customer education. As she talked, her voice rose and she had trouble keeping it even. But she tried. The company had a couple bad years and started cutting staff. Her position was one of the first they eliminated.

Her voice dropped to barely above a whisper. "At least that's what they told me." She paused and sighed. "I think they just wanted to get rid of me."

I couldn't tell whether she wanted me to pursue that so I kept quiet.

Finally she said, "So what it boils down to is I need a roommate or I'm not going to be able to pay the mortgage on this place."

"You seem pretty certain you aren't going to get another job."

"I don't have any college, let alone an MBA. Nobody hires you for the kind of money I was making without an MBA."

I wanted to tell her that employers look for more than a diploma. They look for character and assertiveness, and a little bulldog tenacity didn't hurt either. She seemed to have more than her share of all that, but she wasn't looking for a pep talk right now. She wanted to allow herself the luxury of wallowing in her own misery for a while first. I knew how she felt.

"So. You need a roommate."

She nodded. "This is a one bedroom with a den. There's a pull-out sofa in there. I can sleep on it." I guess she interpreted my silence as reluctance. She was right. "You could leave whenever you wanted to. It would be cheaper than a hotel."

As insane as the idea was, it was beginning to make sense, but there was one point I wanted to air out. "I thought I was scum."

Elaine shrugged. "Actually, what Pam said was that you were a nice guy having a tough time handling the aging process."

"The aging process? Pam never told me she was a certified psychologist."

"She said you thought you could recapture your youth with a self-centered twenty-one-year-old."

"Twenty-three-year-old," I corrected her, then folded my arms across my chest. "She said that, did she?"

"Uh huh. She also said this woman was a ball-crusher."

I shrugged. "I like that in a woman."

She smiled. "You want to try this arrangement for a while?"

I'd like to think I did it for convenience's sake—no apartment hunting, no hassling with landlords over security deposits—but I think deep down, while I knew that there are a lot worse things than being alone, there are also a lot better things too. I figured I could invest a week or so in that possibility. Still, I didn't answer immediately. There was something else to consider here. The woman needed me. More specifically she needed my money. My bargaining position would never be better.

"Who gets the parking space?"

6

IT IS AGAINST my nature to admit that I have made a mistake of colossal proportions. So, as I drove to Harry's lab on the northwest side to give him the photos for analysis, I made a point of not thinking about my new living situation.

I wondered what Diana Hauser did with herself when she wasn't lining her pockets with underwear. Volunteering at the local children's hospital didn't seem a realistic assumption. I only had a couple psych courses, so my knowledge of the subject is pretty meager, but you don't need a PhD to realize that a woman who shoplifts out of her husband's store is executing one of the all-time great look-at-me ploys. But was it working for her? And if it wasn't, what came next? Plop down in the middle of the designer casual section, douse herself with kerosene, and light a match?

When I got to the lab, Harry was bent over a lab table and didn't see me in the doorway. I watched him sprinkle donut crumbs into a cage containing several rodent-like creatures. They could have been mice, gerbils, or guinea pigs. I can never tell the difference. I lurched into the room, Quasimodo-style, dragging one foot behind me.

Without turning, Harry said, "Be with you in a second, Quint."

I stopped. "Dammit, Harry. Next time I'm wearing swim fins."

Harry shrugged and dropped the last piece of donut into the cage. "Quint, you could wear high heels. I'd recognize that size-ten shuffle of yours no matter how you disguise it."

He was probably right. Harry had an uncanny ability to know people by their footstep. I hadn't been able to trick him yet. "Yeah," I said, "but I'm gonna try. It gives my life purpose."

Harry turned and looked at me for the first time. He took a step backward in exaggerated surprise. "Quint. You've changed."

Motioning for him to drop the subject, I approached the rodent cage and peered in. "You always make friends with these little guys before you shoot 'em full of sugar substitutes?"

Harry's expression was sober. "There is no progress without sacrifice."

I looked at him. "Seriously. What are you going to do to them?"

"I feed these gerbils junk food to observe how it affects their ability to procreate. A fanatical bunch of nutritionists wants to know." He gestured toward one of the creatures. "So far, he's sired eighteen litters."

I looked at the animal. "No kidding," I said, not knowing whether, for a gerbil, that was a good record or not. "Nice goin'," I said to the animal. It studied me for a moment and then went back to snuffling for crumbs.

I straightened up. "It's damned near impossible to find a parking space around here."

Harry rolled his eyes. "Quint, you'd have trouble finding a parking space in a mall on Super Bowl Sunday."

"You're probably right," I conceded.

"What's this I hear about you and Maggie?"

"I don't know. What do you hear, and from whom?"

"Nothing really. Maggie called. Figured you guys had a spat."

"More than that. I was replaced with a newer model. So was my car."

Harry grunted in sympathy. "I never thought that was a match made in heaven, even though Carol did. Who's to tell?" He scratched his chin, thinking, then said, "You going to tell me where you're living?"

I crossed my arms over my chest and leaned against one of the tables. "Harry, did you ever do something so impulsive, so devoid of any input from the reasoning part of your brain that you had trouble admitting it to yourself, let alone someone else?"

Harry studied me for a minute before asking, "What's her name?"

I shook my head. "Doesn't matter."

Harry grinned and chuckled. "Wait'll Maggie finds out." Then he became more serious. "She's been trying to get hold of you, you know."

"I know."

He smiled again. "Ain't love grand?"

I shrugged and pulled the letters out of my pocket. "Love stinks. Most of the time."

"Spoken like a veteran of the wars." He turned his attention toward the envelopes. "What've you got for me?"

I handed him Hauser's photos, and Harry spent several minutes looking them over, studying them from all angles as I filled him in on the details. When he was hovering over an experiment or coaxing answers from mathematical equations, Harry seemed much older than his fifty years. His incredibly slow, methodical movements could easily be interpreted as feebleness. Then, when he was explaining the results of an experiment or relating the data behind some new hypothesis of his, he dropped ten years. His gestures became animated and expansive and his barely controlled excitement and enthusiasm were contagious.

He had a more cautious reaction to something he was dipping his toes into for the first time. When Harry looked up from the pictures, it was the Harry I remembered from

48

my days on the police force. He was both excited and reserved.

He held up the pictures. "This is your boss, isn't it?"

I nodded.

"Preston Hauser. Heir to the department-store dynasty." He looked at the letters again. "As I recall, he's married to a beautiful young woman. Restless though."

"Restless?"

He shrugged. "It may be nothing. Hauser was a guest speaker at some university function. He brought his wife, who apparently spent most of the evening in the company of a man more her age. She didn't try to hide it either."

"Do you know who the other man was?"

"No, I don't. But you might ask Carol. She pays more attention to things like that." He laughed. "By the way, I have instructions to invite you over for dinner."

"Please Harry, not yet."

He nodded his understanding and went back to examining the pictures. "So, you want me to see what I can find here."

"That's what you do best, isn't it?"

"Well," he said, ignoring my statement, "just off the top of my head, I'd say you're looking for a right-handed individual with a pretty good telephoto lens and a fondness for nursery rhymes."

"That really narrows it down, doesn't it? You say right-handed because of the direction of the slash through Hauser's neck?"

"And you said you needed me." Harry squinted at the photo. "And I'd guess the slash was made with a razor blade. Aside from that," he continued, "I'm not sure how much I can tell you. I can check for fingerprints but there are probably a number of sets on here already. Including yours and mine. I can do a blood analysis"—he moved the photo under a lab light for a better view—"but I'm not sure how much that's going to help you. Unless it's a rare blood type. But I'll do what I can."

"That's all I'm asking."

"Quint. Does this fall under an obscure clause in your job description at Hauser's?"

"No. I'm doing a little freelance work for Hauser."

"Tell me. How is Hauser taking all this?"

"For a man who's received three death threats, he's remarkably composed."

"Interesting," Harry said.

I nodded.

He peered at me over the top of his reading glasses. "Who do you think?"

I shrugged. "Too soon to tell." I wasn't ready to make educated guesses. "How soon can you have something for me?"

He looked at the schedule on his calendar. "This afternoon soon enough?"

"Perfect."

"You talk to Maddox yet?"

"Yeah, I did," I said, realizing this was my cue to satisfy Harry's curiosity. I explained about Keller's accident and told him what Maddox had said. Harry waited until I was through.

"Don't like the sound of this," Harry said.

I shrugged. "I don't much either, but it's probably nothing."

Harry eyed me. "Right."

It's hard to tell when Irna Meyers is angry. Try to picture a wasp in a snit. When beady eyes and crossed brows are the norm, then I guess it becomes a matter of degrees. This morning, however, Irna seemed more irritable than usual. Was there something there besides fierce protectiveness?

"You don't have an appointment." End of discussion.

"I most certainly do." I tried a show of force, pulling a

small appointment book out of my breast pocket and flipping it open to a page. Any page. "It says right here. Preston Hauser. Ten o'clock," I lied. I replaced the book. "Please. Check with Mr. Hauser. He's expecting me."

Irna glared at me for what seemed a very long time, then finally got up and walked over to Hauser's closed door. She shot me a look that said, "Do you realize what you are asking me to do?" and knocked on the door so softly it was as if she were afraid of waking him. Maybe she was. I didn't hear a response, but Irna apparently did. She entered his office and closed the door behind her.

While she was gone, I took the opportunity to check the appointment book on her desk. She was right. My name wasn't there. Yet Hauser had told me he would have Irna pencil me in. I had the feeling this was an appointment Hauser wasn't anxious to keep. He wanted me to figure it out without his help. Too bad for him. I had some questions that required answers and was willing to push as hard as necessary.

The door finally opened and Irna emerged. "Mr. Hauser will not be able to see you at this time," she said, closing the door. She sat down and gazed at the door to her boss's office before turning her attention back to me. "You'll have to reschedule." She made no move toward her appointment book, but there was a note of apology in her voice that I hadn't thought her capable of.

I interpreted this as an opportunity to be brash. I approached her desk. "Irna. It's very important that I see Mr. Hauser. I think you know that."

She straightened several sheets of letterhead and dropped a pencil into a holder before she said, "Mr. Hauser has experienced a loss."

It was apparent that I was going to have to work for every morsel of information I could glean from this woman. "Did someone die?"

Before she could reply, Hauser's door opened. I turned, expecting to see Preston himself, but instead a tall, elderly woman left his office. She nodded to me and then turned to Irna.

"Call me, Irna, if he needs me." The tall woman shook her head and sighed. "It's such a shame. She was only seven."

"Yes, Mrs. Hunnicutt."

I thought I detected a note of disdain in Irna's tone, but I could have been wrong. The elderly woman left.

"Who was only seven?" I asked, moving toward Hauser's door with little regard for my own safety. I wouldn't have thought Irna could move so fast, but she positioned herself between me and the door before I was able to execute my maneuver.

"Scheherazade."

I needed a bigger hint. "Who?"

"Mr. Hauser's horse."

It was beginning to sink in. "The one on his desk?"

Irna nodded.

It took a minute, and I had to conjure up some long-buried emotions I'd felt when my first dog, Alex, got hit by a car, but I finally understood that the man had a right to grieve in private for a while. Especially if that man's name was on the store's letterhead. I dug my hands in my pockets and assumed my defeated pose.

"Can I reschedule for this afternoon?"

I could barely detect the relief in Irna's tone, but it definitely was there. "Certainly." She consulted her calendar. "Three o'clock?"

"That sounds okay," I allowed.

As I returned to my office, I tried to put the event into perspective. Failing, I allowed myself to speculate. What would Hauser do with the center picture on his desk? Would he replace it or just drape it in black velvet? And the woman I saw leaving his office. Irna had called her Mrs. Hunnicutt. So that was Hauser's big sister.

Lois stopped me as I was walking into my office, leaning across her typewriter to hand me a note. "You had a call." She hesitated. "It was Maggie." She said that like she was expecting an interesting reaction from me.

"Thanks," I said and walked into my office.

The phone and I stared at each other for a while as I managed to transfer my anger and hurt to the block of beige plastic. It was a lot easier to rise above the will to succumb to the telephone than to deal with my feelings about Maggie. I was so intent on fighting the temptation to pick it up and use it that I almost jumped out of my skin when it rang. It was the second button—an inside call. I sighed my relief and picked it up.

"Mr. McCauley, Irna Meyers. Mr. Hauser would like to see you immediately." She paused, but not long enough for me to tell her about the appointment book I had to check. "It's urgent."

Urgent or not, I wasn't going to pass up an opportunity to get some information out of Hauser, so I grabbed my briefcase containing the files.

When I got to Hauser's office, Irna waved me on in. From the look on her face, I expected the worst. I was relieved to see the man standing, hands clasped behind his back, looking out onto Michigan Avenue. He heard me enter and turned. Then he picked an envelope up from his desk and handed it to me.

"This just came."

There was an edge in his voice. I couldn't tell whether he was just nervous about the letter or irritated with me for letting one slip through.

I opened it and removed the contents—a photocopy of a newspaper article reporting on the fatal crash of a private plane. The first paragraph read: "A small twin-engine airplane crashed shortly after takeoff from DuPage Airport, killing the pilot and his passenger. The cause of the crash is still being investigated but is believed to be the result of engine malfunction. Killed were Preston Hauser, 61, owner of the Hauser's department store and president of the Hauser Foundation, and the pilot Nathan Rudman, 33."

It was eerie. Even though I could tell the article had been doctored, standing there talking to a man whose death I had just read about was macabre. Apparently someone had clipped Hauser's name and description from another article, pasted it over the real victim, and gone to some length to make sure most of the cut lines didn't show. At first glance, it looked like the real thing.

"Is this your pilot's name?" I asked.

He shook his head. "No. That must be the name of the pilot who died in the real crash."

To give the item the personal touch, the headline had been rewritten. "Two Die in Plane Crash" had been crossed out and "Fear of Flying Justified" was typed above it. The type appeared to be the same as was used in the other letters.

Hauser sighed, removed his glasses, and rubbed his eyes and face. Then he looked in my direction the way someone does when he is only partially aware of your presence. Whoever was behind these threats had escalated the war. He or she had invaded Hauser's privacy and opened a wound that had never healed well. I wondered if his preoccupation with horses started after he lost his family.

"My dislike of flying is no secret. A lot of people know how my first wife and our son died. But it is often the most efficient means of getting from one place to another and I won't allow this phobia to run my life." He continued, "I'm intending to fly up to Green Bay this afternoon."

"Take a commercial flight."

He shook his head. "No. I won't be dictated to by a madman. My pilot will meet me at DuPage Airport, where we will take off at two o'clock to arrive in Green Bay at four-fifteen."

He gave me the name of his pilot and where I could reach him. "I'll be at the airport before you get there to check out the airplane."

"Are you a mechanic too?"

"No. But I know one." It was time to get down to questions. "Who knows you hate to fly?" I didn't want to use the word afraid.

He shrugged. "My family. My friends. Many of the people here. Some of the airport personnel." He thought for a moment longer. "I've never made much of an effort to hide it. Anyone who is at all acquainted with me could know."

"Okay, Mr. Hauser. I need some information before I can start to piece this together." I pulled the files from my briefcase and dropped them on his desk. "Why these people? Why not others?"

Hauser studied me for a moment before replying. "There was one other."

"Who?"

Hauser removed a manila folder from a desk drawer and, smiling, tossed it across the desk toward me. I looked at him, picked it up, and opened it, just as he hoped I would. I'm so predictable. You could tell that by looking at my rap sheet. It was only a half page long and pretty dull. Of course, it hadn't been updated since I moved out of Maggie's apartment. But everything else was there. The marriage, the divorce, the jobs. All of it. I was relieved in the same way I am when the squad car that has been following me for the last couple miles turns down another street. I really didn't have anything to hide, but I guess I'm as paranoid as the next person. I was also annoyed at the idea of this detective riffling through my private life. Hauser was watching me, amused. No one deserved to be that smug. I flipped the page over, glancing at the back.

"This is it?"

He frowned slightly. "Should there be more?"

Arching one eyebrow, I made a show of reexamining the sheet. Then I inserted it back in the file and dropped the whole thing on Hauser's desk. "No."

Hauser looked from my file to me, then back again, opened his mouth as if to ask a question and apparently thought better of it. He leaned back in his chair, one hand clutching its arm. We were both a little startled when his watch blurted out its tinny beeping noise. He reached into a drawer for his vitamins.

Here we go again.

"Tell me about Judson." I wanted to hear what Hauser had to say about his golden boy.

Hauser removed each of the five vitamins from their containers and poured himself a glass of water. First things first. I shook my head as he offered me one, then he held up a finger motioning me to wait until the ritual was complete. What else could I do? One capsule, two swallows of water, one capsule, two swallows of water, until they were gone. He replaced the containers in the drawer and then looked puzzled, as if trying to recall where he had left something.

"What was that you asked me?"

"What about Judson?" I asked again.

He sighed as if he were about to tell me about a son who had gone astray. "I'm perplexed about Art." Hauser seemed thoughtful as he absently rubbed his right temple. "He's been with me for five years. I hired him directly out of school. We were quite close for a long time." He shrugged and sighed. "One might regard it as rather a father-son relationship. I'm quite fond of him. But lately..." His voice drifted off.

"Lately?" I prodded.

"I don't know. He's rather distant, angry. I give him free rein in the public relations end of the business, but he has always asked my opinion before launching a new project. Lately he's been disagreeing with everything I suggest. Rather obstinate. About seven months ago I loaned him some money to pay off his gambling debts. No interest." Hauser had been stroking the finish of a ceramic coffee mug and now he took a drink from it. "After that he seemed to change. I suspect it was the loan. Some people feel awkward when they are loaned money. You know, rather unsure of how to act toward the person who has provided the loan."

"According to this file he still has a gambling problem."

Hauser nodded. "Once a gambler..."

"If he owes all this money, why do you think he's still walking around without holes in his kneecaps?"

Hauser flicked a piece of lint off the cuff of his jacket. "Perhaps he has found another loan officer."

"Who do you think sent the letters?" I tried the direct approach since my subtle touch wasn't working.

He seemed to have been expecting that question and kept his eyes on me as he took another drink of coffee. I think he was trying to read my mind.

I snatched at the most convenient straw and pushed the issue further. "Do you think Diana is involved?"

Hauser gasped and his eyes widened. I thought for a moment that the question had landed right in the strike zone. Then he cried out and slammed down on the desk face first. The glass toppled, sending ice cubes and water streaming across the leather blotter.

7

WHEN I LOOK back on the moments that followed Hauser's collapse, I sometimes see myself springing from the chair to somehow save the dying man, instead of sitting there stunned for several seconds that will forever be recorded as an eternity in my conscience. Then it helps to tell myself that it wouldn't have made any difference. It helps, but not much.

I sat, frozen to the chair, until Hauser took his next breath. It was labored and obviously required a whole lot of effort. Reaching across the desk, I felt for his carotid pulse. It was faint and rapid. That was when he began breathing convulsively. I pushed him back in his chair so I could loosen his tie and unbutton the stiff shirt collar. His eyes were wide and dominated by the whites. I didn't need a first-aid course to know the man was beyond my help.

"Irna!" I yelled. "Get in here!" I was afraid Hauser would, in his convulsions, swallow his tongue, and I was trying to pry his mouth open. His teeth were clamped shut. Damn that woman. What the hell was she waiting for?

"Irna Meyers! PLEASE."

Maybe she'd been powdering her nose because that last entreaty brought her running. When she saw Hauser, she clamped her hands to her mouth and froze.

"Call an ambulance. This man is dying."

His breathing had slowed and was coming in short gasps now. I looked back at the door. Irna was gone. As I held Hauser's head back to keep his air passage clear, a shudder rippled through his body and he exhaled a long, final sigh. I didn't need to feel for a pulse to know he was dead. His eyes were flat and glassy, as devoid of life as a lunar landscape.

I glanced at the telephone. None of the outside lines were lit. Irna must have called the ambulance already. I picked up Hauser's private line and dialed the police. When I hung up, Irna was watching me from the doorway. Maybe she was afraid to cross the threshold.

Without taking her eyes from Hauser she said, "He's gone, isn't he?"

"Yes." I braced myself for an emotional outburst.

She stared at him for a long time, then, without taking her eyes from him, asked, "What happened?"

"I'm not sure. I think it was something he ate."

Without turning her head, her eyes slowly met mine. It was eerie. "What do you mean?"

I shrugged. "It happened just a few minutes after he took his vitamins."

She turned her gaze back to Hauser and put her hand to her mouth. Then she approached the desk with slow, jerky steps, the way a cat hedges around a suspicious object. If there was going to be an emotional outburst from this woman, it was slow in coming.

She reached across the desk to pick up the overturned glass. I grabbed her hand. "Don't touch anything, Irna. The police will want things just the way they were."

I glanced at the colorful, possibly libelous files on Hauser's desk and realized I had to get them out of here before the police arrived. "Irna, get Roger Munro. Tell him to show the cops where to go, and tell him to make sure no one else comes up here."

Irna's reaction to my order wasn't what I'd call instantaneous. She glared at me as if to ask where I got off telling her what to do. Then, with an obvious effort to collect herself, she left the room.

There wasn't any place in Hauser's office to hide the files so I crammed them back into my briefcase, careful to retrieve the one labeled with my name, as well. I dropped the briefcase next to the chair I'd been sitting in and hoped that Irna didn't speculate aloud as to the whereabouts of the files that had been on Hauser's desk.

I heard commotion outside the office. Seconds later, Fred Morison ushered two uniformed policemen into the room. Irna followed them.

"I thought I said Munro," I snapped, realizing too late that I really didn't have the authority to order Irna around and I didn't need to give this woman any more reason to dislike me. Still, the last person I wanted around was Fred Morison.

"What's going on here?" Morison demanded, then saw Hauser slumped in the chair. "What happened to the old man?" He bounded toward the desk as if he might be able to bring him back to life, though he obviously knew damned well Hauser was dead. Fred never would have referred to Hauser as the old man, even if he were in a coma and there were so much as the remotest possibility that the words could have registered somewhere in the back of Hauser's subconscious.

"He's dead, Fred," I said in a tone I usually reserve for children who are slow to realize that the charm in responding to every sentence with "Why?" has worn very thin.

Meanwhile, I wanted to know what prompted this man, who had been known to turn his back on a shoplifter in the act of pocketing a designer watch in order to avoid the inconvenience of detaining someone, had taken it upon himself to hustle the police to Hauser's office.

One policeman was keeping the curious out of the room and dissuading Fred from touching anything, while the other asked me what had happened. He was very young and visibly anxious to turn this over to a higher authority.

So was I. When the detectives finally arrived, I answered some of the same questions and a few more.

I was talking to a Sergeant O'Henry—fiftyish, with sparse gray hair and small sharp eyes. He examined the scene carefully without touching anything before he began questioning me. I showed him the vitamin bottles and explained Hauser's ritual.

"How long after he took these did he keel over?" O'Henry wanted to know.

"No more than five minutes."

"Hmph," he said, eyes narrowing. He looked at me and then, as if he were making a confession, said, "I take a vitamin C every day. It's my wife's idea actually. She claims it wards off colds. The thing is, you never really know if it does work. I mean, how do you know how many colds you would have gotten if you hadn't popped one of these every day?"

He seemed to need a response, some endorsement of his health plan. "It can't hurt," I said. "Not usually anyway."

O'Henry smiled weakly and shook his head. Then he asked me why I was meeting with Hauser, and I told him I wanted to speak privately. We walked to the window, away from the others, leaving Fred Morison trying to look like he belonged somewhere.

I told O'Henry about the letters Hauser had received and that he had hired me to investigate them. While I was talking, O'Henry unwrapped a stick of gum and stuffed it in his mouth.

Then he gestured toward my briefcase. "That yours?" I nodded, and he didn't pursue it.

"He hired you to find out who wanted to kill him?" He glanced at Hauser's body, then back to me. "Bang-up job you're doing." He spoke matter-of-factly and I didn't think he intended that statement to sound as insulting as it did. But I could have been wrong.

I found myself working very hard to justify my lack of

61

success. "Look, Sergeant. Hauser hired me yesterday, almost two months after he got the first letter. I don't think he ever felt the person intended to kill him."

O'Henry was watching me, listening and chewing his gum. He didn't interrupt, although I was beginning to wish he would. It was difficult to explain Hauser's lack of concern, and somehow I didn't think telling O'Henry, "You had to be there," would cut it.

"He just wanted to know who was sending the letters," I concluded.

O'Henry regarded me for a minute, then turned his head so he could view the scene on Michigan Avenue. It was a messy winter day, and cars sprayed slush as they made their way down the Magnificent Mile. Fred stood next to Irna, talking to her quietly. She wasn't speaking, just nodding or shaking her head.

Without turning back to me, O'Henry asked, "Did Hauser have any theories?"

"If he did, he didn't share them with me."

"Where are the letters?"

I gestured toward one of the detectives who was placing the clipping in a plastic bag. "There is the last one. The other three are being analyzed."

"Oh? By whom?"

I gave him Harry's name. He just nodded, but I could tell by the slight widening of his eyes that he was impressed. Harry was still regarded as one of the best pathologists around.

The police photographer had arrived and was taking pictures of Hauser's body. For some reason this had always seemed to be the worst part of a murder investigation. The final sitting.

It occurred to me that Diana didn't know she was a widow yet. "If you're through with me for now, I'm going to see Mrs. Hauser."

O'Henry raised his eyebrows. "You two friends?" Apparently the Diana and Preston saga was the stuff of which legends are made.

I didn't think his remark deserved an answer. Instead, I wrote Elaine's address on a piece of paper and handed it to him. "In case you need to reach me."

"I'm sure we will," he said, folding it carefully and placing it in his jacket pocket.

The Hausers had two places of residence in the Chicago area. One was in a very high-class bedroom community in a far west suburb. Like many of the homes in that area, the eight bedroom house was situated on a four or five acre lot complete with stables and the requisite number of Arabians. Minus one. They also owned a condominium, which was situated on a very exclusive stretch of Lake Shore Drive.

I was reasonably certain that Diana Hauser would prefer the Limelight to the Hunt Club any day of the week. I was right.

When she opened the door she was wearing a blue-and-white-striped, French-cut leotard, blue tights, and white leg warmers. A mist of perspiration masked her face, throat, and chest. She was an incredible sight as she dabbed at the back of her neck with a towel.

"Why, Mr. McCauley. Did you bring me something?"

Her smile invited me to places I had only imagined, and I tried to keep my voice as noncommittal as possible. "I'm afraid I brought you some news. May I come in?"

She hesitated, trying to read something from my expression, then moved back, making way for me. "What do you drink?" She draped the towel around her neck and walked to a wet bar adjacent to a large window overlooking Oak Street Beach. "Something tells me this is the kind of news that will call for a chaser."

"Nothing for me, thanks," I said and watched her drop a couple ice cubes in a glass and pour herself something from a leaded crystal decanter.

"This is very bad news," I said, not sure whether I was trying to break it to her gently or there was another reason for my hedging.

Diana sipped on her drink. "Share it," she said.

"Preston is dead."

There was a flicker of something in her eyes. I wasn't sure whether it was pain, anger, shock, or some other emotion, but I didn't think it had much to do with what she said next.

"What happened?" she asked; then, without missing a beat, added, "Did he choke to death on his ego?" She turned sharply and looked at the scene from the window.

"They don't know yet. He might have had a heart attack."

"Might? That means it *might* have been something else."

I nodded and waited for her to continue.

She shook her head, frustrated, as if she had just realized there was a game going on here and, if she didn't like the rules, she was going to have to change them. Let her try. The fact that she was up for a game after learning that her marital status had abruptly changed said something; but then so did the fact that she apparently didn't know how Preston might have died. If she had anything to do with it, she would be playing this scene a lot cooler. Unless she was way ahead of me.

She paced back and forth across the room, sipping her drink, as if trying to piece something together. Then she stopped in midstep and turned to me. "Okay, I'll bite. What else *might* it have been?"

"Some kind of poison. Probably slipped into his vitamins."

For several seconds there was dead silence. Then she

started to giggle. The giggles escalated into laughter. I'm not without the ability to know a good example of irony when I see one. And I was aware that if Hauser had bought the farm via a strychnine-laced vitamin B complex, then his death would definitely classify as one of life's zingers. But, given the fact that we were talking about a death here, I'm not sure I would have reacted with unbridled hilarity the way Diana Hauser was doing.

The giggling fit crumpled her onto the floor in a lotus position. Miraculously, she did not spill a drop from her glass. I sat on the edge of a sleek, gray leather recliner, which threatened to engulf me as I waited for Diana to finish her act. It had to be an act because if it were the real thing, she wouldn't have sneaked several glances in my direction to see how she was doing.

I sat there, elbows on my knees, hands folded, smiling politely.

After a minute or two the giggles receded, and in between gasps for breath, she shook her head and muttered, "Perfect. Perfect Preston."

Nice touch, Diana. Just don't overdo.

"Well," I said, rising. "I guess I can leave without fear that you might put a gun to your head or do a half gainer off the balcony."

"Wait," she said as I reached for the doorknob. She stood, leaving the drink on the carpet. "You don't understand how it is, uh, I mean was between Preston and me."

I shook my head. "I guess I don't. Would you care to enlighten me?"

She cocked her head and studied me for several seconds. "Are you always this sarcastic, or do I just bring it out in you?"

She stood defiantly, her weight on one hip and arms crossed, her icy blue eyes doing a number on me.

"Diana, all I know is that a man who hired me to investigate some threats to his life is dead. Even though I barely had time to begin an investigation, I feel pretty lousy about the fact that he died while I was supposed to be helping him. Although I'm sure Preston would have preferred that I had discovered the identity of the person threatening him while he was alive to appreciate it, I still intend to find him or her. And if it isn't the same person who killed him, I intend to keep looking. Now, I had hoped you might be able to help me, that you might want to help me, but I could grow very old trying to figure out what version of the Texas-two-step you're doing."

I gave her about two seconds to respond before opening the door. I was a little surprised when she stopped me.

"That was a long speech for you, wasn't it?"

"Yes. In fact I've just about used up my allotment of words for the day. So if I'm going to stay, you better be doing the talking."

She gave me a brief smile that lingered in her eyes. "All right," she said. "I'll tell you about Preston Hauser." Her eyes had lost their warmth. "You may decide that some obligations just aren't worth pursuing."

8

SHE WALKED SLOWLY across the room, aware of the way she moved and of the fact that I was watching her, and settled into a soft gray love seat. Patting the empty half of the couch, she gestured for me to join her. I opted for the bench that accompanied the grand piano next to the wet bar. The keys were covered and I rested one arm on the lid and tossed the ball into her court.

"Okay. Just what is it about Preston Hauser that is going to make me wish I had told him to plant his ten thousand dollars?"

She raised her eyebrows. "Ten thousand?"

I nodded.

She set her drink on a small table next to the couch. The movement was so abrupt, the ice in the glass clattered and I think the liquid would have sloshed over the side if there had been more than a thimbleful left in the glass. She was about to blurt something out, caught her breath and considered me for a moment, then turned away.

She was composed again when she asked, "What kind of death threats was he getting?"

"Uh uh." I shook my head. "You talk, I listen."

I sounded like a bad Tarzan impersonation. I glanced at my watch. It was almost one P.M., and I was real tempted to pour myself a drink. Considering the grim turn the day had taken, it probably wasn't too early. But I didn't want to give Diana an opportunity to work on her story. I just wanted to listen, take in everything she had to say about Preston before she could think too much. There would be time later to worry about how much of it, if any, was true.

She removed a cigarette from a silver case on the table next to her glass and lit it, inhaling deeply. Then she sighed and gazed at the ceiling. "Where do I start?" She stared out the window at the sky and absently slid a hand under her leg warmer to rub her right calf. "When I met Preston," she began, speaking with a dreamy quality, "I thought he was the most distinguished, intelligent, gentlest man I had ever seen. He made me feel very special. That's something most men don't know how to do, you know." She looked at me and stopped rubbing her leg, allowing my attention to drift to her face. "Oh sure. A lot of men can make a woman feel good, pretty, successful, or whatever it takes to hold her interest. But some men, like Preston, can make you feel like you always thought it would feel when you were a little girl imagining what it was like to be a woman."

As she talked, a Siamese cat—the beige kind with brown on the tips of its ears—with startling blue eyes appeared from behind the couch and approached Diana. She dipped her finger into her glass and offered it, dripping, to the animal. The cat sniffed, then licked the liquid from her finger. It shoved its head against Diana's hand and ran its body against her palm until all that touched her hand was the brown tip of its tail. Then the cat left the room. Maybe these two had more in common than eye color.

Diana paused in her speech and turned back to the sky before continuing. "Good as it felt, that's how bad it felt when it stopped. One day I was a queen, a fairy princess, a goddess, the next day I was trash." She shrugged. "I couldn't walk into a room without doing something wrong." She drained her glass and wiped away the moisture an ice cube had left on the tip of her nose. Then she held her glass out for me to refill. What could I do? I poured the liquor. "But he wasn't consistent," she went on. "I mean, one day he would be cold and distant, watching me for flaws, waiting for me to do something out of line. And the next day he would be all loving and caring again. I felt like one of those stupid little animals they use in laboratory experiments. You know, the ones that bang the lever to get rewarded with a pellet. They don't get one every time, or even every other time, but they keep banging away and maybe the fifteenth time or the forty-third time they get this measly pellet. And that's enough to keep them going another hundred or thousand times, whatever it takes."

"There's a whole system based on that principle. It's called Las Vegas."

She ignored me. "After a while, he stopped the hot and cold treatment and stopped caring, too. That's when I found out it's better to be carped at than ignored."

"You don't impress me as an easy person to ignore. Why would Preston treat you like a queen one minute and a leper the next?"

She gave a little shrug that was more like a sigh. I decided to try the direct approach.

"Was he seeing another woman?"

"Who knows," she said, as if she were telling me she didn't have the time of day. She straightened her right leg and raised it, toe pointed, toward the ceiling.

"Were you seeing someone?"

She smiled. "If you believe the rumors, I have the morals of an oversexed alley cat. I've made the rounds of buyers and junior executives and performed feats with the board of directors that would make the *Guinness Book of Records*."

"Should I believe the rumors?"

"I think that people who believe rumors like that are hoping to become part of the legend. What do you think?"

"I don't know what to think," I said, ignoring the insinuation. "I barely know you, and the few things I do know about you don't exactly fit the classic devoted-wife mold. You shoplift items out of your husband's store. You walk and talk like you've got more on your mind than a good conversation. And, upon learning of Preston's untimely death, you dissolve into a nicely staged fit of giggles. You tell me. What am I supposed to think?"

She lowered her leg from its flexing position. One or more parts of that speech hit the mark. She stood slowly, allowing the towel to slip from her shoulders and onto the floor. Her eyes narrowed. "Get out."

I shrugged and stood. "Whatever you say. But you had better do a little more work on that misunderstood-widow routine. Your next visitor will probably be a police sergeant who is definitely not a game player."

"The relationship I had with Preston is none of your business."

"I know. I just thought you needed to talk."

She crossed her arms over her chest and studied me for a long moment. Then she said, "He got tired of me, okay? Just like he eventually got tired of all his toys and tossed them aside to make way for the new ones. You know, it used to be my picture that was in the middle on his desk. My only consolation in this game we called a marriage was knowing that some day that damned horse would lose the center position."

"Was he seeing another woman?" I asked again, hoping for a straight answer this time.

She let out a frustrated sigh and pushed her hair back in an impatient gesture. "There were a lot of them. No one special. He didn't try to hide it from me. Sometimes he'd even be really brazen about it."

"Is that why you come on the way you do?"

She shrugged and said nothing, but held my gaze while a

slight smile played at the corners of her mouth.

"Why didn't you leave him?"

The moisture on her face had dried, leaving behind a kind of glow, which struck a note of discord. Brides glow. Widows don't. She gazed up at the ceiling as if the answer might be written there, then looked directly at me—or maybe it was through me. I wasn't sure. Once again, she said nothing.

Without breaking her gaze, I asked, "Did you send him those letters?"

"No," she answered immediately and then, just as quickly, realized she had fumbled at a very crucial point.

"How did you know about the letters?" I asked.

"Preston showed them to me." She avoided eye contact as she spoke, then looked at me, daring me to challenge her.

I didn't want to disappoint her. "They were mailed to his office and he told me that Irna and Grace were the only other people who knew about them."

"He lied." She didn't even blink.

"Someone lied," I allowed.

I have no idea how long we would have stood there, staring at each other, so I don't know whether to bless or curse Sergeant O'Henry for his timing. I do know that I was more than a little disappointed when the doorman rang Diana's apartment, announcing the detective's arrival.

As we waited for O'Henry to find his way to the apartment, I wished Diana would change into something that would make her look a little more like a grieving widow and a little less like an aerobics instructor. But I didn't say anything for fear she would just throw a robe on, leaving O'Henry to speculate what, if anything, she wore underneath. I had to settle for being grateful I hadn't accepted her offer of a drink. O'Henry might have been inclined to lock us both up for lack of decorum.

"Look, Diana. There's a lot that hasn't been said here, and I can just about promise you that things are going to get worse for you before they get better. So, if that happens, and you decide you really want to talk—not spar, talk—then let me know." There was a knock at the door before she could respond.

When O'Henry entered the room, he didn't speak at first. He looked from Diana to me then back again, trying to figure out whether we added up. He was holding the small notebook he had been using in Hauser's office. He gave Diana a solemn nod.

"I am very sorry about your husband, Mrs. Hauser. I would like to ask you a few questions, then I'll leave you two to your commiserating."

"That's all right," I said, pretending to ignore the bite in his tone. "I have to be going." I took my coat from the brass rack. It would be interesting to stay around to see how these two handled each other, but I needed to get back to the store.

"Don't go too far," O'Henry suggested.

"I'll try to keep a tight leash on myself." I turned to Diana and said, "If you need anything, be in touch." The hell with O'Henry. Let him think what he wanted.

"Quint." She stopped me halfway out the door. I turned to her. She had paled a little, as if the enormity of the situation had finally begun to have an effect on her. She said, "Thank you," but I think she wanted to say a whole lot more.

When I had left the office to give Diana Hauser the news, I'd handed the reins over to Fred Morison. At the time it seemed easier than finding someone else. I should have gone to the trouble. When I got back to the office, I found that Fred had taken his temporary elevation of duties to heart. He was seated at my desk, sipping out of my coffee mug, deep in conversation with Irna Meyers. When I walked into the room, it was like someone had suddenly turned their sound buttons off. Irna straightened her skirt and Fred slurped some coffee. They stared at me as I approached my desk. "Fred, thanks for watching things," I said.

"Anytime, Quint."

"Are they finished upstairs?"

Fred nodded. "All over except the questions." Then he added, "Who do you think did it?"

"I think I'll leave any speculating to the police," I lied.

Fred shook his head, smiling to himself, apparently reveling in the fact that he could be a part of anything so exciting as a murder.

"How is Mrs. Hauser?" Irna asked.

"As well as can be expected." I thought that sounded noncommittal enough. I really didn't know how to answer the question. What could I say? "Well, Irna, first she laughed, then she felt sorry for herself, then she got reflective. I thought she was going through puberty."

"They asked me how someone could have gotten in there to replace those pills." Irna assumed a defensive position, head high, chest out, hands clasped behind her back. "I told them that Hauser's employees trusted one another. No one felt that locking doors and filing cabinets was necessary."

"Who are *they*?"

She cleared her throat. She didn't want to have to repeat this. "Detective O'Henry and Mr. Griffin."

I looked from Irna to Fred and detected a certain smugness that I had not previously been aware of. I should have been suspicious. "Is there a punch line here?"

The phone rang. Fred answered and, smiling, handed the receiver to me. It was Griffin. He wanted to see me.

I hung up the phone and, without looking up, said, "I can take it from here, Fred," hoping they would both take the cue.

They did. I waited until they both filed from the room before cringing and collapsing into the chair Diana Hauser had occupied the day before that seemed like such a long time ago.

"Quint, thank you for coming." Griffin gave my hand a firm shake before gesturing me into the chair across from his desk. I sat and he straightened the knot in his tie and cleared his throat. I had never noticed how smooth and immaculate his hands were. I wondered if he had them manicured. Somehow that fit.

He folded his hands in front of him and stared at them, shaking his head. "Terrible, terrible waste. Senseless. Why?" Then he shifted his gaze and stared at me. I had the feeling he was testing me rather than looking for an answer. Then he snapped out of it and was business as usual again.

"I understand you were involved in some kind of investigation for Hauser. Something about some letters he was getting. What was that all about?" He asked the question casually, like there was no doubt in his mind that I would fill him in on every detail. He was wrong.

"Hauser hired me as a private investigator. One of the reasons he hired me was because he thought I could keep my mouth shut. He was right."

Griffin leaned forward in a predatory manner and said very slowly, "He's dead now, McCauley. You won't be betraying his trust."

I shook my head. "I'm sorry. I have to respect Hauser's request."

"Very well," he said. "I have other ways of gathering my information."

"That's fine," I said, sure he was speaking the truth.

74

Griffin's composure cracked for a second and a little irritation seeped out. Then he leaned back in his chair, once again totally composed. "Well, I think you know what I have to do now." From the tone of his voice, he might have been discussing the weather. "We've got a problem here. I don't think I have to tell you how ludicrous this situation looks. Not only is our security so lax that someone was able to replace Preston Hauser's vitamins with God knows what kind of poison, but the head of security happened to be sitting right in front of Preston when he took those pills." Griffin shook his head. "Doesn't look good at all. What do you think I should do about that?"

I sensed this wasn't the time to ask for a raise. "I think you've got that figured out."

Griffin nodded to me, acknowledging my perceptiveness. Then he said, "Don't get me wrong, McCauley. I don't blame you personally. Hauser liked to look at this store as a big happy family. He never gave security much thought. But, someone has to be held accountable here, and I'm afraid that someone is you."

When I was fourteen, I was fired from my first job as stock boy at the local grocery. The manager, Mr. Sekera, thought I was helping myself to fresh produce. I felt exactly the same way now as I did more than twenty-five years before—ashamed, hurt, and more than anything, angry. Back then, I was angry because it hadn't been me stealing the fruit and I knew I'd been railroaded. The same bad deal didn't feel any better this time.

"So, I'm elected scapegoat. I think it stinks but I can't say I'm surprised."

"Quint," he said. "You disappoint me. I thought you'd bear up."

"Griffin, you're an ass." I needed that. "Well," I said, rising, "I guess this will give me time to concentrate my efforts on the investigation."

Griffin leaned forward, his eyes narrowing. "McCauley, perhaps I didn't make myself clear. I just fired you."

"Maybe I didn't make myself clear. You didn't hire me to investigate those letters you're so curious about. Hauser did."

"Why don't you leave the sleuthing to the police. You're out of your league."

"Maybe. But you're not the one to knock me back to the minors."

The color was beginning to rise in Griffin's face. "Don't be so sure."

"You know what I find really satisfying about this whole thing? I get this warm feeling inside me knowing that you might wind up working for a woman who steals lingerie out of her own store. I wouldn't mind being a fly on the wall at your next board meeting."

"People swat flies. They are disposed of that quickly and there is never any call for remorse."

I placed both hands on Griffin's desk and leaned toward him. "Your mother could drop dead in this store's every-day-china section and you'd only feel remorse if she took down a display with her." Griffin's jaw muscles were tight so I pushed a little harder. "And don't expect me to get all wobbly-kneed at your veiled threats. I don't jump when you tell me to, I don't buy into your corporate climber bullshit, and"—I smiled—"I don't answer to a woman who is her own store's number-one enemy."

"Get out," Griffin said.

"I was just leaving." I straightened up. "Have fun counting the lingerie."

9

Lois, the secretary for my office group, avoided my eyes as I walked into my office for the last time. The gossip lines had been fast and, this time, accurate.

I stopped in front of my desk and just stared at it, not really thinking anything. "Can I get you something?" It was Lois. She stood outside the door.

"No. Thanks."

She hesitated. "A box?"

I looked at the sum of my personal effects. I'd stowed my briefcase containing the files in the trunk of my car before I'd driven out to the Hausers' condominium. There wasn't much left—a stained bar towel, a battered baseball, a knife, and a chipped coffee mug. I told her I could manage without a box. I didn't hear her leave, but when I looked back at the door, I was alone. It occurred to me that I would miss Lois's quiet efficiency. And her Christmas cookies.

I put the baseball on the mug and the mug on the towel and wished I had taken Lois up on her box offer. I sheathed the bird-and-trout knife, which had never been close enough to either of those species to pose a threat. It had served me well, though, as a salami slicer and letter opener. I stopped to admire its rosewood handle before sliding it into my sports jacket pocket.

"Quint?" It was Art Judson. When I turned toward him, he approached me. "God, Quint, I'm sorry. What a rotten, rotten break."

"Compared to Hauser, I guess I got off easy."

He managed an uncomfortable laugh. "Yes, I guess so." He looked around my office. "Can I help you with anything?"

"No." I gestured toward my pile of belongings. "I travel light."

"Listen, Quint," Art said and, before continuing, stared out the window for several seconds.

He looked, as always, like he'd stepped out of *GQ*. It occurred to me that I could not imagine this man looking sloppy. I couldn't even imagine him eating a hamburger. Every thread of his custom-tailored suit was immaculate, his shoes gleamed, and even though his hands were in his pockets, I was sure his shirt bore the Arthur Judson trademark—monogrammed cuffs. I was able to confirm my theory when, in a gesture of frustration, he ran a hand over, not through, his hair.

Finally he said, "You really must have done a number on Griffin."

"How insensitive of me."

He smiled. "You'll like this. He usually doesn't forget to collect the keys from someone he just fired." When I didn't respond, he added, "Of course, you don't have to give them to me. You could hand deliver them to Griffin himself. It might do you some good."

I thought about that, then decided it was a bad idea. I handed Art the keys. "No. I don't think I want to see him again. Not right now anyway. Tell you what, though. Why don't you tell him I'll send him the key to the executive washroom?"

Art looked puzzled. "But we don't have an executive washroom."

"I know. But maybe just for a second Griffin will think he's been locked out of it all these years."

He chuckled. "You'll do okay, Quint." Then he added, "I hear you were working on some kind of investigation for

Hauser. Was he in some kind of trouble?"

"Are you sure all Griffin sent you for was the key?"

"What's that supposed to mean?" I couldn't tell if Art was genuinely hurt or just faking it.

I shook my head. "Sorry. Guess I'm a little touchy today. I really can't tell you anything about the investigation. It's confidential."

He nodded and paused. "Did it have anything to do with me? Was Hauser investigating me?" He looked right at me when he asked that question.

"Not exactly. Although he did mention that you owed more than a few bucks to some rather unsavory characters." When Art didn't answer, I said, "Are you beginning to wish you had taken him up on his loan offer?"

His laugh was bitter and that surprised me a little. "There are worse things than being in debt to the mob."

"If there are, I don't think I want to imagine them." Art was silent, so I added, "Like what?"

"With a loan shark, at least you know where you stand. Pay up or you die. But with Hauser, he made sure you kept owing him. He never let you pay it off."

I tried to let that sink in for a minute and when that didn't help I said, "Can you be a little more specific?"

He hesitated, as if weighing whether he should tell me anything. "I borrowed ten grand from him last year. Gambling debts again." He shrugged. "Guess I'm a slow learner. Anyway, he loaned me the money—no interest— said he just wanted to help me out. Everything was fine for a couple weeks. Then he starts asking me to do things for him."

"Do things?" I said when he stopped. "What kind of things?"

"Fix him up with women—beautiful young women. He was very particular. At first I didn't mind. I know these things go on. I've been a party in a number of extracurricular relationships. I didn't think much of it except I guess I thought he was kind of crazy. I mean, he's got Diana waiting for him at home. Why does he need something extra?" Art started cracking his knuckles. One at a time. "But I'm not a procurer. I wouldn't have minded introducing him to a woman now and then, but he made me feel like a pimp." Art stopped here and folded his arms across his chest.

I waited.

Finally, he cleared his throat and continued. "Like I said, Hauser liked them young. And innocent. No whores for him. He liked to pick from the Hauser Foundation scholarship candidates. Several of the winners are studying somewhere without a shred of talent." He shook his head and stared out the window before he continued. "I felt like a real lowlife. I'd get friendly with these women—girls really—you know, big-brother like, and then I'd tell them Hauser wanted to see them alone. Some of them didn't even know what was happening until it was over. Some of them knew exactly, but figured it was worth a scholarship."

I thought about what he had just told me, then said, "I'm missing something here. Why didn't you just tell him to take a hike? What was he going to do? Take the ten grand back from the loan shark?"

"It wasn't that simple. By the time I wanted out, I was in debt to him for a whole lot more than ten grand."

"What do you mean?"

"Gambling wasn't a pleasure to me, it was a compulsion. I couldn't stop. Hauser kept giving me money, feeding my habit." He shrugged. "It was expensive for him, but I guess money wasn't a bad exchange for having someone to manipulate. It was a power thing with him."

"But you did stop."

"Yeah. I met someone who introduced me to Gambler's Anonymous, and I finally got the nerve up to tell Hauser he'd have to find another dating service. He laughed at me,

80

said I'd never last. He was going to fire me, but never did. I threatened to tell a few select individuals about his bad habits, but I don't think that worried him any. Hauser considered himself pretty much impenetrable. You know, he hated flying but made a big show out of doing it. Like he wanted everyone to see that he wasn't letting it control his life. He was in charge." He reflected on that before saying, "I wonder who had the last laugh. Anyway, before he got around to canning me, Griffin put in a word for me. I don't know how much difference it made, but I guess it didn't hurt."

"Griffin. Salt of the earth, isn't he?"

Art shrugged and chuckled. "Whatever."

"Have you paid off your loan officers yet?"

"I'm working on it."

"What about Hauser?"

He studied me, trying to read behind the question. "I still owed him."

We both must have heard the noise, because simultaneously we turned and saw Fred Morison standing in the doorway. I had no idea how long he had been there. Apparently Art didn't either.

"Listen, Quint," Art said, straightening his tie and adjusting his jacket. "If you need anything, let me know." I wondered if he appeared as awkward to Fred as he did to me at that moment.

"Let's have a drink sometime." If there was more to Art's story, I wanted to hear it.

"Sure," he said and walked out.

"What was that all about?" Fred said after Art was out of earshot.

"Nothing," I said. "Are you my replacement?"

Fred tried to appear modest. "Yes. I am."

That news brought my situation home harder than the actual firing. It wasn't so much that I felt bad about losing this job. It was just that I didn't feel like starting over. I realize that some overachievers begin law school at forty-five and have a thriving practice going by the time they are fifty. What would Sunday supplement editors use for feature-story material without them? But not me. The day I stopped aspiring to greatness and decided it was okay to be average was a great day for me. I found a lot of freedom in the relief I felt. Who knows; maybe that's why Maggie dumped me. Why latch onto a guy who doesn't care whether or not he makes *Encyclopaedia Britannica* when you could have someone who wanted nothing less than chief justice of the United States? Now they were telling me how much they thought of the job I did at Hauser's by replacing me with Fred Morison. What an epitaph.

Fred didn't make it any easier for me when he said, "Can I help you move anything out?"

"No thanks, Fred. I think I can handle it."

He was looking at the walls now. "My wife made a really nice latch-hook rug that would look great in here. What do you think, Quint?"

"Sunset over the west rim of the Grand Canyon?"

"No." He thought very hard for a moment. "I think it's a Rocky Mountain scene. Real nice though."

I nodded. "I'll bet."

"You never did much with this place—you know, to make it personal, your own place."

"Very perceptive of you, Fred."

"I'm gonna let people know this is my office, I work here, I run this department. When someone walks in here, they're gonna know that Fred Morison runs this place."

I tried to imagine what devices Fred would use to spread his image, what his individual stamp would be. He often talked about all the hunting and fishing he did with his brother-in-law and how the two of them belonged to a survivalist group that met monthly somewhere up near

Lake Geneva. He bragged about the deer, foxes, and rabbits they hunted. I pictured the walls studded with the heads of creatures out of Disney films. Bambi, Thumper, the whole lot of them, doomed to spend eternity watching Fred Morison clean his nails with a pocketknife and pack his pipe tobacco with a large-headed nail.

"Well, Quint, it's been—"

I held up a hand. "Please, Fred, spare me."

"I just don't want any hard feelings," he said.

"There are none. Trust me." As I walked out the door I added, "Take care of yourself, Fred, and don't forget to take your vitamins."

I was trying to leave the place behind me as quickly as possible, so as I walked out onto Michigan Avenue, I didn't notice the stretch limousine pull up to the curb about a quarter block ahead of me. By the time I reached it, a uniformed man had one hand on the rear-door handle.

"Mr. McCauley," he said and I hesitated, not sure, even though I had heard my name, that he was speaking to me. He opened the door and, with a wave of his hand, gestured me into the backseat. I remember what my mother said about getting into strange cars, especially ones with darkened windows. So, even though it was a limo, a white one at that, and I was feeling pretty fatalistic, I peered into the car before taking the plunge.

A handsome, elderly woman wearing large-framed glasses and a red beret sat alone in the backseat. I'd seen her earlier that day coming out of Preston's office.

"Mr. McCauley, I'm Grace Hunnicutt, Preston's sister. I must talk with you. Can you give me a few minutes?"

I glanced at the chauffeur. If the two of them were planning to execute me gangland style and dump me in the nearest landfill, the hired help's expression wasn't giving them away.

"Well," I said to the woman, "time is one thing I have plenty of now." I slid into the backseat, stacking my belongings in the corner. I was facing her and would be riding backward through traffic.

Her smile was strained but gracious. We shook hands. It was warm and dry, and her grip surprisingly firm.

"I'm sorry about your brother, Mrs. Hunnicutt," I said.

She glanced quickly out the window, her eyes blinking rapidly behind the bifocaled lenses. "Thank you. And please call me Grace." She paused, and cleared her throat. "It's never easy to lose a sibling. But when it is the little brother you spent a large portion of your youth getting out of scrapes, well, it seems as though I let him down."

"I know how you feel," I said.

"Yes," she regarded me, "you would, wouldn't you?" Then she quickly added, "Don't misunderstand me, there was nothing you could have done. I realize that."

Then she said, "Drive, Marshall," and we pulled away from the curb.

"Does he know where he's going?" I asked.

"It's not important," Grace said, smiling, and added, "Would you care for a drink?"

She pushed a button and a well-stocked bar appeared. A couple hours ago it had been too early in the day to drink, especially with Diana Hauser, but a lot had happened since then. I poured myself a scotch.

"I'd like a vodka, please," she said.

We sipped on our drinks and gazed out the window at the passing scenery. Watching the traffic and the pedestrians through shaded windows was like standing behind mirrored glass. It evoked a curious blend of omnipotence and voyeurism. I turned to Grace. She was definitely a Hauser, those same cold, gray eyes and the Hauser carriage. Even seated, you could tell she was a tall woman, and although she might never have been conventionally beautiful—her nose was a bit too broad and her face too long and narrow—she had an elegance about her that stood up pretty well to time. She wore her silver-gray hair short and feathered beneath the red hat.

She finally broke the silence. "I know you were working for my brother and I know why. In fact, I was the one who suggested Preston hire you. I'd like you to continue investigating those letters. I will, of course, pay you."

I shook my head. "That won't be necessary. Preston paid in advance. I don't think I've exactly given him his money's worth yet." She nodded.

"I only wish I had been able to convince Preston earlier to get help." She sighed and looked out the window. "I want to assist you. I will do anything I can to find the person who did this." She turned back to me and smiled. "I can be very useful. There was very little about my brother's affairs that I didn't know. For that matter, I'm sure I know more about the store and its people than Preston ever cared to."

A thought occurred to me. "Were those your notes in the suspect employees' files?"

She looked away briefly and I'm not sure whether the smile was triggered by pride or good-natured embarrassment. "Preston used to tell me that I have more sources than a gossip columnist. Perhaps I do. At any rate, that inept detective Preston hired needed all the help he could get. You will find that I have a great deal of knowledge that will also be very helpful to you. I only ask that you keep me informed." She looked out the window again. "When Preston died, the Hauser name died. Whoever is responsible must be made to pay."

"Do you have any ideas?" I asked.

She smoothed the suede on her handbag, watching the nap go light, then dark again. Finally she said, "Let's just say I have my suspicions. But I have no proof and, at this point, I would rather not influence your investigation."

"What is your opinion of Diana Hauser?"

She looked up from her purse. "My dear sister-in-law? Diana is very much like a pedigreed Blue Himalayan cat I used to own. Lovely to look at, but adept at very little aside from preening. That is not to say, of course, that my brother's wife is not capable of doing whatever is necessary to make her happy."

"What makes Diana happy?"

She drained her glass of vodka and said, "If you have to ask me that, you're not as smart as Preston thought you were."

"Maybe I am, maybe I'm not. But I don't think Diana is that simple to classify."

"Perhaps not," Grace conceded. "I do tend to give her credit for very little aside from taking up space." She sighed. "When Preston married her, it was all very sudden. They met in California and were married within a few weeks. When he brought her home, I was very hopeful. I thought perhaps the reason he had married a woman so young was to ensure the continuance of the Hauser name. It wasn't long before I realized that Preston's wife was not exactly brimming with maternal instincts." She paused. "There isn't very much left to the Hauser family name, Mr. McCauley. I want to know who threatened my brother and who carried out that threat."

"What about the police?" I asked. "Are you going to have the same talk with them?"

She gave me a curious glance, as if she were trying to tell if I was being a wise guy. I did my best to imitate the chauffeur.

"Having the police prodding into one's personal life in order to solve a crime is, at best, a very awkward situation. It's like . . ." She hesitated, searching for a comparison.

I tried to help. "Sort of like using nuclear weapons to rid

your garden of gophers." Grace lifted one eyebrow. "You accomplish the initial objective, but the side effects can be brutal."

She smiled and nodded her head. "Precisely. I'm glad to see that you understand, Quint. Also," she continued, "I don't know whether I can count on the police to keep me informed."

"You seem pretty certain that I'm going to need your help."

She laughed slightly. "Perhaps I'm a bit overconfident, but I think you will realize that I'm your best and only reliable source for information concerning the Hausers." Reaching into her purse, she said, "I can either be reached at the store or at one of these numbers." She handed me a card with her name and two numbers written on it. "One is my apartment and the other is Preston's estate in Wayne."

I nodded. "Who's going to run the store?"

She smiled. "Mr. Griffin fancies he is. I have news for him. I may not have the Hauser name anymore, but I have the Hauser blood." Her tone became more serious. "I know you have been fired by Griffin. I don't feel that move was deserved. Given a little time, I may be able to reinstate you as security chief."

"It's not that important," I said.

"What is important?" she asked.

"Finishing a job."

Grace nodded. The car pulled over and stopped in almost the same spot where I'd been picked up. "Thank you, Quint."

I smiled. "For what?"

"For listening to an old woman. And for easing my mind. You're competent. But you probably aren't adept at this sort of thing yet so promise me you will be cautious."

These Hausers had more in common than their posture. Like Preston, Grace had the ability to deliver a compliment and slam dunk you at the same time.

She continued. "I also feel I can trust you. There aren't many people I can say that about anymore."

She tapped on the window and the door opened. I glanced up at the chauffeur and said to Grace, "He's good. Don't let him go."

I stepped out onto Michigan Avenue, mug and baseball in hand, and watched as the limousine, carrying its anonymous occupant, slid into traffic.

10

ELAINE WAS PLANTED on the sofa. She had on argyle socks and the blue, ratty-looking robe. The room was hazy with smoke, and cigarette butts erupted from the blue ceramic ashtray on the coffee table. Elaine was leaning over it, squinting one eye to keep out the stream of smoke she was exhaling. She held the cigarette poised, trying to find a space large enough to extinguish it in.

"Allow me," I said, taking the ashtray with one hand and her cigarette with the other. I doused the butt under the faucet and, after checking to make sure nothing was smouldering, emptied the ashtray. I replaced it on the table.

"Thank you," she said, dropping in the match she had just used to light another cigarette. She coughed and waved the smoke out of her face. Then she offered me one from the pack.

"No thanks. I'll just stand here and breathe for a while."

She nodded and turned back to the game show in progress on television.

"Mind if I open a window?"

"Good luck," she said.

I walked over to one of the windows and immediately sized up the problem. "These windows don't open."

"I know."

I examined the window that did not open. "We're on the twelfth floor, aren't we?"

"Uh huh."

"Then why is there a dead fly on the windowsill?"

"I'm not sure," she said, tearing her attention from the TV and giving my question serious consideration. "I think it adds character to the room. A little mystery." She gave it another moment. "Sort of like the leopard they found dead way up on Kilimanjaro. What was it doing all the way up there?" Her voice drifted off, then came back. "Stiff as a carp."

I nodded. "Just the metaphor that came to my mind too. So," I turned to her. "Have a good day?"

"Yeah. Great. I love relaxing." Then, as almost an afterthought, "How about you?"

"Oh, not too eventful." I sat in one of the utilitarian chairs. It was surprisingly comfortable. "My boss dropped dead while I was talking to him. Probably poisoned. His wife laughed when I told her, then insisted that she didn't do it. The police detective assigned to the case probably suspects that the widow and I are having a torrid affair. Then the general manager decided that if the head of security allowed the owner of the store to be murdered in his presence, there was no telling what else he might do. So he fired me."

At first, Elaine didn't respond. She just stared at me for several moments, analyzing the veracity of my statement. Apparently satisfied, she dropped back to her reclining position and stared at the ceiling. Finally she said, "Are you?"

Somewhere along the way I had lost the thread. "Am I what?"

"Having an affair with the widow? She sounds like your type."

When I didn't answer, she sat up, pulled her legs up to her chest, and wrapped her arms around them. "Were you really fired?"

"Yep," I said, nodding.

"I'm sorry," she said, and I could tell she meant it. Then she seemed to consider what I had just told her. "Who was killed?"

"Preston Hauser."

She let that sink in. Then she said, "Wow," without much enthusiasm.

I nodded. I was going to tell her not to worry about my keeping up on the rent, at least for a while, but she didn't seem to be thinking about money. We both sat there, in a comfortable silence, for several minutes.

Then I said, "Unemployment makes me hungry."

"I know what you mean." She dismally surveyed the crumpled potato chip bag and empty candy wrappers strewn around the couch.

"Do you like Guinness stout?"

"Never had it."

"Why don't you get some pub-crawling clothes on. I'll treat you to the taste sensation of your life."

While she changed, I called Harry.

"Damn, Quint. What did you get yourself mixed up in this time? I thought you had a sedentary desk job."

"Not anymore."

"What do you mean?"

"They fired me."

"That's tough."

"Yeah, well, that's the breaks. Anyway," I continued, trying to get Harry back on the track, "did you find out anything about those letters."

"Some. But not a lot. A few sets of prints. Yours and Hauser's are probably on there. I'll need sets of anyone who touched these letters."

"Make sure you get a set of Diana Hauser's."

"Well, your policeman friend, Sergeant O'Henry, is tending to those tasks."

"Did he give you the fourth letter?"

"Yes. I'm still working on that one. It's great to be doing freelance work for the police department. I'm going to enjoy sending them the bill."

I laughed. Harry had considered himself underpaid when he was with the department.

"What about the blood?"

"Ah, now that's interesting. It's really going to narrow down your list of suspects." Harry was enjoying himself now.

"Okay, Harry. Spit it out."

"The cat did it."

"The cat?"

"Yes. The cat. Smeared across Preston Hauser's person is cat blood."

Harry's use of the word "person" was like a finger jabbing me in the side. Sometimes you forget that an investigation is more than a puzzle.

"Anything else you can tell me?"

"Not yet," he said, catching my mood. "Quint, are you going to tell me where you're living these days?"

"If you need to get hold of me, the number is 555-4897."

"I've got time if you want to talk," he said.

I looked up as Elaine walked into the living room from the hall. She wore faded jeans, western-style boots, and a bulky sweater. Her legs were long and slender and she wore the jeans like they were a second skin. Her hair was thick and had a lot of curl in it so it fanned out against her shoulders.

"I can't talk now, Harry. I'll stop by your lab tomorrow."

The White Hart looked and felt like an English pub. From the shingle above the door bearing the sign of the buck's head, to the dart boards on the walls, it did justice to that fine tradition, as a great place to go for a little friendly conversation or for solitude. You could get both here. In addition to Guinness, served at basement temperature, you could get several brands of British ale. You could also order hot sandwiches and sometimes they even served meat pies and bridies.

Elaine was about to experience her first Guinness. I told her it took a discriminating individual to appreciate the taste. She assured me that she was every bit as discriminating as I was and took a sip.

"This tastes like motor oil," she grimaced, then quickly added, "but good," and had another swallow.

By the time she finished the half pint, she decided it was growing on her. I ordered two more when our sandwiches came.

"Can you do anything besides be a security guard?" she asked, biting into her corned-beef sandwich.

"Let's hope so."

"Do you have a degree?"

I shook my head and swallowed a bite of beef. "I went to Northern for two years. English major." I shrugged. "Never knew what I'd do with it, but I liked studying literature. Then I drew a low lottery number. Got drafted."

I told her about Vietnam and my stint with the First Cavalry. She kept firing questions and I kept revealing more about my past—flying helicopters, the police force, taking time off to bum around.

Finally I interrupted her barrage. "What is this, Elaine, twenty questions?"

She nodded, nibbling on a piece of corned beef that had fallen out of her sandwich. "I've still got about fifteen more. Was there ever a Mrs. McCauley?"

"Yes. In fact there still is." Elaine stopped chewing and I went on before she could interject. "She's a lovely lady. Lives in Downers Grove with my father."

Elaine rolled her eyes and called me a smart ass. She smiled when she said it though.

"Actually, there was another one, for about four years."

"What happened?"

"I had her bumped off. She asked too many questions."

Elaine took one of my cigarettes. "Where is she now?"

"California last I heard. Isn't that where people go to start over?"

She lit the cigarette and drew in the smoke. Rubbing her finger over a pair of carved initials in the table, she said, "Yeah, but it doesn't always take."

"So I hear."

"What did you do after Vietnam and before the police force?"

It had taken Maggie a month to find out what Elaine had learned in two minutes. "I pitched in the minors."

Her eyebrows shot up and she abruptly swallowed. "Really? Where?"

I named a town outside Kenosha, Wisconsin.

"What was it? Double, triple A?"

"Double."

"Tell me about it. What was it like? Why did you quit?"

I leaned back in the chair and pushed my hands in my pockets. I hadn't thought about the minors for a long time. She had hit on a few of my very best years. The early ones were especially good, when I moved steadily up to a double-A team and thought I wouldn't stop until I hit the majors. I was a little surprised that it felt so good to remember those times, and she seemed to be listening.

So when she said, "What was your ERA?" I was off.

"Around three."

"That's good."

"I was consistent." I nodded to myself. "On rare occasions, dazzling."

She leaned forward. "Did you ever pitch a no-hitter?"

I felt like she had read a copy of my life. "Where did you get these questions?"

94

"Did you?"

I recited it to her as I recalled it. "It was top of the ninth, two out. The crowd was on its feet. You could hear the wind in the flags. I was one batter away from a no-hitter. And I felt good. Really good. I knew I could get this guy out. It was my last season. I knew I didn't have whatever it took to make the majors, but I figured if I could get this one guy out, I'd have one really fine memory to take with me, one I could keep tucked away and pull out when I needed a shot."

She nodded slowly. "What happened?"

My memory traveled a little farther and the spell broke. I shrugged and drained the mug of stout. "He hit the ball out of the park and they gave it to me as a souvenir." Now I remembered why I hadn't thought about this for so long. "I clutched."

After studying me for a moment, Elaine said, "Sometimes failure is easier to handle than success."

I didn't want to think about the depth of that statement. Not now anyway. "Yeah, well, in the grand scheme of my life I guess it didn't make much difference."

She didn't say anything.

I settled up our tab and we walked out into the bitter January night. It had been snowing pretty hard and a couple inches had accumulated already. The snow muffled the city noises, leaving the night bright, calm, and silent. I felt good. Considering the events of the day, I hadn't thought that possible.

Somewhere on the way to the car, Elaine's mittened hand found its way into mine. That felt good too.

11

I DECIDED THAT the snow was a lot more appealing when it was highlighting Elaine's hair than when I was trying to drive in it. The roads were slick and we passed a couple fender-benders on the way to the apartment. Elaine was going to see about getting me my own parking space. In the meantime, her yellow Mustang remained warm and secure underneath the building. What could I do? Insist that she be the one to play musical cars with the auto population on the north side? I would never be able to look my mother squarely in the eyes again. I dropped Elaine at the entrance to our building and promised to call if I thought I wouldn't make it back from finding a parking place before morning. She smiled and shook her head.

I weaved up and down side streets. It was worse than usual because of the weather and the streets that were snow routes were off limits for parking. I found myself musing over my new living arrangement. I knew it was too soon to get involved with anyone. It had only been a couple of days, although it seemed a whole lot longer, since Maggie had shown me the door. I was still seeing a lot of things in terms of Maggie, and here was Elaine. Without any obvious effort, she was slipping into my thoughts as surreptitiously as her hand had slid into mine. Maybe I shouldn't worry about it. But then again, maybe I should. Maybe I was experiencing the rebound effect and Elaine was the unfortunate third party. Maybe Elaine was just being nice.

A very small parking space saved me from further self-analysis. I wedged my Honda in between a large Plymouth and an old Volkswagen and, because there was no traffic and the streets seemed better for traveling, started walking down the center of the street. It was to be a long four blocks.

I heard the car before I saw it. Its headlights were off and it seemed to come out of nowhere. While its origin might have been questionable, its destination wasn't, and that destination was definitely me.

The car came from behind me, and the skidding noise it made in the snow before the tires caught caused me to jerk around. It was almost on top of me when I dove between two cars, into a space that I hoped was larger than it appeared. It wasn't. A jolt of pain shot through my knee as I jammed between two bumpers. I tried to extricate myself. The killer car made a hurried three-point turn at the end of the block, then roared back toward me. This time its brights were on.

With a painful jerk, I yanked my leg from between the bumpers and propelled myself with my good leg toward the parkway. I landed face first with a mouthful of snow as the big car smashed into the two cars. The impact pushed one of them onto the parkway. It landed less than a foot away. Time to move. I heard, rather than saw, the car retreat as I pushed myself up off the ground.

For the first few steps, I wasn't sure my knee was going to hold. It felt like an ice pick was digging around inside it. I hobbled down the sidewalk, keeping an eye out for the car and looking for an escape route. Maybe the driver had given up, figuring he had lost the advantage of surprise. No such luck.

I was near the end of the first block when the car came from around the corner, roared up over the curb, and slammed onto the sidewalk, its brights blinding me. Figuring I'd be better off in whatever protection the buildings and yards offered, I hobbled as fast as my knee would allow into the narrow space between two four-story apartment buildings. The car screeched to a stop, and a door slammed.

I quickly inventoried my assets and wished I had been using my old army-issue blade for a letter opener instead of the bird knife. I had to assume that if this person or persons had set out to kill me, they brought the equipment necessary to accomplish the job. Strange. A few minutes ago my pursuer was a big malevolent piece of machinery with no human qualities, just a big, mean hunk of metal. Somehow, knowing there was a person trailing me was a lot scarier. I took the knife from my pocket and drew it from its sheath. The three-inch blade didn't seem enough to make even a pigeon real edgy, but it was better than nothing.

There was an alley behind the apartment building but I rejected it as too well lit and too obvious a way for me to go. It was incredibly quiet and white behind these buildings and the snow was such a fine powder that I could move without a noise. Slinking through these yards, knife drawn, I felt like my presence desecrated the serenity.

Strange. Being stalked by some faceless enemy through the snow and alleys on the north side of Chicago wasn't all that different from being stalked by some faceless enemy through a rain forest on the other side of the world. In Chicago, you could put a hand on a building or a car—some symbol of civilization—but it wasn't there for you. The differences were only incidental. Bird and insect noises were replaced by the sound of distant cars with bad mufflers. You crept through the shadows of the buildings the same way you crept through the trees and tried to keep the whole thing impersonal.

I figured there was only one person. I heard only one car door shut.

I could probably make my way back to Elaine's by cutting through backyards and parking lots and by praying when I crossed the streets, but I wasn't sure I wanted to do that. Some people wanted me dead and I was real curious about their identity. If my current pursuer had a gun, I wasn't about to try to overpower him, but if I could get a glimpse of him, then that might be worth the effort. If he didn't shoot me, that is. I crouched behind some bushes near the gate to the alley and waited. The snow was falling harder now, and I had to keep mopping my eyes and face with my jacket sleeve. I realized there was sweat mixed in with the snow.

He appeared between the two apartment buildings, not making much effort to move quietly. Apparently without checking for tracks in the snow, he turned and walked through the yard, keeping close to the back of the building. Then he kept on walking toward the next one. He wasn't doing a very thorough job. Not that I was complaining, but I couldn't help but wonder how bad he wanted to find me.

My crouching position was causing my knee to fire frequent pain messages to my brain. I tried to ease some of my weight off of it and when I did, my foot slipped and I fell back against the chain-link fence. It clinked and groaned, and I froze.

My stalker stopped moving and turned in my direction, his gun drawn. He began moving toward me and I prayed he was just following a noise and not a sighting. He approached the bushes from the side opposite my hiding place. As he neared, I was able to get an idea of his size. He was big, a large frame carrying a lot of weight. He stopped, and I thought for a moment that he had made me. Then he stepped a couple feet closer to the bushes and close enough to a light in the alley to come partially into its illumination. He had either blond or gray hair, worn long. I could barely make out a beard and a small, sharp nose.

I tried to make myself smaller and realized that wasn't going to do me much good. In a few feet he would be standing right next to me. If he saw me, I would be the easiest game he ever bagged. Right now, I had a small advantage. I held my breath.

He hesitated again, listening and waiting. Then he glanced back at the space between the buildings. I hoped he wasn't waiting for reinforcements. A couple more steps and he was no more than two feet from me. I put the knife between my teeth, and hoped that two things would not happen—I wouldn't swallow the damned thing and I wouldn't have to use it. Taking a deep breath, I lunged at him from my hiding place and my knee buckled under me, throwing me off balance. Unable to hit him head on, I grabbed for his legs and he went down with a surprised grunt.

I reached for his arm, trying to wrestle the gun from his hand before he got a good grip on it again. Apparently he never lost it, because he smacked me in the face with the barrel and let out a yelp as he sliced his hand across the blade I was still clenching. He dropped the gun and grabbed his hand. I moved back, crouching, and took the knife in one hand while I groped for the gun with the other. The side of my face felt numb.

He cursed and lunged at me, reaching for my throat. I flew backward into the snow and tried to block him with my left arm, but I couldn't hold his weight. Instinctively, I brought my arms in to protect myself. He fell against me, impaling himself on the knife. His hands were at my throat. It was a long two seconds before his eyes flew open, registering surprise.

He pulled away from me, bellowing. Staggering backward, he groped at his chest with one hand, looking at the red expanding stain as if he couldn't figure it out. Then he looked at me and, putting two and two together, charged.

This time I was better prepared. I brought my legs up, and as he came down on me, I pushed him away from me, acrobatic style. He flew back and landed hard on the ground. He didn't move.

I went over to him, feeling the ground for his gun on my way. I didn't find it. He seemed to be out cold and that didn't make sense. There wasn't enough time for that much blood loss. I felt for a pulse. It was there, but faint.

I didn't know how deep a knife had to penetrate a large person before finding a crucial organ, and I didn't know how long it would take a man his size to die from blood loss. All I knew was that I was kneeling there, wiping the blood from the knife, wondering if it would ever come off.

Then I saw the cinder block beneath the back of his head. The impact had knocked him cold.

I looked at the back of the apartment building and considered waking someone up and calling the police. There weren't any lights on, but then this kind of scene is best viewed from a dark room.

I began to go through his pockets. Who was this guy? He looked vaguely familiar. Before I could find any identification, I heard a car coming down the alley and dropped any plans I had for sticking around. It might not be this guy's friend, but then it might. I made my way into the next yard and waited to see what the car was going to do. It slowed, then stopped one building away from the yard I'd just left. A car door opened and closed. The motor was still running. I took this as my clue to leave and started back to Elaine's place, staying clear of the alleys and the middle of the streets.

In spite of the cold, I was sweating, and I was starting to feel sick in the stomach, I put the knife back in its sheath. What an intimate weapon, the knife. But then, that's what killing someone is—as the man says, up close and personal, not like dropping out of the sky to pick up wounded men.

Bullets from invisible snipers would ricochet off the side of the helicopter and you'd fire back at a battalion of trees. It was as if the trees were doing the shooting and you wondered what you had done to make them to kill you.

Tonight had been closer—and a lot more personal.

12

I WAS GLAD Elaine's apartment building didn't have a doorman. I'm sure he would have viewed me as a suspicious character. And I was exactly that in torn pants and bloody jacket.

I was relieved to arrive at Elaine's door without running into anyone. I used the key she had given me, and the door opened onto a sight I wasn't ready for.

I thought I was in the wrong apartment at first. There were no lights on, but the illumination that spilled in from the hall showed me cushions off the couch and piles of papers and books strewn over the living room. Part of the shelving unit had been overturned.

"Elaine." I spoke in a normal voice at first, and when there was no response, I shouted. "Elaine!"

Then I saw a familiar-looking object next to the planter just inside the door. I bent down and picked up Elaine's purse. Oh God, I thought. She walked in on this and they didn't want any witnesses. Oh, God, please no.

I left the door partially open and moved into the kitchen, using what little light there was to make my way. Elaine kept her .38 in a kitchen drawer. Right now, a gun would be easier for me to use than a knife.

I removed the gun from the drawer. The apartment was so quiet, I thought I could hear the walls breathing. It felt empty. I thought of Elaine and where she might be and what might have happened to her and then I pushed any ideas I had from my mind. I didn't need a muddled head.

An object blocked the light for a moment. I spun around, dropping into a crouch, arms extended and gun pointed at the figure that stood frozen in the living room, out of the light.

I swallowed hard. "Don't move," I said, feeling like I had just ordered the Statue of Liberty to stay put.

"Quint?" A very small voice sounded both scared and hopeful.

"Elaine?" My voice wasn't much above a whisper.

"Yeah," she said. Then, "What are you doing?"

"I'm protecting the castle."

I got up and switched on the kitchen light.

Elaine stood in the middle of the mess in the living room, unharmed, hair tousled, hands in the pockets of her jacket, and all I wanted to do was hold her. So I did. Her head fit under my chin and I could smell the cold in her hair. She wrapped her arms around me, pulling me closer. I hadn't thought that possible.

After a moment she said, "Are you still holding the gun?"

I placed the gun on the coffee table and touched her face with my hand, as if the feel of her skin would verify her existence for me.

I stepped back and looked at the room.

"What happened?" I asked.

She noticed my disheveled appearance and before she could speak I said, "You first."

She took her jacket off, looked around for a place to put it, and dropped it on the floor. Then she replaced a cushion on the couch and sat down. "Well," she began, "when I got up here, I noticed someone going through the stairway door. I thought that was strange. No one takes the stairs from the twelfth floor unless the elevator's broken, and I had just used the elevator. I didn't think much of it until I opened the door and saw this." She gestured toward the

104

mess. "I was so mad I didn't think twice before tearing down those steps." She shrugged a little self-consciously. "I guess it wasn't a real bright thing to do, but I don't think he saw me. I didn't get much of a look at him either. By the time I got outside the building, he was getting into a car. I got part of the plate number. *BRE* something. I couldn't make it all out, but it was a dark car—dark and big."

"A '76 Monte Carlo," I said. "It now has a bashed-in grill."

She gave me a quizzical look. "Friends of yours?"

"We've gone a few rounds. You sure they didn't see you?"

"Yeah. He was carrying something though. It looked like a briefcase."

"Did you get a look at him?"

"Just his back and then just for a second. Big. He was wearing a khaki fatigue-type jacket. Long hair. I think it was kind of blond."

That clinched it. I didn't want to think about what might have happened if Elaine had arrived a minute earlier. The driver of the car must have seen Elaine get out of the car and me drive off in search of a parking space. After the big guy got back to the car, he and his buddy decided it would be great sport to track me and see if they could eliminate me by making me another routine road kill. Or by more conventional methods.

One thing bothered me a lot. How did they know where I was living? It would have been easy enough to follow me here, but there are fifteen floors of apartments. They had to know which one to go to. They had to know Elaine's name, and I didn't like that notion a bit. Who knew I was living here? I had given Sergeant O'Henry the address, and Harry my phone number. Pam. Pam?

"Is something wrong?" Elaine interrupted my puzzling.

"No. I was just thinking."

I checked and wasn't surprised to find that my briefcase, containing the files of Hauser's suspects, was missing.

"Can you tell if anything of yours was taken?"

Elaine tossed her hair back and laughed. "Not much to take. All my jewels are on loan to the Art Institute."

We both laughed a little, which eased the tension that comes from expecting to walk into a familiar scene and not finding it.

Then I realized that something didn't fit. I glanced at my watch. It was two-fifteen.

She caught the gesture. "In case you're wondering how all of that could have taken an hour." She walked over and picked her keys out of the planter that stood just inside the door. "Just where I left them before charging off after the bad guys. I've just spent forty-five minutes tracking down the maintenance man to let me back in."

"Did you leave him in a good mood?"

"Never found him. I came back here, hoping you'd show up."

She sat still for a minute, thinking. Then she started picking things up—a book here, a record album there. It was, at best, a half-hearted attempt. After a few minutes, she sank down on the floor, cross-legged. She sniffed and blinked her eyes rapidly.

"Bastards," she said.

I sat on the floor next to her, keeping my sore leg straight. "It's my fault."

She nodded. "I know." Then she looked at my torn pants. "I'm afraid to ask what happened to you." She paused. "Tell me."

"Well, that army-issue Wild Bill Hickok character and his chauffeur made a concerted effort to run me over. When that didn't work, Mr. Hickok switched to a more conventional weapon—a .38. So there I was, behind a dark apartment building, making tracks in the snow that a pack of cub scouts could follow, and all I had for a weapon was a knife I kept in my desk to open mail and butcher an occasional salami." I stopped. I didn't know how Elaine would react to the rest of the story. And that mattered a lot to me. I watched for some reaction from her as I continued, "I might have killed him, Elaine. He fell on the blade, but I was holding it and it was pointed in his direction."

When I finished she didn't say anything for a while and I couldn't read her thoughts from her expression. Finally she spoke. "Are you sure he was dead?"

I shook my head and explained about the arrival of someone, presumably his accomplice, at the scene.

She watched me and her whole body seemed tense and rigid. It was like she was waiting for me to pin this whole thing on myself. And she wasn't about to let me do that. "It was you or him. Would you rather it turned out the other way?" This woman could have a very good effect on a person's life. "Did you even know that someone wanted to kill you?" she prodded.

I shook my head.

"Well then," she said, as if that proved everything. I was inclined to let her convince me. She continued, "You must be getting somewhere on this. Someone thinks you're a threat."

"I wish I knew enough to be a threat."

She looked at me and didn't say anything. Her expression was impossible to read. Her hair was tousled and her eyes were bright. I held her gaze for too long and the moment passed. I turned away first.

"I'd better leave in the morning." I paused and added, "If I were a real gentleman, I'd leave now before they send in the next assault."

"But you're not going to, are you?"

I shook my head and sighed. "I've got to make a phone call."

"The police?"

I nodded.

"Do you think they'll believe you? I mean, that it was self-defense and all? Wasn't that Sergeant what's-his-name suspicious of you anyway?"

All those thoughts had already passed through my mind, but I knew it would be better in the long run if I came forward now, rather than waiting for them to find me. Then it *would* look like I had something to hide.

We had just about finished picking up the living room, righting the bookshelves and cleaning up spilled ashtrays, when Sergeant O'Henry arrived. It was after three A.M. He looked like a man who hadn't been awake for very long.

"I had a feeling I'd run into you again real soon," he said to me.

I introduced him to Elaine and he gave me a look that was a mixture of suspicion and admiration.

"You got any orange juice?" he asked Elaine.

"Pink grapefruit all right?"

"Great," he said. "Didn't have a chance to brush my teeth."

I nodded in understanding and wished he'd get on with this. I'm sure that was the intended effect. Elaine brought him the glass and he drank half of it.

"Who are you?" he said to Elaine.

Elaine crossed her arms over her chest, raised her chin an inch or two, and said, "I live here," like she was daring him to make something of it. I looked at her and smiled slightly. So Elaine was a closet rebel. I liked that.

O'Henry studied her for a moment, apparently deciding whether to pursue her statement. Then he turned back to me. "You *both* live here?"

"You can reach me here."

He shook his head and sat down. "You wanna tell me what happened?"

108

Elaine and I sat down, and I narrated the entire incident. He didn't interrupt me once and would occasionally jot something down in a small spiral notebook. When I got to the part about the knife, I placed it, still in its sheath, on the coffee table. O'Henry leaned over, squinting.

When I had finished, he said, "So you don't know who this guy was?"

I shook my head. "Like I said, he looked familiar."

O'Henry nodded, thinking. He was starting to annoy me. There's a very thin line between being cryptic and being a jerk and he was getting close to crossing it.

"Okay, O'Henry. Who was he? Preston Hauser's illegitimate son from a night of passion with an Amazon?"

"I don't know," he said. "Before you called, no one had reported the incident or complained about a fight or a body in their backyard. I'm still waiting for a confirmation that you didn't dream the whole thing."

I rubbed my eyes and tried to think. Maybe the guy's friend had taken him somewhere or maybe he'd left him there for the neighbors to discover over coffee in the morning.

The phone rang and the three of us looked at it like it was the jury marching in with the verdict. Elaine answered. "It's for you." She held the receiver out to O'Henry. He drained his juice glass and took the phone.

Elaine returned to the couch and sat next to me. We exchanged looks but I'm not sure if either of us had any idea what the other was thinking.

O'Henry didn't give away much of the conversation. Every now and then he'd say, "Uh huh," or, "Yeah," and would occasionally jot something down. Once he said, "You don't say." Then he said, "Oh yeah," with his inflection rising on the second word and he looked at me as he spoke into the phone. "You sure about that?" Then he chuckled and said, "Yeah, I guess that's true. Anything else?" He listened for a moment, then said, "Yeah, sure," and hung up.

Flipping the pages of his notebook, he walked back to the chair. Elaine and I looked at each other and this time I was sure we were thinking the same thing—"Quit milking the audience, O'Henry," or something to that effect.

"Well." O'Henry finally looked up from his notes. "There's a body all right, and it's dead. Right where you left it. Does the name"—he glanced at his notes, affecting a dramatic pause—"Carl Bonkowsky mean anything to you?"

The name was, like his face, vaguely familiar. But I couldn't connect the two. I told O'Henry that.

"Would it help if I told you he worked at Hauser's?"

I leaned forward, elbows on knees, and stared at the floor. He worked at Hauser's. I clicked off the departments. He wasn't in security. He wasn't a sales clerk, nor an administrative employee. Suddenly it clicked. I looked up at O'Henry and Elaine. "Shipping. He worked in shipping."

"Bingo," said O'Henry. Then he shook his head. "Seems like working at that place could be worse for your health than smoking."

I recalled seeing him around the store, but he was someone I had never had any personal contact with. Until tonight that is.

"Tell me, McCauley," O'Henry continued. "Did you leave anything out of your little story?"

"Like what?" I said sharply, wanting him to come out with it.

He cleared his throat and consulted his notebook again before saying, "Like the fact that before you left, you sliced him from ear to ear?"

13

ELAINE LOOKED LIKE she was about to tell O'Henry just what he could do with this nugget of knowledge, but I placed my hand on her arm.

"I didn't tell you because it didn't happen."

"How do you explain it then?"

I tried. "There were two of them—Bonkowsky and a driver. Whoever was driving was doing his damnedest to smear me all over the pavement. I don't have a lot of trouble picturing someone like that dispatching a partner who's too beaten up to move. Especially if he didn't trust him to keep his mouth shut."

O'Henry didn't respond. I kept talking. "We're not talking about nice people here."

That scenario made sense. I knew it and I was pretty sure O'Henry had already considered the possibility. So why did I feel like the celebrity suspect in one of those *Columbo* TV shows who overexplains every inconsistency?

"Besides," I went on. "I'm not denying the fact that I killed the guy, or at least seriously injured him." I probably should have shut up there and then, but my off button wasn't working. "It was him or me. Do you want me to make excuses for surviving?"

O'Henry shifted in his chair and went into a thoughtful mode. He sighed. "What I can't figure out is why you're right in the middle of all this. I'm assuming the attempt on your life and Hauser's murder are connected. So, it occurs to me that you may know something you're not telling me."

He punctuated that statement with a long pause. Then he said, "What is it?"

Elaine and I looked at each other and came to a silent decision. "There were some files," I said.

O'Henry leaned forward. "Now we're getting somewhere. What files?"

I explained how Hauser had given me the files and how the private detective who compiled them had been a hit-and-run victim—a fact which, since earlier tonight, I was convinced was not coincidence.

"Where are the files now?"

I opened my mouth and Elaine interrupted. "Let me tell this part."

O'Henry nodded to her with a gesture that was a bit too gracious. She told what had happened after she returned to the apartment. He jotted down the partial plate number. Then he looked back at me.

"You want to tell me what was in those files?"

I shrugged. "Can't remember too much. Actually it seemed like a lot of merciless digging into personal lives."

"Can you give me an example?"

"Sorry. I didn't have much of an opportunity to look them over before they were stolen."

O'Henry nodded like he didn't believe one word of that, which was okay. There was no way he could prove or disprove my statement.

"Was it the kind of information you could blackmail someone with?" he asked.

That had occurred to me, and although Hauser might have had some questionable habits, I didn't think blackmail was one of them. "I don't know," I lied.

O'Henry sighed again, put his notebook back in his pocket, and stood up slowly. "I could charge you with suppressing evidence. It might stick too." He hesitated, thinking, and shrugged his shoulders as if answering himself. "Maybe I will. Maybe I won't." He turned back to me. "I want you to come in this afternoon to make a statement." He shook his head in a long-suffering gesture. "I have to discuss you with the DA."

Elaine jumped from her seat on the couch, surprising both O'Henry and me. "Why? It was self-defense. Can't you see that? What was he supposed to do?"

"That's okay, Elaine," I said, standing.

"No, it's not." Her face was starting to redden. "Quint didn't have to call you guys, you know. And you would have spent days spinning your wheels trying to figure out who killed that thug."

O'Henry held up his hands in a quieting gesture, but Elaine would have none of it. "Now you're saying he might be charged with something? Well, tell me. With what? Defending himself?"

I knew that my making a statement and O'Henry's chat with the DA were standard procedures, but it did make me edgy. "It's really no big deal, Elaine," I said, trying to convince myself as well.

Elaine's jaw tightened as she clamped her teeth in a controlled effort to keep her mouth shut.

"By the way," O'Henry said, preparing to leave, "in case you're interested, we have the coroner's report on Hauser."

It's strange how quickly an attempt on your own life can make you forget about the successful attempt on another person's life. "Poison?" I asked.

O'Henry nodded. "Cyanide. Enough to stiff a moose." He looked at me. "Whoever replaced the capsules wanted to make damn sure he didn't take a regular one. All the capsules on the top were packed full of the stuff." He shook his head as if he were trying to fathom human nature. He probably did a lot of that.

"Let me know if you have any flashbacks about those files, okay?" he said as he was leaving.

I closed the door behind him and turned to Elaine. She was picking up books and slamming them into the bookcase. Apparently she hadn't heard the last part of our conversation and was still fuming over O'Henry's distrust of me. Without looking at me, she said, "I'm sorry. The guy just made me so damned mad."

"It really wasn't his fault. He was just following procedure."

She looked at me sharply. "Do you always let people walk on you and then apologize for them? I don't understand that kind of attitude."

I wasn't sure what I had done to incur this diatribe, but I knew I didn't want to go a round with Elaine too, so I kept my mouth shut.

"That's it. Just stand there and take it. Be Mr. Nice Guy. See how far it gets you."

I ran a hand through my hair, trying to figure out how to respond. There had to be more to this. I couldn't think of what to say. She brushed past me on her way out of the room. Then, I heard her bedroom door slam.

I lay down on the couch, using one of the back cushions for a pillow and tried to sift through everything that had happened in the past couple days, but I had trouble holding a thought for more than two seconds and pretty soon I couldn't tell my thoughts from my dreams.

When I woke, something was tickling my nose. At first I thought maybe it was the smell of coffee, but when I opened my eyes there was a remarkably ugly purple-and-orange afghan covering me. I sat up, my back feeling the effects of sleeping in one position on a soft couch. Elaine was standing over me with a mug of coffee.

"Black?" she asked.

I nodded. "Thank you," I said, taking the mug from her. "And thanks for the blanket."

She smiled. "Ugly isn't it?"

I shrugged and took a sip of coffee. It was strong, hot, and revitalizing.

"I made it in 1970. The afghan." As if that explained everything. Maybe it did.

"What time is it?"

"Noon," she said. "You want some scrambled eggs?"

I nodded. "That sounds great."

My knee was stiff and still hurt, but I could walk on it without too much discomfort. Elaine gave me an Ace bandage to wrap it with. I showered and shaved; and, when I came out, ate one of the most delicious meals I have ever had the pleasure of enjoying. Everything is relative, of course. Not that the eggs weren't terrific, but I was also somewhat euphoric about still being alive.

We didn't talk much during the meal. I was trying to figure out where I'd be living. I couldn't stay here. Elaine had already been too much imposed upon by my life.

After we ate she made another pot of coffee. We just couldn't get enough of the stuff. She wore a pair of gray, large-framed glasses and the steam from the coffee caused them to fog up. She giggled and waited for the fog to clear.

Then she looked at me and said, "I'm sorry about the abuse last night."

"Forget it."

We both knew I would say that. But I still wanted to know what prompted her outburst. She wasn't ready to tell me, though. Maybe she wasn't sure herself. I wasn't sure about a lot of things either. Like, why I was beginning to notice little gestures and movements of Elaine's—for instance, that when she sat down, even at the dining room table, she would fold one leg under her and sometimes, when deep into a thought or conversation, would sit cross-legged; or that she carried an elastic band in her pocket the way some people carry change and when her shoulder-length curly hair got in the way, she whipped it back into a ponytail. But I wanted to know more than what I could pick up through observation.

"Tell me about you," I said.

She shrugged and smiled. Her auburn hair seemed more vivid than ever against the white turtleneck she wore. Why hadn't I noticed her dimples before?

"Like what? Born and raised in Chicago. Only daughter of a mechanic. Mother died when I was three. Dad remarried two years ago. Nice lady. I'm real glad for him. Two brothers. One's a lawyer and the other is a teacher. I'm the only one who didn't go to college. I was determined to prove it was possible to get somewhere without a college degree. And I did." Her laugh was humorless. "Just couldn't stay there." She took a sip of coffee and lit one of my cigarettes. "There you have it. My life in a nutshell. Think we can sell rights to the networks?"

"Maybe. Ever been married?" That might have been too personal, but I wanted to know.

She shook her head.

"Why not?"

"Because I seem to have a real knack for finding men who aren't very good for me. You know, the kind who let their neuroses run their lives."

"At the risk of sounding like Dear Abby, there are a lot of decent men out there."

She studied me for a moment before answering. "All the nice ones are busy bestowing their affections on the women with neuroses."

"Touché," I said.

We cleared off the table, and I washed while she dried.

"Do you remember what was in those files?" she asked.

"Not as much as I'd like to. A few things. Not many specifics. Actually, a lot of the real meaty stuff was supplied by Grace."

116

"Grace?"

"Preston's elder sister."

"Meaty stuff?"

"Yeah, mostly on people in management. You know, dirt like how so and so's in debt to the mob. Another guy was arrested for statutory rape. Things like that."

"Colorful management team you have," she said.

I shrugged. "He was her little brother. You know how that sibling business works."

"I've got a little brother. I can't see myself doing that for him." She crossed her arms over her chest. "But I guess I can't see him asking me to either."

"Your brother probably doesn't need as much help as Preston did."

"Maybe not." But before I could pursue it, she said, "You know more than you admitted to O'Henry, don't you?"

I nodded.

"Why didn't you tell him?"

"I think Hauser was way off-base with some of his suspicions. I also think Grace's fact-finding was a bit too zealous. I don't want to put a decent person's reputation at risk because he looked cross-eyed at Hauser one day. Besides, Hauser never really got specific about any of them. I think he was just fishing."

"Can you tell me anything? Maybe it would help to puzzle it out with someone."

I hesitated at first, not because I didn't trust her, but because I didn't want to get her involved. But then, she already was involved. I told her what I remembered and we batted around motives for each of the suspects. None of them seemed very likely.

"Do you remember where Griffin's friend lives?" she asked, referring to the general manager's frequent visits to a certain apartment building.

"No. Only that it was on Sheridan Road."

"That narrows it." She put the last plate away and folded the dish towel. "Do you think it might have been Griffin?"

I shrugged and thought about that for a minute. "Maybe. If he did kill Hauser, then that would explain why he fired me. He didn't want me snooping around."

"What are you going to do about it?"

"Well, I'm wondering if the late detective Ray Keller kept copies of the data he collected on cases."

Elaine's eyes widened. "Where would they be?"

"I'm not sure. Maybe he had a partner. Maybe his wife cleaned the place out. Maybe she threw them away. Hell, it's a long shot but it's a start."

"Can I do it? Look for the file copies?" She was like a kid asking for a pony.

Before I could answer, the phone rang. Elaine answered it, "McCauley and Kluszewski Investigations."

I rolled my eyes heavenward, but I smiled too.

"One moment please," she said into the receiver, then handed me the phone. "It's the grieving widow," she announced none too softly.

"Hello, Diana," I said.

There was a hesitation. Then she asked, "Was that your roommate?"

"What can I do for you?" I said, instead of answering.

There was a pause again. "I need to see you. It's important."

"What's the matter?"

"I'm upset. That miserable Sergeant O'Henry is trying to do a number on me."

"What do you mean?"

"I'm sure he thinks I killed Preston." There was something that sounded like a small sob, but I couldn't be sure. "Quint, you know I didn't do it. Don't you?"

I didn't know how to answer that, so once again I avoided the question.

She said, "I have to talk to you. It's important." Her voice wasn't shaky anymore.

"Where are you?"

"I'm at the house in Wayne." She gave me the address, then added, "You know, sometimes I just need to get out of the city."

"I'll be there in a couple hours."

"Thank you, Quint."

"Is she the black-widow type?" Elaine asked after I hung up.

"It's real hard to place Diana Hauser into any category," I said, "but it wouldn't be entirely out of character."

The phone rang again. This time Elaine used a more conventional greeting. She shrugged as she handed the phone to me. "This one doesn't say who she is."

"Hi, Quint." Images leapt at me over the line. "It's Maggie." As if she had to identify herself. If she was surprised to hear a woman answer, she didn't let on. But then Maggie wouldn't. "I got your number from Harry," she explained.

"Oh," I said, always ready with a clever rejoinder.

"There's a letter here for you. I mentioned it to Harry and he said it might be important."

"Can you describe it?"

"What do you mean? It's just a letter. I didn't read the postmark or try to steam it open."

"Okay, okay. It may be important. Can I pick it up now? Will you be home for the next half hour?"

Elaine stopped wiping off the kitchen counter. "I don't know," she said. "If I'm not, I'll leave it in the mailbox."

As I hung up, I was experiencing some very mixed feelings. Part of me wished Maggie would be there, and part of me hoped she was as far away as she could get in a half hour. Part of me hoped the letter was the final phone bill from the apartment I'd left two years ago catching up with me, and part of me knew that it wasn't.

14

MAGGIE'S MAILBOX WAS empty. The little piece of tape with my name punched on it had been removed, but hadn't been replaced yet.

I climbed the two flights to her apartment, wondering if the fact that I was able to park in my old space was significant or simply a matter of good timing. I stared at the door for a minute before knocking. It was odd, being on this side of a door I used to consider, more or less, my own. I felt like a stranger, or worse, a solicitor. I had turned in more than my share of keys these past few days.

She opened the door and for a minute we just stared at each other. She looked terrific as usual. Her short, dark hair complemented her small features, and she was casual in a pair of khaki corduroys and a tight-fitting, black, V-necked sweater.

"Come in," she said.

The place hadn't changed, but that shouldn't have been surprising. Why did I have to keep reminding myself it had only been a few days? There didn't seem to be anyone else here.

I turned to Maggie. "Where's your young lawyer friend?"

"Gone," she said, brushing past me on her way into the kitchen. She pulled a jug of burgundy from the cupboard and set out two glasses. "Care for some?" she asked, pulling the cork from the half-empty bottle.

"Sure," I said. "You mean gone as in 'Quint McCauley is gone' or gone as in 'He's just recharging his batteries'?"

She finished pouring the wine and handed me mine. We clinked glasses. "To old friends," she said, and we drank.

Then she set her glass down. "It didn't work out."

I waited and she added, "I got tired of debating with him."

"At least you gave it everything you had." I shrugged and added, "Maybe you ought to give up on the idea of choosing a partner from one of your own kind. You need an easygoing noncompetitive type."

"Like you," she said.

I shrugged again.

"Are you still available?" she prodded.

"Are you kidding? My life has been one whirlwind since I walked out the door."

She studied me. "You didn't answer my question."

"I know." I wasn't trying to be evasive or mysterious. I simply didn't know.

"I think maybe I was a bit hasty in asking you to leave." She sipped her wine and sat in a chair at the small kitchen table. I remained standing. "You were good for me. I didn't realize that until you were gone." She smiled. "How does the song go . . . 'don't know what you got till you lose it . . . ' or something like that?"

"Sounds like a lot of songs." I also thought that two days wasn't enough time to know how someone likes his eggs cooked, but I didn't ask about that.

"Maybe."

Another sip of wine and she was still watching me, waiting for some kind of response to let her know how she was doing. I couldn't give her one, because I didn't know. She was no less beautiful, alive, or desirable than she had been three days ago, but something rang hollow. Top of her class in brains, looks, and personality, a lot of flash and class, but not a lot to chew on. Three days ago I hadn't noticed that.

121

"So, McCauley," Maggie said, trying a different angle. "What have you been up to these last few days?"

"Not much," I said, not wanting to go into it.

"That's not what I hear from Harry. I understand you're out of work."

"Just temporary."

"Need a place to stay?"

When I didn't answer she said, "Okay, Quint, I guess I owe you a little groveling? Why don't we pick up where we left off? It's only been three days. Come back. Please."

How could I tell someone who placed an emotional price tag on every action and had trouble discerning shades other than black and white that I didn't want groveling? I cleared my throat and jammed my hands in my jeans pockets. I noticed that her wine had an unpleasant aftertaste.

"I hear you have a letter for me."

She plunked her glass on the table. I wasn't trying to irritate her. I'm not sure what I had wanted on my way over here, but, at this point, I just wanted to leave. The situation was sour, like the wine, and I didn't feel inclined to try to change it.

Maggie handed me the letter and at first I thought there must be some mistake. This letter should have Preston Hauser's name on the front, not mine. I recognized the type and the innocuous white envelope with no return address. I swallowed hard. That was definitely my name there on the front.

"What's wrong?" Maggie asked.

"When did this arrive?"

"Today. Why? What is it?"

I wasn't intentionally ignoring Maggie, but I had a lot on my mind at the moment. Apparently she didn't see it that way.

"Look, McCauley. This strong, silent bit is wearing thin. Either talk to me or take your stupid letter that's giving you palpitations and get the hell out of here."

122

I opened the envelope and removed a letter and a photograph. I looked at the photo, then the letter, and I could almost hear the ice cubes clinking in my veins. I was finally able to empathize with my client. Then I looked at the photo again and something clicked. I pocketed the envelope and its contents, said to Maggie, "I've gotta go," and walked out of her apartment.

Maggie's nostrils flared when she was really mad—one of the few gestures that was totally unflattering to her.

It felt good to get out of the city, and it was a fine day for a drive—sunny, cold day, with yesterday's snowfall sparkling like gems. As I was driving, it occurred to me that Maggie hadn't noticed my mustache, or lack of it. She hadn't even looked at me funny. Interesting.

There's not much to Wayne except the vast, expensive homes set on vast, expensive acreage. And there were almost as many horses as people.

The Hauser estate was immense and the driveway long enough to make me wonder if they had ever considered putting up a gas station. There was a white-fenced paddock on either side of the driveway, but both were empty today and the snow fresh and untouched. The setting looked like a Christmas card.

A maid ushered me into what she called the sitting room, where Diana Hauser waited for me. Intended or not, the effect was stunning. The room was white, with white carpet and furniture, a few chrome pieces, and white drapes framing a huge bay window that looked out onto the snow-covered expanse of lawn. Diana Hauser stood in front of this window and turned toward me as I entered the room. She wore a blue silk pants outfit, all one piece with a plunging vee for a neckline, vivid against the stark white.

"Thank you for coming, Quint," she said, throwing her arms around me and holding on longer than necessary. I gently moved her away. She looked a little hurt and confused. "What's wrong?"

I shook my head. "It's been a long couple of days." She smiled like she didn't have any idea what I was talking about and sank into a cushion on the couch. Sighing, she stared out the window. Finally, she said, "I don't know what to do."

"Bored?" I asked, realizing as I spoke that there is a time and place to be a smart ass and this probably wasn't it. I shook my head and sat in a chair next to the couch. "I'm sorry. What can I do to help?"

She turned toward me, apparently forgiving my attitude. "I don't know. That Sergeant O'Henry has been harassing me. I came here from the city because I thought he'd leave me alone if I were harder to get at. I was wrong. He was here this morning."

"And what did the good sergeant want?"

"He wanted to know what I was doing last night. He wouldn't say why."

"Did you give him an answer he was happy with?"

She shrugged. "I was here. Alone. I watched a movie, cried, and got drunk on vodka martinis."

"What was the movie?"

"I don't remember the name of it. It was something with Arnold Schwarzenegger playing some barbarian."

"That narrows it," I said. "Sounds like a real tearjerker."

"It wasn't the movie that made me cry. You sound like O'Henry. Whose side are you on, anyway?"

"I'm on Preston's side. Remember, he's the one who's paying me."

She lit a cigarette with an ivory-trimmed lighter, then dropped it with a clatter on the white marble coffee table and said, "That's rather mercenary of you, isn't it?"

"Maybe. What else did O'Henry say?"

"What difference does it make," she snapped. "The guy's a jerk."

124

"That may be true, but he's a jerk you're going to have to deal with."

"Why did he ask me what I was doing last night?"

"Didn't he tell you?"

She impatiently tapped an ash off the end of her cigarette, then crushed it out. "Oh, he said something about some guy from the store getting killed. Wanted to know if I knew him."

"Did you?"

"No," she said, agitated. "He worked in shipping. Why would I know him?" She stood abruptly, walked over to the window, and stared at the snow. "Now, not only does he think I killed Preston, he thinks I killed some shipping clerk."

I joined her at the window, pretending to be absorbed in the view. "He doesn't think you killed the shipping clerk. He knows who killed him." I felt her turn toward me so I continued, "I did."

Her mouth dropped slightly, and I was pretty sure this was news to her.

"Why?" she said.

"Because he tried to kill *me*."

That appeared to take her unawares too, but she seemed more confused than shocked. "Why?" she finally asked.

"That is the key question, isn't it?"

She went back to the couch and sat, shaking her head. "I don't get it."

"Don't get what?" I said. "Why someone other than you would want me dead?"

She stiffened slightly. "What the hell are you talking about?"

I took the photo and the letter from my pocket and threw them on the coffee table. "I wouldn't call this fan mail, would you?"

She moved the two items around on the table with a bright red nail, as if not wanting to touch them.

I picked up the letter. "I like this. A bit of the old sod." I read the verse aloud:

> "There once was a man named McCauley,
> Whose nosing around wasn't jolly.
> His employer's demise
> Didn't cut him to size,
> And it turned out to be his last folly."

Diana gave me her best blank look.

"It's not bad," I said. "Probably wouldn't win a limerick contest, but then there's really not much you can do with McCauley. Too bad I'm not from Nantucket."

I exchanged the letter for the photograph. "And not a bad likeness of me."

Diana gave me a wry smile. "Nice try, Quint." She leaned back in the couch, arms folded, in control. "What makes you think I sent them?"

"This." I held the photo up for her to see. "It was taken Wednesday. The day you asked me to lunch."

"You're really grasping at straws, aren't you? That picture could have been taken any time."

I had hoped she would say that. I shook my head and sat next to her, holding the photo so we could both see it. "No. It had to be Wednesday." I paused for a dramatic effect. "I know I'm not likely to make the list of Chicago's best-dressed men, but I would never, unless I had no choice, wear a brown striped tie with a blue tattersall shirt." I paused. "On Wednesday I had no choice."

She gave me a frozen look. "You're basing this ridiculous accusation on the premise that Quint McCauley would never clash?" She was amused.

"One other thing." I tapped my naked upper lip. "If it wasn't taken yesterday or today, it had to have been taken

126

20 years ago. That's how long I had the mustache."

Her look hardened and after a moment she said, "So. Someone took a picture of you on Wednesday. Prove it was me."

"All right," I said. "The bullseye drawn on the picture is a nice touch. And it's made even more effective because of the crystal-ball distortion of the picture. To create this extreme a distortion, you need a fisheye lens." Diana's eyes narrowed. "On Wednesday you were using a fisheye lens."

"Just a coincidence," she said, sounding less sure of herself.

"Maybe," I said. "But it's enough of a coincidence to arouse O'Henry's curiosity. That doesn't take much, you know. And I'm willing to bet a lot of police, armed only with a search warrant, would find, probably right in this house, the typewriter that produced this thoughtful message. I'd also be willing to bet that Siamese of yours has recently suffered a cut paw or maybe an ingrown claw. What do you think?"

"I think you're a bastard," she said, her eyes filling.

Sighing, I leaned back in the couch. I guess I didn't expect her to thank me.

We sat there for several minutes that seemed a lot longer. The chrome grandfather clock in the corner of the room ticked off each second. I didn't have all day, and I wasn't sure why I was being so considerate of a woman who had mailed me a death threat.

I looked at her as she continued to stare out the window. Her mind could have been a million miles away, but her eyes weren't telling. Someone had to keep this moving.

"Why?" I asked her.

Finally she turned toward me. It was as if she just realized, after all this time, that I was sitting there next to her. "Oh, I don't know. It just sort of happened."

"Can you expand on that a bit?"

She sighed. "I was sitting here one day, reading the paper and I saw that picture of him with the winner of one of the Hauser Foundation grants and I thought to myself, 'Well, there's one more life that son of a bitch is going to control.'" She shot me a significant look. "It takes more than talent to win one of those, you know." Then she turned back to the scene at the window. "I was so disgusted I threw the paper across the room and went to make myself a drink. When I came back, Samantha, my cat, was sitting on the newspaper, licking and chewing at her paw." She smiled to herself. "Samantha was the only living creature in Preston's life that he had absolutely no control over. Anyway," she continued, "I noticed she had torn a claw and it was bleeding, rather badly. I had one of the maids take her to the vet. Then I noticed Samantha had bled all over Preston's picture." She nodded to herself as if confirming a suspicion. "I thought he looked good with blood smeared all over his face. That's when I got the idea."

"And you decided to launch a mail campaign?"

She shook her head slowly. "Not really. I don't think I really planned past that first letter. Then I saw how upset it made him. He never mentioned a thing, but I knew from the timing that it had to be the letter." She shrugged slightly. "I liked the way it made him distracted and nervous. I was controlling *him* for a change, and it felt good. So I sent him the second one. I finally had a way of evening up the relationship. For once he knew what it was like to be manipulated— to have someone playing the puppetmaster."

"Diana, no one ever controls another person without that person's permission."

She looked directly into my eyes, then turned away and said, "I needed him. Sometimes I hated him and sometimes I adored him. But there was never one time when I didn't need him."

"What was it you needed? His money?"

"Are you kidding? I come from money. I can't even conceive what it's like not to have it." She paused. "No. It was him I needed. He made me feel alive. He controlled my moods. When he was doting on me, he was incredible. When he wasn't, well . . ." Her voice drifted off.

"Did you kill him?"

She looked at me like she was trying to figure out if I was kidding or not. "That would have been a stupid thing for me to do, wouldn't it?" Her voice rose. "I wanted his goddamned attention. How much attention am I going to get from a corpse?"

Death. The ultimate distraction. I was moved by her sentiment. "You said you needed him. Did you love him?"

"What's that got to do with anything?"

I shrugged. "Maybe I'm old-fashioned."

"People don't love each other anymore. They use each other. They enter into this contract that says, 'I'll play the lead in your script if you play the lead in mine. And whatever you do, don't ad lib.'"

"What was your role?"

"I was the young, beautiful, charming hostess who complemented him and made him the envy of his friends. He pampered me, gave me gifts, made me feel special." She sighed. "But in the end, he didn't keep his part of the bargain. He began to ignore me, not all the time and not consistently but enough so he knew it bothered me. And he knew how to manipulate me by giving and withholding his attentions."

"His ignoring you. That wasn't part of the rules?" I asked, intrigued by this game, but glad I had never played it.

She continued as if she were explaining some very elementary facts to a slow learner. Maybe she was. "Nobody ignores me." There was a touch of incredulity in her voice and she placed a hand over her breast. "Could *you* ignore

129

me?" She really expected me to answer that.

"Not when you're tossing lingerie in my in-basket."

She stood and walked over to a chrome liquor cart. Without bothering to ask if I wanted anything, she dropped a piece of ice into each of two glasses and smothered the cubes with the contents of a crystal decanter. It looked like scotch. She tasted hers before handing one to me.

"I have trouble controlling myself around men I find attractive. I think Preston liked that about me. I'm very demonstrative."

I wished she hadn't said that.

She combed a few stray strands of hair away from her face with her fingernails. It was all in place now. Resting one arm on the back of the sofa, she turned toward me. At first she didn't speak, just sat there in that provocative pose, sipping her drink and studying me with those icy blue eyes.

Finally she said, "What about you?" Another sip. "Are you always this cool?"

"Yes," I lied. "Always."

She set the drink down and moved closer. The light fragrance she wore made me suddenly thirsty, and I took a large drink of the scotch. She stroked my face with the back of her hand and watched me. It occurred to me that this was the second time today a woman had advanced on me. My defenses were weakening.

"Always?" she asked.

I took hold of her wrist, which felt very small and fragile, and moved it away. She slid closer still, pressed her mouth against mine and moved her other hand down to my thigh. She was warm and soft and her body touched and pressed against mine in all the right places. There were a lot of good reasons for calling an abrupt halt to the activities, but I didn't really want to hear any of them.

My mental dilemma must have been similar to the one

experienced by some primeval ancestor when he tried to convince himself that climbing up out of the muck and breathing the air of reason was a good idea. Why bother when the muck feels so damned good?

Despite myself, I poked my head up for air. Score one for the lizards. "I still need to know a few things. For example," I continued before she could interrupt, "why send *me* a letter?"

Her smile both mocked and tempted me. "I hoped you scared easily." She leaned back against the couch cushion, still smiling. "I think maybe I was right."

It was my turn to stare out the window.

When she spoke again the humor was gone. "Did I break the law?" She was watching me as if she had just asked a profound question.

"Assuming you didn't kill him, I don't know," I said, then began to think out loud. "Maybe assault. But no. That's so nebulous any lawyer could get you off. Besides, I think Preston would have to file suit. Not too likely." I clicked off a number of offenses in my head and came up with the only one that I thought might stick. "Illegal use of the mail."

She touched her fingers to her lips in an effort to suppress a giggle.

"However," I added, "if you combine that offense with murder . . ."—I shook my head—"you just might spend the rest of your life licking postage stamps on death row."

"I told you, I didn't kill him," she said as if stating the obvious. "I had no reason."

"How do I know you didn't kill him so you could smoke with your coat on?"

"I said I didn't kill him."

"Then who did?"

"It could have been a lot of people." She cocked an eyebrow, slipping back into her playful role. "Even you."

"Who else?"

She took a drink, then began twirling the ice cube in her almost-empty glass. "Doesn't his dear sister Grace have any theories? I can't believe she's keeping a low profile right now. She's probably busy dropping hints that Preston's young widow did him in." Diana drained her glass.

"Not to me," I said. "She just wants to know who killed him."

Diana's laugh was dry and without humor. She peered into her glass, looking for a drop she might have missed. "That's the first time we've agreed on anything since I thought Preston was going to sell the store."

"Preston was going to sell Hauser's?"

She shook her head. "Not really. Apparently it was just one of those momentary whims of his. It passed."

"Who do you think had the most to gain through Preston's death?"

"That would be me, as far as money goes. But like I said, I don't need it. As for my life, well, I guess I had the most to lose in that department. Whatever I was with Preston, I'm much less without him."

I picked up the picture and the letter from the coffee table, pocketed them, and stood up.

Diana was fiddling with the ends of the silk sash tied around her waist. She didn't look at me when she said, "What are you going to do?"

I didn't answer because I wasn't sure yet.

"Are you going to tell O'Henry?"

"No," I said, not sure why. Maybe I believed her or maybe I just wanted to. "He doesn't have to know. Not yet anyway. However," I added, taking in her beauty and her wiles and realizing I wasn't totally convinced there wasn't a black spider sporting an hourglass at the core of her soul, "if anything unfortunate happens to me, he will know."

She nodded. "That's fair."

132

I walked to the doorway but looked back when she called my name. Her arm rested on the back of the couch and she spoke to me over her shoulder. "You don't have to leave, you know. What happened earlier, that wasn't all part of the act. I really don't want to be alone now. I'd like you to be here."

I almost stayed, and I might never have regretted it. Instead, I just shook my head, said, "I'm sorry," and left.

Chalk up another one for the lizards.

15

IT WAS AFTER seven when I got back to Elaine's. She had whipped up a spaghetti dinner I could smell ten feet from the door. We split a bottle of Cabernet and stuffed ourselves on garlic bread, spinach salad, and spaghetti with meat sauce that was wonderfully rich with garlic.

I told Elaine most of what had happened. She listened, without interrupting. When I finished she said, "Do you think Diana Hauser killed her husband?"

I thought about that for a long time before answering. "She might have. I get the feeling she lives her life on the edge a lot. It probably wouldn't take much to push her over. But then I don't know that she really had a motive. She didn't need his money. Her family has plenty, or so she says. And I really think she did need him, or thought she did. She wanted to torment him, to make him feel like he wasn't as in control as he thought he was, but I don't see anything there that would be a motive. I mean, how can you continue to torment someone when he's dead? But, as of now, she's the only viable suspect, as they say." I sipped on coffee that tasted faintly of cinnamon.

Elaine said, "You ready for dessert?"

"Are you kidding? There's no place to put it."

"I think you can find room for this." She left the room and returned in a few seconds with a brown envelope, which she plopped down in front of me. "Enjoy," she said.

I could tell by her impish grin that she wasn't going to give me a clue so I pulled out the contents. There were seven manila files. I looked from the contents to Elaine, then back again. I opened the first one. As far as I could tell the information was the same. I flipped through the rest. They had all been in the stolen group of files: Frank Griffin, Hauser's purposeful general manager with an unswerving eye for attractive women; Larry Duane, Hauser's department head who was under surveillance for suspicion of running a dogfighting ring; Byron Noble, a buyer with an unswerving eye for attractive men; Art Judson, Hauser's PR man with a bad gambling habit; John Harrison, head of maintenance, who had spent a couple years at Joliet State for assault and battery; Tom Cassidy, who apparently took a personal interest in promoting the careers of the ladies of the evening and had been arrested, though not convicted, on statutory rape charges; and, of course, everyone's favorite former security head: me. As I thumbed through the familiar names, I could hardly believe I had them in my hands.

"What is this?" I said.

"What does it look like?"

"It looks like Hauser's files, but that doesn't make any sense." I looked through them again. "These *are* Hauser's files."

Elaine nodded. "You're not the only one who had a busy, productive day."

I was awestruck. "I guess not," I said and added, "And you had time left over to put together a feast. God, what a woman. How did you do it?"

"Well," she said, leaping into it, "after you left I started doing some digging. I found out that this detective of Hauser's, Ray Keller, lived with his mother."

"How did you find that out? Police records?"

"No. Phone book. I looked up his number and dialed it. Actually there were several in the directory. I just figured if someone answered to the name Ray Keller or if he was out

135

then I could disqualify him because he wasn't dead."

"Flawless logic."

"I thought so. Anyway, I think it was the fifth number and this woman answered. She got kind of upset when I asked for Keller and she wanted to know who I was. I lied." She looked a little ashamed. "I said Keller had been doing some investigating for me on a very personal matter. She told me he was dead and I pretended to be very upset. Distraught. Well, Mrs. Keller—Carmen—she's a real motherly type. She became concerned about me. So I told her that Keller had some information on my husband, who was cheating on me. But I told her that my husband and I were trying to make a go of it again and I wanted to be sure no one ever saw those files. Well, she invited me over. That's where I spent the afternoon." She paused. "That's also where I got the recipe for the spaghetti sauce. And the files."

"I'm speechless," I said. "She just gave them to you?"

"Well." She shrugged. "She spent all afternoon talking about Ray and what a wonderful son he was. She showed me pictures, drawings he made in grade school." She shook her head sadly. "I felt like such a jerk. I mean, I knew I was being deceptive, and this was such a nice lady. I figured the least I could do was listen to her. She showed me all his files. Apparently he worked out of that apartment. She said I could take anything I wanted. She had all she wanted to remember Ray by in her own memorabilia." She sipped her coffee. "She also thinks the police didn't investigate Ray's death thoroughly enough. She thinks someone killed him. She can't believe her son would ever be drunk enough to fall into the path of a car."

"What do you think?"

"I think Mrs. Keller is genuinely convinced, but I also think she's a mother who loved her son very much. And maybe she doesn't want to believe that her son died for no good reason. Still, it's hard not to take her side. When I left she asked me to come back soon. And she said she hoped my marriage worked out." Elaine shook her head slowly. "What a miserable thing for me to do."

I was touched by her guilt. Most people don't feel that deeply. "Hey, Elaine." I put my hand on her shoulder. "You made the woman's day. And you didn't just sit there and listen to her go on about her son because you wanted those files. You cared enough to listen."

"She was so lonely. Her son was all she had. Now he's gone and she's got nothing." She sighed. "And I lied to her."

"Yeah, well if these files tell us anything, they may tell us who killed Hauser and Keller."

She grabbed the top file and flipped it open. "What are we looking for?"

"Anything that could be a big enough secret to warrant killing two, maybe three people."

"Ah," Elaine said. "This one. We may be able to eliminate this one immediately." She looked at me. "Did you kill Hauser?"

"No."

"Well, that's good. We can narrow it to six now." She continued to read my file.

"A real page-turner, isn't it?"

She yawned, then something she read made her giggle.

"You got to the part about me living in sinful bliss with a woman young enough to be my daughter. I feel the need to point out that I would have been a very young father."

"Maybe that's why Hauser hired you. He could relate to a man who liked younger women."

I shrugged. "Who knows?"

"I suppose," Elaine said, "that a woman of thirty-one would be over the hill for you."

"Not if she were rich."

Elaine whacked me on the head with my own file and

glanced at the name on the next file. She gasped. "Oh, my God."

"What? Oh my God what?"

"This is incredible," she said as she scanned the contents.

"A hint, Elaine. I need a hint."

"Does Pam know that Art has these gambling debts?"

"Why should Pam care?" I asked, but the answer was dawning on me. "Pam and Art?"

"Don't look so shocked. Pam's got a lot going for her."

"I know that, but . . . Art Judson? They just don't seem a likely couple."

Then I recalled Pam's attitude toward me. It wasn't like she was snubbing me, but more like she had gone on to something else. And Art had mentioned meeting a woman who was helping him get it together. Pam could do that.

"I feel like I'm invading someone's privacy," she said, continuing to leaf through the folder. "You don't think Art could have killed Hauser, do you?"

"I think it's possible. What do you think?"

She paged through the file again. "God, this is all real hard to believe."

I waited for her to elaborate.

"It says here that Art was once in debt some twenty thousand dollars, but that someone gave him the money to pay off the debt. Doesn't say who. Then it says that he is quite the womanizer. Went through beautiful, very young women like there was no tomorrow." She shook her head. "God, poor Pam. She's really hung up on the creep. Now he owes a bunch of money to some guy named Lorenzo."

I sat up. "Paul Lorenzo?"

She glanced at the paper. "Yes. Why?"

"That's interesting."

"Why?" she repeated.

"Paul Lorenzo owns Lorenzo Trucking, which was recently given the trucking contract for Hauser's."

Elaine's eyes widened.

"I heard that Hauser hit the ceiling when he found out that Griffin hadn't renewed the current trucker's contract and had given Lorenzo the business without even asking for bids." I wondered about Art's loyalties. And about Griffin's connections.

Elaine closed the folder and placed it in its own space on the table. "These are the 'maybes.'"

We went through each of the remaining five folders, jotting notes and downing several cups of coffee. When I opened Griffin's file a photograph fell out.

"Hello. What have we here?" I picked it up off the floor. It was a picture of a young, very attractive woman in the company of a blurred man who might have been Griffin.

Elaine leaned forward. "Let me see." I showed her the picture.

"Who is that?" She squinted at the photo, trying to bring it into focus.

"I think it's Griffin. But I don't know who the woman is. What's strange is that I don't remember seeing this picture in the files Hauser gave me."

Elaine took the picture from me. "Overdoes the make-up, don't you think?"

"I hadn't noticed."

"And if she's a natural blond, I'm Princess Di. I'll bet she's one of those part-time models."

"Are you finished?" I asked.

"I guess so." She replaced the picture in the folder and tossed the whole thing in the maybe pile.

When we finished with all of them, Elaine looked at her notes and then at me. "You go first," she said.

"I eliminated four. Harrison spent two years in prison, and although it's not something he would want anyone to know about, it's a matter of public record. Duane is break-

139

ing the law with his dogfights, but I don't think he has whatever it takes to kill a human being."

"Scum," Elaine muttered. "Who else?"

"Cassidy. He likes hookers. Big deal. So do a lot of men. And the statutory rape charge never stuck. He's not in a very powerful position within the company, either. Not a lot of leverage for blackmail or a lot to lose if someone were to find out. And Noble has never tried to hide the fact that he's gay. Doesn't flaunt it either. He and Griffin don't get along at all—Griffin thinks there's something wrong with you if you don't have a wife and at least one mistress—but I don't think Noble had any problem with Hauser. He's a valuable employee." I put down the sheet of notes. "What about you?"

She scanned her notes before answering. "Close. I didn't eliminate Duane, though, and I considered eliminating Griffin."

"Why Duane?"

"I think," she said, flipping through his folder, "I think it was largely a matter of wishful thinking. Justice." She looked up at me. "He wouldn't get the chair for running a dogfighting ring, but maybe he would if he had killed Hauser." She dropped the folder on the table. "I guess that's not very logical."

I picked up Duane's folder. "We'll put it with the maybes. Why not Griffin?"

"Well, apparently he does have a mistress, but you can't prove it by that picture. Keller may have been okay as an investigator but he was a lousy photographer. All the others evidence seems kind of flimsy."

I nodded. She might be right.

"Why do you think he's a possible?" she asked.

"He wouldn't get the chair for firing me, but maybe he would if he killed Hauser." We both laughed. "No," I said. "It's more than that. Maybe it's because his is the only file that is so sketchy and vague. All the others have done specific things that can be pinned on them. Griffin hasn't. Maybe he has a mistress and maybe he hasn't. I just think there is more to it than meets the eye or his file wouldn't be here. Besides, Griffin runs Hauser's. It's possible that he could benefit from having Preston out of the way. Also, I'm beginning to think that Griffin's influence at Hauser's went a lot deeper than most people realized."

Elaine nodded. "Okay. That narrows it down to two—Griffin and Judson." Elaine rose and began clearing the table. "So, where do we start tomorrow?"

I collected my plate and the spaghetti sauce dish. "Elaine," I said. "You've been an incredible help already. In fact, I guess you could say you've given me a place to start. But, I can't get you further involved."

She stopped rinsing plates and wiped her hands on the back of her jeans. "What do you mean? I already am involved. Somebody trashes my home and I take it personally." I didn't say anything and she added, "I want to help."

She meant it. But I had the feeling things were going to get a lot worse before they got better. Already I wasn't playing real smart. I should have told O'Henry everything. Dumped it all in his lap and gone on with my life. Elaine shouldn't have to pay for my stupidity.

"I know you do," I said. "But I can't let you because I can't let anything happen to you, and I don't know any way to make sure of that except to keep you out of this."

I left the room to get my suitcase, which I had never completely unpacked. We had moved my suitcase to Elaine's bedroom before O'Henry arrived the night before. Elaine was still in the kitchen while I got my things together. I shoved my belongings into the suitcase, snapped it shut, and turned. Elaine stood in the bedroom doorway. Her arms were crossed in front of her and she wore her defiant look.

"You have to let me help," she said. "If you don't, I'll do it on my own. I know enough already to do that."

"Why is this so important to you?"

She cleared her throat before answering. "Because I think I'd be good at it, and I want to prove to myself that I don't need a multimillion dollar company behind me to succeed. Because it feels good to do something for myself and not for the company. Because I don't want you to leave."

That last statement hung in the air between us.

Dropping my suitcase to the floor, I approached her. She didn't move and, this time, neither one of us turned away.

I pushed her hair back off her shoulders and traced the curve of her throat with my thumbs. She tilted her chin upward in response. We kissed, quick and gentle at first, like we were testing the water. Finding it agreeable, she pushed her hands up under the back of my sweater as I moved mine down the front of hers, touching the rise and fall, the hardness and softness of her breasts.

Locked in an embrace, we pulled each other down onto the carpet, fumbled with sweaters and zippers and hooks and laughed at the awkward moments, until we were finally as close as two people can be.

Later, we lay on the carpet, still twined around each other, feeling the chill of the air as it evaporated the sweat from our bodies.

I thought she was reading my mind when she said, "I wonder how the bed works."

We moved onto the bed and made love again, more slowly now, taking time to explore each other and allowing the sensations to linger.

I woke in the early morning with the light of the moon on the bed and watched Elaine as she slept—her skin smooth and white, her breathing deep and even and her face peaceful in repose. Then, selfishly, I nuzzled her awake until her protests dissolved into sighs.

16

EARLY MORNING HABITS are the hardest for me to share with another person. When you think about it, that doesn't make much sense. But there you have it. I was a willing recruit in a decade that endorsed casual sex, but I never got used to the strangeness of waking up with someone for the first time. Anxiety builds with the new smells, morning noises, first words that sound like frog talk, and with the knowledge that your partner, in the heat of the night, never got a really good look at you. You both know you don't look quite the same as you did in the dark.

The sweat of passion has dried and left your hair matted and oily and your face is lined with pillow creases. It is painfully obvious that your membership to the health club expired a long time ago. Sometimes I think such moments are the first real test of a relationship. Anyone can enjoy a night of lovemaking, but to hold onto that heady feeling you get when you know you'd do it again and enjoy it even more—well, that's not always easy. You need the right combination of personalities, and luck has a lot to do with it too.

This morning my arm was asleep. As it began that excruciating tingling, I thought about how I'd almost left last night. If I had, would this ever have happened? Maybe. Maybe not. I felt like a selfish bastard that Elaine might be in danger because of her proximity to me, but then she hadn't exactly given me the bum's rush either.

That's it, Quint. You work hard enough at this, you'll

convince yourself you're here by popular demand. Yours and hers. I sighed. Tonight I'd really have to leave.

"What are you thinking?" Elaine spoke.

I studied her for a moment, thinking this wasn't painful at all. Gathering her in my arms, we nestled together for a few minutes, not needing to talk.

Finally I said, "I've got to leave, Elaine. Sleeping with a target isn't good for your health. Trust me."

"Quint," she said, "what makes you think you're the only target here? I mean, whoever tried to kill you may very well think I'm a threat too. Or is there something you haven't told me?"

I didn't want to tell her about the letter I had received from Diana. I was beginning to think it was pretty stupid of me not to turn her in. I didn't want someone agreeing with me. If Diana really did decide to carry out her threat, would she know where to find me?

"Who knows I'm living here?" I asked.

Elaine thought for a moment, then said, "Pam. Who else did you tell?"

"I think she was the only one. Harry only has the phone number. Whoever broke in here to get those files had to know the apartment number."

She propped herself up on an elbow so she could address her question directly to me. "Are you saying Pam broke in here?"

"No. But do you think Pam might have mentioned it to Art?"

Elaine lay back against her pillow, staring at the ceiling. Finally she said, "We'd better talk to her."

We were discussing our strategy over Cheerios and English muffins before I realized we had passed through the morning ritual with relatively few awkward moments.

Elaine called Pam to tell her we needed to see her. On our way over, Elaine didn't offer any directions to Pam's

145

place, and I didn't ask for any either. I did ask Elaine if Pam had been surprised to hear from her. "Or did she assume it was a transatlantic phone call?"

"Oh, no. I called Pam the day after I returned. I told her about my new boarder."

"Was she amused?" I asked.

"I'm not sure that's the word I would use."

I passed a truck and it sprayed slush on the windshield.

"Starting to thaw," I said, activating the washer.

"I can't imagine what you two want," Pam said as she ushered us into her studio apartment. She studied our faces, as if she hoped to read something from our expressions.

She said, "I was sorry to hear how Griffin, uh, let you go," and shook her head. "It doesn't make sense to me. Morison is totally ineffectual. From what I hear, he doesn't know what he's doing."

"Thank you, Pam. My ego needed that."

She shrugged. "It's the truth. Coffee?" We both accepted.

"It made Irna's day, though," Pam went on, as she measured coffee and filled the machine with water. "The way she's copying him with memos and filling him in on procedures, you'd think they were planning to take over the store."

"Yeah," I said, grateful that someone else had noticed their collusion. "What is it with those two? Being small and mean is like a religion to Irna. And if she's finally decided to be nice to someone, why, for God's sake, would she choose Fred Morison?"

Smiling, Pam removed mugs from a cupboard. "You don't know?"

"I guess not. What don't I know?"

"Fred Morison is married to Irna's only daughter, Myra."

"You're kidding."

"Nope."

I looked at Elaine. "I've just figured it out. Irna killed Hauser to make me look incompetent so Fred would be made king of security."

"Try again" was all Elaine said. Pam just laughed.

We made small talk while the coffee brewed, as if we all knew something uncomfortable was about to be said and none of us was anxious to get to the saying of it.

Elaine and I sat on the studio bed, and Pam removed a slumbering gray tabby from an overstuffed chair. The cat stretched its front half, then its back, regarded us with nearly closed eyes, and ever so slowly walked toward the kitchenette. We all watched the sequence, perhaps a bit too intently. The cat glanced over its shoulder at us before nuzzling into its bowl of food.

"Well," I said. Pam looked at me, waiting. "Well," I repeated. Elaine poked me in the ribs. I didn't know how to say this without sounding accusing. "Does anyone besides you know that I am staying with Elaine?"

Pam set her coffee cup down. "No. Who would I tell?"

"What about Art?" I asked.

Pam glanced sharply at Elaine. "So much for my private life."

"Pam, please. This is very important," Elaine said.

Pam sighed. "Well, yes, I told Art. I mean . . ." She looked from me to Elaine and back again. "What's this got to do with anything?"

"Anyone else? Did you tell anyone else?" I asked.

Pam shook her head. "I don't think so."

"Do you know if Art might have told someone?"

"You'll have to ask him," Pam said, her voice rising. "Quint, Elaine, what's going on here? Has Art done something? What's going on?"

"Did Art ever mention anything about some files on key people at Hauser's?"

"No, he never mentioned any files. And dammit I want to know right now why you're asking."

This time Elaine spoke. "Someone broke into my apartment two nights ago and took some files Hauser had given Quint. We're just trying to figure out who knew he was there and that he had the files."

"So you think it's Art. Just because he's got a history of gambling you think he's capable of doing something like that. For God's sake, Quint, Art's a friend of yours. He confided a lot in you the other day. I know. He told me."

"Pam, I'm not saying he did anything. I'm just wondering if he might have told someone. Griffin?" I might have imagined it, but it seemed like that name caused a slight widening of her eyes but she didn't say anything. I continued, "Maybe it just slipped out in conversation. I mean, my living with Elaine is not a state secret. It may not be the most conventional arrangement, but . . ." I decided now was a good time to shut up.

Pam sighed. "I don't know. Why don't you talk to Art? Why did you come to me in the first place?" She leaned back in her chair. When she spoke again it wasn't to anyone in particular. "I've been really good for him. That's what he told me. And I believe him." Then she looked at me. "Why are you trying to cause trouble?"

"Believe me," I said, "I'm not. Is Art home today?" Pam nodded and I said to Elaine, "I'm going over there myself." She didn't argue. I figured Art would be more willing to talk if it were to me alone. Elaine must have agreed.

I had never been to Art Judson's place, but I had a pretty good idea of what to expect—high-tech toys, heavy masculine furniture, sculptures and paintings selected by some interior designer who put it all together. I wasn't far off. The only detail I hadn't anticipated was the body-building equipment that turned one portion of the living room into a health club.

Even casual, Art was immaculate. I'm not sure you should trust someone who wears jeans that don't show any signs of fading. He was getting ready to go to another health club when I arrived.

"Why bother?" I asked. "Haven't you got everything you need here?"

Art laughed. "It's kind of hard to do laps here." He glanced at me. "What club do you belong to?"

"Art," I said, "the last club I belonged to was the one where they give you merit badges for helping little old ladies. I think I lack the incentive."

"Feeling great is incentive enough for me," Art said.

He offered me some kind of bottled water, which I refused, and we sat in the furniture part of his living room.

"Still looking into Hauser's death?"

I nodded.

He shook his head, slowly. "Why bother, Quint? It's not like the guy was a prince. He used people—strangers, family, friends—it didn't matter to him."

"Not a very admirable quality," I conceded, "but I didn't know that was a capital crime."

"Knock it off, Quint. Haven't you figured it out? Everyone else has."

"Maybe I missed something."

"What it's going to boil down to is that Diana Hauser bumped him off."

"Why?"

"His money. What else?"

"She might have done it, but I don't think her motive was money."

"You sound like you don't want to believe that the beautiful Diana Hauser could have done such a nasty thing. Sounds like you've fallen under the old Hauser spell. Can't say I blame you. Also can't say you'd be the first. She's got lots of men doing lots of favors for her."

"So I hear. Like who?"

Art smiled.

"You know," I said, "it seems to me that Diana Hauser is the subject of a lot of accusations with very little concrete evidence to back them up. She is supposed to be sleeping with enough men to warrant a revolving door on her bedroom, but I have yet to hear one name. People say she married Hauser for his money, yet she comes from a lot of money. What does she need Hauser's money for?"

Art studied me, still smiling. "You *have* fallen for the old Hauser mystique. I should know." He paused. "You want a name? Try mine."

I swallowed. "You and Diana? When?"

"About a year and a half ago."

It wasn't easy to tell if Art was lying. I suspected he had a lot of practice at it. "Did Preston ever find out?"

He shrugged. "The way Diana told it, he wouldn't have cared even if he had known."

"What happened between you two?"

"She was a little flaky for me," he said, holding up the glass of bottled water. "I don't put things in my body that aren't good for me. I keep myself fit. Why would I want to be associated for any length of time with a person who seriously messes with my mental health?"

"For the same reason you piled up a sizable gambling debt—addiction. It's hard to get over something like that. How did you do it?"

When he responded, I wasn't sure whether he was answering my question or changing the subject. "Like I said, the lady is weird."

"How so?"

He sighed and gazed out the window. Although it was thawing outside, the temperature in here was beginning to get a bit chilly. Art's features hardened and he spoke as if recalling an unpleasant experience. "She's very, very pos-

150

sessive, except when she feels she's losing the advantage."
He turned toward me. "Then she becomes obsessive."

"Go on," I said.

Art took a drink of his bottled water and grimaced as if
he'd just downed a shot of moonshine. "God, Quint, it was
weird. She was demanding one hundred percent of my
time. I mean, I couldn't ask that of her. Oh, no. But she
wanted exclusive rights to me. She was pretty blatant about
it too. At a couple of those fancy Hauser Foundation din-
ners that some of the Hauser staff attended, she practically
paraded me in front of Preston." Art shrugged and chuckled. "It didn't seem to bother Preston too much." Shaking
his head he added, "He was another weird one. Anyway, I
had a couple dates with one of the women's-wear buyers."
He looked at me and asked, "Do you remember Anna
Kimball?"

"Vaguely. She was only at Hauser's for a short time,
wasn't she?"

Art nodded. "Here's why. All of a sudden she started
getting phone calls in the middle of the night—nothing
really threatening, you know. Someone would just hang up
or listen to Anna say hello over and over. One day Anna
found her tires slashed. She thought it was a neighborhood
gang. She lived in one of those mixed areas. No sooner did
she replace the tires than it happened again. This time she
moved and unlisted her number, but she kept getting the
phone calls. No more slashed tires but one day she returned from a business trip and found messages like 'Art
Judson isn't worth dying for' smeared in lipstick all over
her mirrors." He paused and drained his glass of water.
"Her landlord said some woman claiming to be her sister
desperately needed to drop something off. He couldn't
give much of an identification. From his description it
could have been Diana or a dozen other attractive blonds.
He wasn't even sure when I showed him a picture." Art

shrugged. "Anyway, Anna apparently agreed with the writing on the wall, so to speak. We stopped going out."

"How did it end between you and Diana?"

Art laughed without humor. "Not long after Anna and I split, Diana dumped me. It was as if she just wanted to show me who was running things." He sighed. "Good riddance, I say."

That took me a minute to digest. "Listen Art, I just talked to Pam."

He crossed his arms over his chest. "Why did you need to talk to her?"

"I just needed some information. She said she told you where I am living now."

Art smiled and relaxed a little. "How's that working out? Elaine's really something, isn't she?"

I mumbled a noncommittal response.

"Are you two sharing more than an apartment?" He gave me one of those knowing winks that I thought went out with leisure suits.

"Art, let's pretend for just a minute that we're not in a locker room."

"Sorry," Art said, then added, "You may be the only living male to have seen her out of her business suit."

"Did you tell anyone where I am living?"

Art stopped laughing and went into his thoughtful mode. "You mean anyone like Diana?"

"For starters."

Art shook his head. "Diana and I haven't shared so much as a word for quite some time."

"Anyone else?"

"I didn't tell anyone. I mean, no offense Quint, but who cares where you're living?"

"Someone who didn't want me poking through some very informative personnel files."

"What files?"

"The ones that someone wanted bad enough to break into Elaine's apartment to recover them, and the ones that someone considers important enough that it might be neater to have me out of the way."

Art shook his head and leaned forward. "What are you talking about? Someone tried to kill you?"

"Hard to believe. I'm such a likable guy."

He didn't argue or agree.

"Pam said she told you where I was living. Who did you tell?"

Art opened his mouth as if to speak, then hesitated.

"Talk to me, Art," I urged.

Staring at the floor he said, "It's probably nothing." Then he looked up at me. "But for whatever it's worth, Griffin was asking about you. I think it was legit. He needed to know where to send your last check."

"Wouldn't payroll be the ones to track me down?"

Art shrugged. "Maybe he was just helping out."

"Sure, that must be it. Griffin's such a conscientious type. I'm sure he wouldn't sleep if he thought I got chiseled out of my last paycheck."

Art chuckled.

"How well do you know Griffin?"

Art shrugged. "We aren't close friends or anything, but we play a little racquetball. Why?"

"Do you know if he fools around?"

"Probably. You'd understand why if you had seen his wife." Art grimaced. "Ouch."

I took the photograph of Griffin and the woman that Elaine and I had found in the file. It wasn't particularly clear, but you never know. "Ever seen her before?"

Art examined the picture, then handed it back to me saying, "Nope. Never." He spoke evenly and held my gaze, but he had looked at the photo a little too long and with a little too much interest for someone who made no connection. "Nice looking, though" was all he said.

I pocketed the photograph. "How do you like working for Grace Hunnicutt?"

Art laughed. "If she doesn't watch herself, she's going to wind up like Preston." He waved his hand as a disclaimer. "I didn't mean that. But the lady's not making friends. People like Griffin are used to having no one to answer to. Preston was just there in spirit. Grace likes to get her hands into things." He shrugged. "We'll see. Maybe the old lady'll give the place a little life. It could sure use it. Hey, Quint. Why don't you come to the health club with me? I can bring guests. Couple games of racquetball'd probably do us both some good."

I stood up and put my jacket on. "Gosh, Art, I left Elaine back at Pam's place. Thanks anyway." I put my jacket on, preparing to leave.

"Glad I could help," he said, then added, "Uh, Quint. I'd appreciate it if you didn't repeat the Diana Hauser episode to anyone, especially Pam."

"Don't worry," I said, resisting an impulse to tell him to take good care of Pam. Then I remembered I wasn't in any position to talk.

As I walked to my car, I decided I needed a place to think. The White Hart was open for lunch on Saturdays and that seemed a good spot. Over a plate of shepherd's pie and a glass of Guinness I debated my next move.

Griffin? No. I wanted to know more about his friend on Sheridan Road before I approached him. Diana? If what Art had told me was true, she was capable of some pretty strange behavior. Strange enough to put Elaine in jeopardy. Strange enough to kill her spouse?

17

As I DROVE back to Pam's I debated again whether it was safer for Elaine if I stayed with her or away from her. If I were with her, she might get in the way of anyone trying to kill me. On the other hand, if her association with me had already placed her in jeopardy, then perhaps it was better I stayed around. I'm not exactly a lethal weapon, but I'm better than nothing. Then I decided that maybe I should discuss this with Elaine before deciding her life for her.

Pam and Elaine were eating popcorn and watching *The Scarlet Claw* when I returned. I sat on the edge of the couch and reached into the bowl. It was almost empty.

"I can make some more," said Pam.

"No, thanks," I said. "Not for me anyway."

Pam looked at me, trying to read my expression, before she asked, "How's Art? What did he tell you?"

I knew this question was inevitable, but I hadn't come up with a good response. "Art's okay. He was helpful."

"Did he break into Elaine's apartment?"

Her tone was sharp this time and I felt rotten because I was making her work so hard for information. But there wasn't much I *could* tell her.

"No. I'm sure he didn't," I said, adding, "You've been good for him Pam." I told her that partly because it was true and partly because I hoped to derail her from her line of questions.

She allowed me a small smile, partly, I suspect, because she appreciated the observation and partly because she knew exactly why I'd chosen this moment to say it.

"Well," I said, rising, "I've got some things to do." I turned to Elaine. "Do you want to stay here, or can I drop you off at home?"

"Where are you going?"

"A little legwork. Door-knocking."

"I think I'll join you."

"This isn't going to be exciting, Elaine," I warned her. "In fact, it probably won't even be productive."

"I want to go," she said, shrugging on her down jacket.

I looked at Pam. "All part of our madcap life-style."

"Yeah, and all we used to do was go to the movies."

"Where we going?" Elaine asked as we got into the car.

"We'll start at the bottom of the apartment building on Sheridan Road and work our way to the top, trying to get an ID on this woman. If we're really lucky, the minute we get there we'll run into a doorman who will say, 'Oh, yes, of course, that's Mary Smith, apartment 5E.'"

As it turned out, we weren't lucky, not even remotely. No doorman, and it was a high-rise with twenty floors. The process was very time consuming. We only had one picture, so we couldn't split up. And even though it was a Saturday afternoon, a lot of people weren't home. We didn't get more than a 'She looks vaguely familiar' until we hit the tenth floor. It was late afternoon and almost dark. A short man around thirty with receding sandy-colored hair answered the door to apartment 1015. He opened it as wide as the chain would allow.

After glancing at the picture, he looked from Elaine to me and said, "When are you going to leave that poor woman alone?" and started to close the door.

My foot jammed it open again. For a little guy, he had a lot of strength and I was glad I wore boots.

"Wait a minute," I said. "Please. Can you just tell me who she is?"

He studied us for a moment with small narrow eyes that looked like two slashes when he squinted. "Melinda Reichart. And your verb tense is wrong."

This guy was going to make me earn every shred of information. "What are you saying?"

"Don't you people talk among yourselves? There must have been a dozen policemen down here asking questions."

"Questions? About what?"

"You're not a policeman, are you?"

"No. Does that make a difference?"

"It does to me. Now I know I don't have to talk to you."

He applied pressure on the door, pressing it into my boot. "Please remove your foot. I'm not impressed with strong-arm tactics."

Elaine, who had been standing behind me, stepped forward. "Please, sir. My sister has been missing for three years now. We think this girl might know her. Won't you help us?"

She was so convincing I almost believed her.

The little man chewed on his lower lip and gave it serious thought. Finally, after heaving a resigned sigh, he said, "You won't get any help from her. They found her dumped in an alley about two weeks ago. Shot to death."

Elaine gasped.

"Hey, I'm sorry," the little man said. "But you asked."

"Do you know if the investigation turned up anything?"

He shrugged and rolled his eyes. "It's not like the police go out of their way to keep me informed, you know."

It was becoming increasingly difficult to be civil to this guy. "I just thought you might have heard something, or, seeing as you two were neighbors, I thought perhaps you would have paid some attention to the news accounts of her death."

Another sigh. There was a little whine in it this time.

157

"Robbery. They said it was robbery. Her wallet was taken out of her purse."

"Was anyone arrested?"

"Not that I know of."

"What apartment did she live in?"

"Ten-fourteen." He gestured at the apartment across the hall.

"Did she have any friends who might be able to tell us something."

"How should I know?" he snapped.

"Please," Elaine said. "Maybe they knew Marla. My sister."

"It's not like I knew the woman or anything." Elaine's pleading look must have begun to wear on him. "Look. She only lived here for a couple months. She kept to herself. She had a pretty regular gentleman caller, but I don't think she spent much time socializing with her neighbors." He shrugged. "I asked her over once. She just said no. Didn't bother to make up an excuse or anything. Just no." He added, more to himself than to us, "Why is it that people who are that good looking are always so unpleasant?"

"You don't have to be good looking to be unpleasant," I said. "Can you describe her 'gentleman caller'?"

"Not really," he said. "I didn't pay much attention. He usually came late at night and only stayed a few hours. Probably married."

"Probably. Well, thanks for your help." I removed my foot from the doorway. He continued to peer out at us, nose barely above the chain.

We tried 1012. No one was home. But we had better luck at 1016. A tall, plump woman in her thirties with wire-rimmed glasses and long, straight brown hair answered. That was when we heard our little friend from across the hall close his door. The woman peered past us toward the noise.

158

"Nosy little asshole," she said. "If you're sellin' something or spreading the good word, I warn you I'm an atheist with all my cash tied up in stocks."

I said, "We're just looking for information. Did you know Melinda Reichart?"

She was chewing a large wad of bubble gum and snapped it a couple times before answering. "Not so's I'd care to admit it."

"Why not?"

"She was a snotty little bitch. I'm sorry she's dead, but she didn't add much to the quality of the human race, if you know what I mean."

"I guess I don't. What were her less than endearing qualities?"

She looked from me to Elaine, then back again and opened the door farther. "Why don't you two come on in. This might take a while."

We walked into the place, and I thought I must have stepped back two decades. Plastic, colored beads separated the kitchen from the living room. Black-light posters and a reproduction of a Grateful Dead album cover were the focal point above the couch. The room smelled of incense, and a string of smoke rose from a cone-shaped piece of the stuff sitting in an ashtray next to a marijuana cigarette. The woman caught my observation and smiled, apparently unconcerned. The couch was piled with books and computer printout paper. Elaine and I sat on two of the many large cushions covering the floor.

"Why do you want to know about Melinda?" The woman interrupted my inspection.

Elaine jumped in. "We're trying to locate my missing sister. I think she knew Melinda."

The woman studied Elaine for a moment. I wasn't sure whether she believed her, but she was apparently satisfied with the story. "Melinda said she was a model. I think she was probably a hooker. Too skinny to be a model."

I didn't think that was possible, but the point wasn't worth arguing.

She continued without my prompting her. "She used to have all sorts of men over there. All hours of the day and night. Now I really don't give a shit if she was getting laid by the Bears' entire defensive line, but she had this holier than thou attitude that really grated on me. Never acknowledging your presence unless she needed something. Like once her phone was out of order and she came over here, sweet as can be, and asked to borrow mine."

"Did you let her?" Elaine asked.

The young woman shrugged. "Why not? Just 'cuz she's a bitch doesn't mean I have to be one too."

"I don't suppose you happened to hear what the call was about?" I asked.

She smiled conspiratorially. "It's a small place. Hard *not* to hear."

"And?" I prodded.

"Probably one of her johns. Or tricks. Or whatever they call them. Must a' had a scheduling problem. She was saying something like 'No. You can't come over. He'll be here. I can't tell him not to come. I told you how he is.' Somethin' like that."

"When was that?"

"Couple weeks ago."

"Right before she was killed?"

"Around then."

"Did the police ever ask you about her?"

"A cop came by and I told him she had some boyfriends but couldn't be specific. The cop was kind of a jerk." She shrugged to herself, as if that were a given. "A lot like Melinda, in fact. Stuck up."

"Do you know what guy she was referring to when she made that phone call?"

160

She considered the question before answering. "There was some guy who came over that she used to fight with. Couldn't tell what they were saying. Just loud voices."

I showed her the picture of Melinda and Griffin. "Was that him?"

She studied it, then handed it back to me. "Might've been. That's not a very clear picture. I mean you can see her highness all right, but that guy . . . well, that could be him. I mean, he looks like one of them, but I don't know if he's the one she used to go rounds with." She shrugged. "Sorry."

"That's okay," I said. "You've been a big help."

Opening the door for us, she turned to Elaine. "You really looking for your sister?"

Elaine met her gaze. "No. But it is important."

"That's what I figured. Good luck," she said and we left.

We drove back to Elaine's place in silence. I was thinking about what Art had told me and what we had just learned about Griffin's girlfriend. This was getting to be a very uncomfortable situation. Diana Hauser could be more of a case than I had figured, and Griffin was keeping company with a woman who wound up dead in an alley. Maybe it was time to see if the police were interested in what I'd turned up. Maybe the police had turned up something I could use. Maybe it was time to give Griffin a call.

Elaine broke the silence. "You think Griffin killed her?"

"I don't know. But even if he didn't, I'll bet he's not too anxious to publicize the fact that he was keeping company with a future murder victim."

"What did Art tell you?"

I didn't answer her right away. Then I said, "I need to sort this out first."

Elaine nodded and turned to watch the scenery. "I have to pick up a few things at the grocery. What do you feel like for dinner?"

We felt like red meat so we selected a couple of good cuts of tenderloin that would go nicely with a bottle of Cote du Rhone Elaine had been saving for a special occasion.

She smiled and said, "Last night was special. I don't want to put you under pressure or anything, but I expect tonight to be even better."

I told her I'd try to live up to her expectations.

When we got to the apartment building, we parted temporarily. Elaine took the bottle of windshield-washer fluid down to her car in the heated garage and I brought the bag of groceries up to the apartment.

The phone was ringing as I put the key in the lock and, just like it could see what I was doing, stopped as I reached for it.

I put most of our purchases away, leaving the steaks out on the counter, and decided to give Frank Griffin a call. I found his home phone number in the file that the late detective Keller had compiled. It was six-thirty on a Saturday night. Maybe I'd interrupt his dinner.

A woman answered.

"Frank Griffin, please," I said.

"Who's calling?"

I told her and there was silence for almost a minute. Finally she came back. "I'm afraid Mr. Griffin is unable to come to the telephone. Can I take a message?"

"This is very important."

"I'll ask him to return your call as soon as he is able." God, the woman was as spontaneous as an answering machine. I gave her my number, confident Griffin wouldn't even have to bother throwing it away.

"Damn." I hung up the phone.

I opened a beer and carried it to the window that only yesterday I had discovered overlooked Wrigley Field. Three more months till the season starts, I reminded myself, then realized that in just over a month they'd be

162

starting spring training. I allowed myself a moment of nostalgia.

"This was in my car," Elaine announced as she entered the apartment. She carried a container roughly the size of a shoe box, bound by heavy twine and tied on top in a crude bow. I set the beer down and took the box from her.

Elaine's full name, last name misspelled, was printed in black marker on the top. The box was fairly light and as I shook it gently, something shifted inside.

"It's not ticking," I said.

"I don't think I like this," Elaine said, then rummaged through a kitchen drawer until she pulled out a pair of scissors.

I held my hand out and she slapped them into my palm. We stared at the box. I had set it on the dining room table. It wasn't moving and seemed to stare back at us, taunting and menacing.

"Maybe it's just my cosmetics order," Elaine suggested.

I cut the twine and removed it. Then we looked at each other and simultaneously held our breath. I counted to three and removed the lid. Elaine's reaction was instantaneous. She clapped her hand to her mouth and turned away.

"Oh, God," she gagged. "Get rid of it."

I slammed the lid down and held it there for several seconds, then removed it again slowly, wanting to confirm what I'd seen. I was right. Maybe I can't tell a gerbil from a guinea pig, but I know a rat when I see one, even when it's been partially eviscerated. The creature, in its day, had been a big one. This bloodied, disemboweled condition could have been the work of a cat. The carcass lay on a bedding of grass and straw and it reminded me of the sort of coffin a child would rig for a deceased pet, sending the animal on its way into eternity in comfort. The stench was overwhelming. I replaced the cover once more.

Elaine stood with her back to me. "When I turn around, I want that thing to be out of here, and no sign left that a gutted rat was on my dining room table. You got that?"

I briefly considered arguing for a fingerprint analysis, but Elaine read my mind. "I don't care if Preston Hauser's prints are all over the damned box. I'm counting to ten and it better be gone by the time I get there."

I was out of the door before she reached three and out of earshot when I dumped the creature and its cardboard coffin down the trash chute, with probably a couple digits to spare.

When I closed the apartment door behind me, Elaine was standing in the kitchen, arms folded across her chest like she was trying to get warm. "Shit," she said, "I hate those things." The phone rang and Elaine, still wrapped in that thought, answered.

"Hello," I heard Elaine say. A few moments of silence. "Hello. Hello." Elaine gave me a puzzled look. "Is anyone there?"

She shrugged and turned to hang up the receiver. I made the distance across the room in three steps and grabbed it from her hand before she replaced it on the hook.

"Listen, Diana," I said and heard a click.

I fumbled for my wallet where I'd stored Diana's phone numbers. I dialed her Chicago number first, not sure of what I was going to say if she answered, but as sure of the identity of the person behind the gift as I'd been sure of my photographer. There was no answer.

"Who are you calling?" Elaine asked. "What's going on?"

Without responding, I dialed the number in Wayne.

Grace answered. "I believe Diana is in the city tonight. Can I help you with anything?"

I hesitated, tempted to tell her about tonight's incident, but I wanted to cool off first. "Maybe. But it can wait."

164

"Perhaps after the funeral tomorrow," she suggested, and I agreed to talk to her then.

I hung up and turned to Elaine, who was waiting for an explanation. She deserved one, but I wanted to relax the mood a bit before we started talking about Diana Hauser.

"In a minute," I said, moving into the kitchen. "First, do you like your steak—?" I broke off in mid sentence, seeing Elaine's color pale about two shades. I congratulated myself on selecting the perfect entrée to follow an appetizer of rat entrails.

I put the steaks in the refrigerator and withdrew a bottle of Chardonnay. "If we get hungry, I'll open a can of chicken noodle soup."

18

ELAINE SIPPED HER wine while I finished the can of beer I'd opened.

Neither of us spoke for several minutes. Finally, Elaine asked the question that I'd been considering. "How does Diana know who I am and where I'm living?"

"The only thing I can figure is that she followed me to you. Then maybe she saw you in your car." I shrugged. "She may not know what apartment you're in. Otherwise, why not leave her gift by the door?"

Elaine nodded. "That's true." She took a healthy swig of wine and poured herself another glass. "That makes me feel a little better.

"You're pretty sure Diana did this. Does your conclusion have anything to do with your conversation with Art?"

I looked at her and once again realized that there was no lying to this woman, and she wouldn't tolerate evasive answers for very long either.

I cleared my throat. "Apparently Diana Hauser is not totally in tune with reality."

"No kidding. But you knew that already, didn't you?"

"I figured she was a little flaky, but it's beginning to look like she could be dangerous."

Elaine's eyes widened. "You think she killed Hauser?"

"I don't know." I drained the beer and crushed the can in my hand, a sure sign that I was considering a situation from all angles *and* that they don't make cans like they used to. "For someone who insists she didn't do it, she sure doesn't mind drawing attention to herself. Seems to me if I were under suspicion I'd be making a concerted effort to keep a low profile. It's just too obvious. Even for Diana, who isn't exactly known for her subtle ways."

"Okay, Quint. What did Art tell you?"

"The woman is jealous to the point of being psychotic." I told her about Art's fling with Diana and about her reaction to his dating another woman. "The lady doesn't handle rejection well."

Elaine eyed me. "Did you have an affair with Diana Hauser?"

I shook my head.

"Did you *almost* have an affair with Diana Hauser?"

"No," I said. "Evolution prevailed." I waved off her bewildered look. "Trust me. It never happened."

"But she came on to you."

"I guess you could call it that."

Elaine sank into the sofa and put her feet up on the coffee table. "I'm glad I never wasted all that psychic energy on men who rejected me."

"That's the point," I said. "If her reaction to Art's rejection is typical, then it doesn't follow that she would have killed Preston. I mean, she retaliated against Art's new friend. Not against Art. And, if Diana sent the rat-in-a-box, she was lashing out at you, not me."

"Maybe she didn't know whom Hauser was rejecting her in favor of."

A thought hit me. Whom or what. "Oh my God," I said aloud.

"What? Oh my God what?"

I recalled the news Hauser had received the morning of his death. With all the events that had occurred since then, it had slipped my mind. "Hauser had a picture of this prize Arabian in a frame on his desk. In fact, he had more kind words to say about the horse than he did about Diana."

Elaine shook her head. "That's weird." Then she added, "Don't tell me she iced the horse." She giggled as if she knew that was a silly notion.

"Someone might have. It was young and apparently healthy, and it died. Maybe it had some help."

Elaine considered that for a moment, then said, "Do they do horse autopsies?"

"Beats me," I said. "I don't even know what they do with horses after they die. Somehow that never really seemed important to me. I think I'll see what I can find out about Scheherazade's untimely death at Hauser's funeral tomorrow."

"Maybe they'll take care of them both at once," Elaine said.

"What do you mean?"

"Maybe they'll bury Preston on top of his horse." Elaine giggled.

"Christ," I said. "I knew Diana was a bit flaky. Now I'm not so sure about you."

Elaine giggled again.

I leaned back, feeling suddenly very tired. "If Diana did the horse in, it doesn't follow that she would kill Preston before he had ample time to suffer over his loss. What would be the point?"

"I don't know, Quint." Elaine paused, thinking. "It doesn't seem like Diana Hauser has predictable behavior patterns." She shook her head. "She sounds like a real fruitcake. Maybe she has voices in her head telling her to do these things."

"Yeah," I said. "The little voices that told her to lift silk lingerie may have escalated the war." I glanced at my watch. "It's late," I said. It really wasn't that late, but I was thinking there were better things to do with Elaine than sit on the couch and analyze Diana Hauser.

Elaine placed an argyle sock–clad foot on my thigh.

"What do you want to do now?" she asked, smiling.

I put my hand on her foot. "Well, like I said. It is late."

She nodded.

"You wanna work on the floor exercises we were practicing last night?"

We did. Only we skipped the part on the floor. Still, we were both tired, and when the telephone rang at one-thirty, we were sound asleep. Elaine fumbled for the receiver on her nightstand and in my sleep-blurred mind I prayed it wasn't Diana Hauser. I came to regret that prayer.

Elaine mumbled a few words and sat upright. "Pam. Calm down. I can't understand you. What are you saying?" She listened. "Are you sure?" A shorter pause. "We'll be right over. Call the police." She pulled the telephone cradle over onto the bed and pushed the button down. Without turning to me, she said, "Art's dead. He's been shot."

When we got to Art's apartment, Pam was in a state of shock, but she was a whole lot better off than Art. He lay sprawled on the gold shag carpet. A dark stain had blossomed beneath him. His eyes were open, staring into an eternity that held nothing but empty space.

Pam was huddled in the corner of Art's couch, hugging her knees to her chest and whimpering. Elaine tried to calm her, but Pam just shook her head and brushed off Elaine's gesture.

I crouched in front of her. "Pam?"

She looked at me and stopped shaking her head. "Oh, God." She buried her face in her hands, sobbing, and finally allowed Elaine to put an arm around her shoulders.

She hadn't been able to call the police like Elaine told her, so I did, and specifically asked that O'Henry be notified. Then I turned back to Pam, whose sobs were subsiding a bit. "Can you tell us what happened?"

She shook her head. "I don't know. I found him like that." Gulping down a sob, she took a deep breath and attempted to collect herself. "He . . . he was supposed to come to my place tonight, about nine. At ten-thirty I started calling him. I got real worried. I almost called you guys. Finally, I came over here." She moaned, burying her face between her knees and chest. "I found him like that," she finished, her words muffled. "Oh, God, why? What did he do?"

"Did you call us right away?" I asked, trying to narrow down the time of his death.

Her head bobbed up and down. "I think so."

I didn't want to push her too hard, but I wanted to question her before the police arrived. "Pam, did Art still have a lot of gambling debts?"

She jerked her head up and snapped, "I told you before, he wasn't gambling anymore."

"He told me that too. I just need to know if he might have owed someone enough money to make them want to settle the debt this way."

Pam wiped her eyes with the cuff of her sweater. "No. He was paying them off."

"You're sure?"

She nodded. "He still owed a lot, but he was paying."

"Where was he getting the money to pay off the kind of debts he had?"

"I don't know. I never asked. All I know is that he kept saying 'I can see the light at the end of the tunnel.' "

Good old Art always did have a way with words.

The police arrived within a few minutes and the usual procedures followed—questions, photos, and analyses. They told me O'Henry was out of town but would be back in the morning. Elaine took Pam back to her apartment. The sun was coming up when I finally put the key in the door to Elaine's place.

170

I set the alarm for ten and didn't exactly feel rested when it went off, but I wanted to be sure I didn't miss Hauser's funeral. I figured his murderer would be there, whoever that might be.

Diana Hauser looked stunning in black, but then that's what I expected. She wore a raw silk black dress accented by pearls partially visible under her silver-fox coat. A wide-brimmed black hat framed her face. The service was brief, and afterward, before the procession out to the cemetery, she spent a few minutes accepting condolences.

I approached her and she glanced from side to side as if seeking an escape route. Finding herself hemmed in, she turned to me, her smile appropriately strained as she held out her hand. "Thank you for coming, Mr. McCauley."

I took that hand and held it as I spoke. "You seem to be holding up all right."

As a response, she raised her shoulders in the merest shrug. "One does what one has to."

I nodded. "I understand you've found an effective solution to the rodent problem. They make very thoughtful gifts." Her smile froze and she tried to pull her hand from my grasp. I held on and leaned forward so I could speak into her ear. "One more move like that and that coat of yours isn't going to be fit to dust furniture with." Then I stepped back and released her hand. She didn't reply, but met my gaze with a cold, hard glare.

Having said what I'd come to say, I nodded and moved on.

At the burial, she sat with Frank Griffin and his pudgy wife, Theresa, on one side and Grace Hunnicutt on the other. I stared at Griffin and when he finally glanced my way, I smiled and nodded. He turned away quickly without acknowledging me.

I didn't have any trouble attracting Sergeant O'Henry's

171

attention. He stood with his hands shoved deep into his overcoat pockets and his shoulders hunched against the cold. He wasn't wearing a hat and his ears were turning red. He nodded to me, but I turned away.

There'd been a break in the frigid spell we'd been having and the temperature was in the mid thirties. It was still cold and I think everyone was in a hurry to get Preston in the ground. Preston's passing had rated news coverage and several photographers were busy snapping the grieving friends and relatives, especially the beautiful, young widow.

When the minister finally said his last words and the group broke up, I made my way over to Griffin. "If you'll allow me a minute of your time, Frank, I won't give you grief for not returning my phone calls."

"I'm afraid I can't talk to you now, McCauley," he said, taking his wife by the arm and leading her toward the row of cars. "Why don't you make an appointment with my secretary?"

"I don't have anything to say to your secretary."

"Well, I don't have anything to say to you," he replied and turned away from me.

"I'm sure you don't now," I said, "but I have some information you may find interesting. Some information I'm sure you'll want to comment on."

He hesitated and I knew I had him. "I'll only be a moment, Theresa," he said to his wife, who smiled and nodded.

Griffin and I stepped away from the group. "All right, McCauley. Tell me what you have to say and don't waste my time."

"The files," I said.

"What are you talking about?" he said and then laughed.

That was my first clue that I was getting warm. If he didn't know what I was talking about, he would have left me standing there talking to thin air.

"A woman named Melinda Reichart. To be more specific, a dead woman named Melinda Reichart. I think we'd better talk."

He glanced at his watch, glanced at his wife, who was doing her best not to appear out of place, standing by herself in the dwindling crowd, then turned back to me. "McCauley, I don't know what you're talking about, but I'm not about to have you questioning me about strange women in front of a distrusting wife." He glanced at his watch again. "It's two o'clock now. Meet me in my office at five-thirty." He regarded me for a moment, his breath steaming in the air. "I'm not a pleasant man to cross."

"You're not a pleasant man to share breathing space with," I said. "See you at five-thirty." I turned and spotted the white limousine parked along the curving cemetery road and walked toward it. Marshall, or whatever his name was, held the door for me and I slid into the back seat like I was used to the treatment.

Grace had removed her dark glasses and replaced them with bifocals. Her black hat with its veil lay on the seat next to her.

"How is your investigation coming, Quint?"

"I've made some headway," I said. "Can you tell me something?"

"I'll try."

"Did Preston's horse, Scheherazade, die of natural causes?"

She regarded me for a moment before answering. "As a matter of fact, she didn't. According to the autopsy, she had been given a lethal injection of tranquilizer. Why do you ask?"

"Is it common to give a horse an autopsy?"

"Yes. Especially when the horse is young, healthy, and heavily insured."

"Any idea who killed it?"

"No. The killing was senseless. In fact I was going to ask you to look into it. That horse represents a sizable investment." She stared out the window, in the direction of her brother's grave. "Preston was so fond of that animal. He was extremely upset when I told him of its death. It was as if someone knew what would hurt him the most." Then she murmured, "The unkindest cut of all."

"Tell me something else," I said. "Yesterday a female friend of mine received a box with a disemboweled rat in it. Do you think Diana's capable of something like that?"

"Oh, how awful." Grace dwelled on the image of the rat a moment before considering my question. "Diana?" she said. "Well, I'm not sure. I hate to think that anyone I know could be capable of such a thing."

"Does that include Diana?"

Grace was silent for a while. Finally she swallowed and said, "I don't know. Diana is capable of some very strange behavior, but disemboweled rats? How could anyone bring themselves to do that?"

"It's possible that a cat did the disemboweling part, but it would have needed help getting the thing into a box and tying it up. Cats don't have an opposable thumb."

Grace smiled briefly. "You know, it would be fairly easy to find a rat in that condition in the stable area."

"The house in Wayne?"

She nodded. "I'm not saying I think she did it, but she would have had the opportunity." She seemed to tangle with a thought for a moment. Then she said, "Do you think she might have killed Preston?"

I couldn't tell from her expression whether she was hoping for a yes or no answer.

"I don't know," I said. "She might have. But if she was hurting things she was jealous of, it doesn't make sense for her to kill Preston."

"Perhaps not," Grace mused.

"What was their relationship?"

She smiled and considered that before answering. "It wasn't very good. She wanted to have her cake and eat it too, as they say."

"What do you mean?"

"Oh, she wanted Preston's adulation, but she also wanted the attention of any other man who looked vaguely interesting. And, believe me, she wasn't very fussy. One man was not enough for dear Diana, and Preston wasn't the sort to put up with that for very long."

"From what I gathered, Diana's behavior was a grandstand play for attention."

Grace shook her head. "I don't think so. Oh, she might have been angered by the fact that Preston was becoming bored with her, but she wouldn't let that get in the way of her liaisons."

"Was Preston considering divorce?"

"He mentioned it in passing. Although I don't believe he ever took any action."

"Was Preston considering selling Hauser's?"

She was obviously taken aback by that question, but recovered quickly. "Where did you hear that?"

"Was he?" I prodded.

"No. Definitely not." Her response was terse and invited no further discussion.

"That's not what Diana told me."

Grace emitted an exasperated sigh and shook her head. "That woman has a gift for making mountains out of molehills."

"Then you're saying that Preston never considered selling the store?"

"That's not what I said." She paused, apparently to collect her thoughts. "Preston went through a phase where he thought he was tied down by the store, that he wanted to be free to pursue whatever interest grabbed his fancy.

Diana was quite concerned. She suspected that those other interests might not include her."

"Was she right?"

"Possibly. At any rate, it was just a whim of Preston's. It passed."

Grace studied me for a moment, then said, "Correct me if I'm wrong. You are looking at all the evidence you have and most of it points to Diana. But you are not totally convinced it was her. Is that correct?"

I nodded. "I guess so."

"What would it take to convince you?"

"A threatening letter addressed to the horse. Membership to the poison-of-the-month club. A signed confession." I shrugged. "Wouldn't take much."

"Well," Grace said, "as I told you before, if I can answer any questions or get you any information, please don't hesitate to call me. I'll do the same for you."

A few moments later I was watching the white limousine wind its way down the road toward the entrance to the cemetery and almost jumped out of my skin when a voice behind me said, "Can I get a lift from you?" I whirled around. It was O'Henry. Just what I needed.

"How did you get here?" I asked.

"My wife dropped me off. We just came from visiting her sister."

I studied the stocky man. "You really take a lot for granted, don't you?"

"Only when I think I'm right about someone."

"I'm parked over there." I gestured toward my Honda. What else could I say?

19

DRIVING OUT OF the cemetery, O'Henry asked, "Have you had lunch yet?"

I looked at him. "You buying?"

He grunted something that I interpreted as a yes, and I instinctively drove to the White Hart.

We both ordered sandwiches and Guinness. O'Henry took a long swig. "Great stuff," he said. Perhaps I'd misjudged the guy.

He devoured half his sandwich and sprinkled vinegar on his french fries. He tasted one, added a little more, tried another, and nodded in satisfaction. Finally he said to me, "Don't you think it's time we started pooling information?"

"Why would you want to give me any information?" Once a skeptic, always a skeptic.

"Two reasons." He had drained the glass of stout and waved the empty glass toward the bartender. "One. I figure that's the only way I'm going to get any information from you. And two. You check out all right, even though people around you are dropping like flies, and I think you play both ends against the middle when it comes to women. Also, to tell you the truth, I'm not convinced you don't have something going with that Hauser woman."

I didn't answer. I figured at this point anything I said might get me in trouble.

"You think she killed her old man?" he asked.

I waited until the bartender exchanged O'Henry's empty glass for a full one. Then I said, "Maybe. I think Diana

Hauser is probably very unstable, but I don't know if she's the best suspect."

"There's a lot of evidence that says she did it."

I wasn't going to fall for this. "Like what?"

O'Henry smiled.

"I'll show you mine if you show me yours?" I asked.

"Something like that."

"Okay. You first." I lit a cigarette and placed the pack on the table.

"Well." O'Henry leaned back into the booth, glass in hand. "She needed Hauser's money." He punctuated that with a long pause, watched for my reaction. He picked up my cigarettes and removed one from the pack while he waited. "You mind?" he asked. I shook my head. He lit the cigarette and absently pocketed my matches.

"What does she need his money for? From what I hear she comes from money."

"The family inheritance, and it is a big one, doesn't apply to her anymore."

"Oh, really?" This was getting interesting.

"Really. She didn't stand to inherit a penny from her father. Apparently she posed in the altogether for one of those men's magazines, and Daddy didn't like it one bit. Wrote her out of his will so fast she didn't know what hit her. Some people think that's why she married Preston."

"For the money or because she was looking for a replacement for her father?"

O'Henry shrugged. "I hadn't thought of it that last way. Guess there might be something to that."

"And if she married Preston as a father replacement, then the scenario that says she killed him for his money doesn't work."

"Maybe not, but I'd need some convincing there." He leaned forward. "Now. You tell me something I don't know."

I considered this. I could tell him about the rat, but that

was personal and bound to make him more suspicious of my relationship with Diana. If I told him that Diana wrote the letters, he'd have to charge her. If I didn't, I'd be real close to withholding evidence. Besides, I was starting to like the guy.

"She sent him the letters."

He raised his eyebrows.

"She says she did it for attention, the same way she lifted underwear out of his store. He was ignoring her. That was how she fought back."

"She stole stuff from her old man's own store? Her own store?" He added, more to himself than to me, "That's not even stealing."

I shrugged. "You had to be there."

"I guess," O'Henry said.

He drained his Guinness and waved for another. I finished my first and nodded my thanks as the bartender brought us two more.

"It's too neat, too obvious."

O'Henry nodded. "I used to feel that way. Then I remembered that sometimes it *is* obvious because the murderer doesn't, for whatever reason—stupidity, conceit—the murderer doesn't think he or she will get caught."

I didn't say anything. He had a point.

Finally O'Henry said, "Okay. If you don't think she's the best suspect, then who is?"

"What about Griffin?"

O'Henry raised his eyebrows and didn't respond for a minute. Finally he asked, "Why?"

This opened a whole new set of decisions for me. Should I tell him about the files and put everyone who gave Preston Hauser the creeps under suspicion? But if I wanted to enlist O'Henry's aid for this afternoon, since I wasn't at all sure I wanted to go see Griffin without any backup, then I'd have to tell him something. I decided to test out how little I could reveal and still be effective.

"Let me just tell you a few facts. Then you have to talk for a while. I'm way ahead of you in dispensing information. First, it looks like Griffin had a mistress named Melinda Reichart. Very beautiful and also, as it happens, very dead. Shot in what was officially listed as a robbery. I'd be real curious to see if the bullet that killed Melinda and the one that killed Art might have come from the same gun."

"I was going to get to Art. Looks like that wasn't a mob hit. He owed them money but he was paying them off. They usually don't blow away paying customers."

"Bad PR," I agreed, swishing the stiff foam around in the glass. "Any idea where Art was getting the money to make those paybacks?"

O'Henry shrugged. "Hauser and him were pretty buddy-buddy."

I shook my head. "Not anymore. That relationship was dissolved some time ago."

"What are you thinking?" O'Henry squinted at me and ran a hand over his mouth. "Blackmail?"

"It happens," I said. "If he knew about Griffin and Melinda. Even if he didn't know she was dead, if he knew Griffin was having an affair, Griffin might be willing to pay to have him keep his mouth shut."

"You think maybe Art got too greedy?"

I shrugged. "It's possible. I wouldn't put it past him. A debt like that can make you do some pretty desperate things." I considered again whether to tell O'Henry about my meeting with Griffin for later in the afternoon and decided it might be to my benefit to have some assistance. Griffin didn't have a lot of conscience to struggle with when eliminating members of the human race. "I mentioned the woman to Griffin at the service this afternoon. He's concerned enough to want to hear more."

"Oh yeah?" O'Henry was way ahead of me. "What if we

wire you. Where you meeting him anyway?"

"His office at five-thirty."

"Okay. I'll have ballistics check on those bullets and see if we can get a match. You going straight home, or whatever it is you call it?"

"Not right away. I have to stop and see someone first. I'll be there in an hour."

He glanced at his watch. "Two-thirty. I'll call you at four. If it looks like we might be onto something, we can have you wired up before you go to Griffin's." He finished the glass of stout and wiped his mouth with a paper napkin. "I'm still not convinced that the lovely Mrs. Hauser didn't engineer the whole thing."

"To tell you the truth, neither am I."

I dropped O'Henry off at the station and drove over to Pam's. I figured Elaine would still be there. She was. Pam was in pretty good shape, considering. They had been talking for a while when I arrived, and the strain of listening and comforting was beginning to show on Elaine. She looked relieved to see me.

"Have you talked to the police?" Pam asked. "Do they have any idea who killed Art? They won't tell me anything."

"Pam," I said, trying to sound convincing. "They don't know anything yet. It's really too soon."

I could tell by the look Elaine was giving me that she didn't believe me, but if Art had been killed because he was blackmailing someone, I wanted to be damned sure of my facts before I laid that one on Pam. Meanwhile, there was one other thing I wanted to check out.

"Can I use your phone, Pam?"

"Sure," she said like it couldn't possibly make any difference.

I wasn't sure where I'd find Grace Hunnicutt after her

brother's memorial service, but I had a hunch she'd be minding the store. I was right. I had to give my name before getting through to her. When she came on the line, she sounded like she was greeting an old friend.

"Quint," she said. "It's good to hear from you. What can I do for you?"

"Well, I hope you can clear up something for me."

"I'll try."

"How much did you know about Diana's financial situation before she married Preston?"

"Well." She paused as if giving my question careful consideration. "Her father owns a very successful law firm on the West Coast. I believe she is an only child so I suppose she stands to inherit a sizable fortune. Why do you ask?"

"Do you know anything about a falling out she had with her father?"

There was silence for several seconds, and when she spoke again it was with great reserve. "What are you talking about?"

"Well, I have heard that Diana was cut off from her father's inheritance. It doesn't matter why, the point being that she didn't stand to gain a penny from him."

"What?" was all she said.

"Grace." I was still not quite comfortable calling the wealthy matron by her given name. "Do you think that Preston would have married her if he had known that?"

"I . . . I." She seemed genuinely disconcerted. "I don't know. Forgive me, Quint, this news has really caught me off guard. I don't know what to say. Preston never said anything to me about Diana's, uh, misfortune. He usually did confide in me. I don't know what to say."

"That's all right," I said. "Sorry I dumped this one on you."

"Oh, please, Quint," she said quickly, "don't apologize. I admit I am a little shocked, but I want to be able to help you find whoever did this to Preston. If that means a few shocks in my life, well, I can certainly live with them."

"Okay, Grace, thanks."

"Can I do anything to help?"

"No, but please, don't tell Diana what I just told you."

"I doubt she'd be able to grasp it anyway. I'm not sure that very much of reality is seeping into Diana's life at this point. She is quite beside herself."

"Have you called a doctor?"

"Oh, yes. The family doctor knows what is going on."

"Well," I said, "keep me posted."

"I will," she said before hanging up.

Elaine watched as I replaced the phone in its cradle. "So it's beginning to look like the beautiful, wealthy widow might have had murder on her mind."

I sighed. "I don't know. Are you going to be here for a while?"

Pam had gone into her bedroom to lie down.

"A little longer. Why?"

"I've got to stop at the apartment. I thought if you weren't going back there for a while I'd take advantage of your parking space."

She smiled. "Be my guest."

I didn't tell her what O'Henry and I were cooking up. I figured I'd keep her informed on a need-to-know basis, and she didn't need to know that I had a date to keep with a prime suspect.

My Honda slid into Elaine's parking spot like it belonged there. I decided I could get used to that. There were a lot of things about Elaine that were very pleasant getting used to. I got out of the car with my coat draped over my arm.

Maybe I was thinking about the intensity of the few days we had had together. Maybe I was thinking about the list of suspects in Hauser's death. Or maybe I was reveling in the fact that not only did I have a parking space, it was in a garage—a heated garage no less. Whatever the reason, I wasn't one hundred percent attentive to the present, and I didn't have so much as an inkling that anything was out of order until I heard a footstep behind me. I started to turn, but before I could, a blinding explosion went off inside my head.

As I started to reel into the blackness, it occurred to me that this might very well be the end, and that there must be something seriously wrong with my priorities if my last conscious thought was to be that I was dying in a heated garage.

20

AT FIRST I thought I was dead, and eternity must be a sensory deprivation tank—the joke at the end of the universe. Then it occurred to me that I shouldn't be smelling grease and that whatever was jabbing me in my right shoulder didn't belong in a vacuum. Besides, I hurt too much to be dead.

A tequila hangover was the only thing I could think of that might inflict this kind of pain, but I didn't remember drinking myself into this state. In fact, I didn't remember anything. I rubbed the back of my head where the pain seemed to originate. There was hardness and swelling that hadn't come from the contents of a bottle, but maybe from the bottle itself. Was that it?

The garage, the noise behind me, the light and then the dark—sounds like you got clubbed, Quint. Now the hard part. Where was I? I was beginning to recognize the odors and the movement. New carpet and car smells combined with greasy rags. A car trunk. We were moving, and my guess was, from the consistent speed, that we were on the open road. Even with a garbled head, I knew I'd have been better off with the tequila hangover.

Whose car was this? Griffin's? My head was clearing a little, but not much. I wasn't tied up. Maybe I was supposed to have been hit harder. Maybe I was supposed to be dead. I felt for the object that was jabbing me. It might be something I could use for a weapon. Jumper cables. Great. If he held still long enough, I could wire him up and cause his batteries to implode. I took one of the clamps in my hand and hefted the metal. These were the heavy-duty kind. Maybe I could use them after all. Maybe he'd figure I was still out and wouldn't expect me to come out swinging when the trunk opened.

Right. Just like Gene Autry. On second thought, maybe I shouldn't do anything real stupid until my options were depleted. Maybe all this frantic scheming was a wasted effort. Maybe I wasn't ever going to get out of this trunk at all. He was going to sink both me and the car in some desolate scummy pool of water in the middle of northern Illinois. They'd find what was left of me months later, when the sun had dried up some of the water and the stench was so bad that even the frogs refused to sit on the car and croak. Maybe.

It was cold in the trunk; yet, despite the fact that I wasn't wearing a jacket, I was sweating. Curled up like a fetus with my legs cramping and my head throbbing, it occurred to me that being locked inside a small trunk was probably a lot like being buried alive. I swallowed a lump of nausea, forcing myself to think, but that was difficult and hardly mattered anyway. There was no way in hell I could plan what I was going to do next.

I had to believe that the trunk would eventually be opened. That was the only way I had a future. And wasn't that logical? Otherwise, why didn't he just finish me off in the garage? Why go to the trouble of hauling me off this way if he didn't want some information out of me? And, if it was Griffin, it didn't take a genius to figure out what he'd want to know before eliminating me for good.

The car slowed and after a sharp right turn, the ride became bumpy. Were we getting close to our destination? I felt around for something other than jumper cables, but the trunk was clean. I thought of my pigeon knife back on Elaine's coffee table. Elaine. Somehow the thought of never seeing her again bothered me more than anything, and let's face it, Quint. Someone didn't dump you in a trunk, transport you to God-knows-where only to chat for a few minutes, then drop you at State and Madison with a quarter for a phone call.

The car stopped. I estimated we had traveled about a mile on this road. A door slammed shut and I heard footsteps crunching in the snow. It had to be Griffin. I grabbed the jumper cables. You never know. A key slid into the lock and I gripped the cables harder. The key turned and the lid opened. My eyes adjusted quickly to the fading afternoon sun, and I released my grip on the cables. The man towering over me, holding what looked like a .357 Magnum, was not Griffin. He was too tall, too massive, and too black.

He grabbed me by the collar and jerked me out of the trunk. My feet hit the ground and I had to grab onto the edge of the bumper. I felt dizzy and slightly nauseous, while the big man continued to hold onto my collar. He towered over me by at least six inches and seemed to be waiting for instructions. I glanced quickly at my surroundings. We were on a small dirt road that ended in the middle of nowhere in the middle of a heavily wooded area. My head cleared a little as another car door opened and shut. This time I recognized the voice.

"Well, well, Quintus. Not quite the meeting you had planned, eh?" Griffin stepped into my line of vision. "Doesn't say much for the head of security to let himself fall into a mess like this, does it? Thinking about the little woman? Let your mind wander? Or are you simply too inept to realize how high the stakes are here?"

He studied me for a moment, sizing me up, nodding to himself. Then he turned to the big guy with the gun. "Take him away from the car, Deke." Deke wrapped a huge fist around my arm and dragged me toward the trees. When we had gone about twenty feet, Griffin said, "This will be fine."

The big man threw me down in the snow at the base of one of the trees. The snow had started to melt, and the cold wetness revived me a little. Meanwhile, Griffin watched, hands in the pockets of his camel's hair coat, smiling his approval. The day was fading fast and I could barely see the car from my position.

Griffin walked up to me, smugness smeared across his face. His associate stood next to me, gun pointed at my head. He appeared to be a man of few words and, I hoped, even fewer brains.

"You should know by now," Griffin began, "that I do not tolerate blackmail." He paused, maybe hoping that I would start pumping him with questions. The captive audience. I shifted in the snow and rubbed the back of my neck.

"Art Judson was a friend of yours, wasn't he?" I think we both knew he wasn't changing the subject.

I shrugged. "Yeah, sure."

He smiled. "He was also a loyal Hauser employee, wasn't he?"

"That's the way it seemed."

"Would it surprise you to know that he was also in my employ? That he was a man who could be purchased with limited funds?"

"Is that how you buy loyalty, Griffin? A bullet in the chest?" I glanced up at the man holding a gun to me. "You listening, Deke?" The big man shifted slightly.

Griffin laughed, apparently enjoying himself. "I reward loyalty generously. I punish betrayal quickly."

"Judson was blackmailing you," I said. Enough of this waltzing.

He nodded. "And Ray Keller." He paused, apparently allowing that to sink in. "No one, and I mean no one puts the screws to me."

188

I wasn't at all flattered by Griffin's sudden urge to confide in me. It didn't say much for my life expectancy, but I wanted to keep him talking. The longer he talked the longer I lived and the longer I had to come up with a way out of this mess. Besides, I figured I'd earned the right to know.

"Why did you kill Melinda Reichart?"

"Because she was an oversexed little tramp who didn't know her own place." He removed a pair of black leather gloves from his pocket and put them on, slowly easing each finger into place, all the while continuing his speech. "Imagine a woman like that even thinking we had a future together. Thinking I would cave in to her material desires by threatening to tell my wife about our affair." He paused and considered his last statement. "It wasn't the threat of blackmail. I couldn't care less if my wife knew about that affair. Theresa knows enough to look the other way." He smiled. "She's had a lot of practice. It's amazing how much people will tolerate in order to retain the status quo. You see, what Melinda did was to assume that she could intimidate me into leaving my wife. No one intimidates me."

"That's not the way I hear it," I said.

Griffin raised his eyebrows.

"In fact, I'll bet you killed her because she told you to get lost, and the only thing you handle worse than intimidation is rejection."

Griffin approached me and crouched down so we were eye level with each other. "You're wrong," he said, staring into my face like he was trying to read something there. Then he stood up, walked away, did an abrupt about-face, and said, "The end is near, Quint. Very near. I wouldn't make any groundless accusations if I were you. They might tend to hasten your demise. And you're still hopeful you're going to get out of this alive, aren't you?" He was smiling again. "One never knows."

It was getting colder, but I was still sweating. I didn't pay much attention to that, however. I was too busy trying to figure a way out and wondering if this was when I should request a cigarette and blindfold. But even though my brain was working, it wasn't producing.

"What about Keller?" I asked, still stalling. "My guess is you had Keller killed because he ID'd the girl in the photo after she wound up dead. He added up two and two and decided to supplement his income."

Griffin shook his head as he recalled the late detective. "Dim-witted gumshoe. I decided that if he was smart enough to put it all together after Melinda's death, then just about anyone could. But he was way out of his league. Judson too. He should have been content with the money I was paying him to spy on Hauser."

That made sense. Hauser knows about Griffin, so Griffin has him killed. Art needs another source of income. He pushes his luck with Griffin so Griffin has Art killed.

I recalled Art's gambling debt. The controversial shipping contract Griffin had arranged. "Were you fronting for the mob?"

Griffin smiled. "No. My connection with the mob is only peripheral. We occasionally exchange favors." He gestured toward the gunman. "Deke here is on loan from them."

I acknowledged Deke's credentials with a nod. "Is it safe to assume that you finished off Carl Bonkowsky?"

His smile was deceptively pleasant. "He was mostly gone. Not much worth saving."

"Enough about us," Griffin interrupted. "Let's talk about you. Who besides that little friend of yours has seen my file and the photograph?"

"Detective O'Henry," I lied. He knew about them, but I hadn't shown them to him.

"Not likely," Griffin said. He began pacing back and

forth in front of me, using the space like a stage as he explained my simplemindedness to me. "I had you followed after Hauser's service today. You entered the White Hart without the file." He stopped pacing long enough to pull a manila folder out of his coat. "This file." He smiled. "We removed it from your trunk while depositing you in our trunk."

In addition to enlightening me, Griffin was doing something else for me. He was giving me resolve. I had no idea how I was going to get out of this, but I was sure of one thing. There was no way I was going to die at the hands of this pompous asshole.

He pulled a photograph from the file. "This is what's causing all the trouble, isn't it?" He showed it to me so I would be sure to realize it was the real one, then he tore it into quarters and stuffed them into his pocket.

"I feel confident that once I eliminate you, my troubles are over. There is the matter of your little friend, but I'm having her taken care of, too." He smiled. "She's in for a big surprise when she returns home." I looked from the big man pointing the big gun at me to Griffin gauging my reaction with his hands deep in his pockets. "I have to tie up all the loose ends," Griffin continued. "You understand, I'm sure. I don't know what method my employee intends to use. I like to leave that sort of thing to his imagination. It never pays to stifle creativity, and he's very good. Elaine may take an unfortunate tumble down a flight of stairs, or perhaps she'll be the victim of a staged mugging with a fatal blow to the head." He paused and stared at me for several seconds. "Or maybe a murder-rape." He nodded to himself. "Yes, I bet that will be it."

I felt something inside me go numb and come alive again at the same time. Using the tree as a support, I pushed myself up. Griffin watched my slow progress, smiling. I felt dizzy at first and grabbed a small branch. It cracked and broke under my weight. I started to go down and Deke reached with his empty hand to grab me. I reacted without thinking. Before Deke got hold of my arm, I brought the small branch up with both hands, scraping it across his face. He uttered more a cry of surprise than pain but lurched back a step and I lunged for his legs, trying to topple him. He landed next to me. I spotted the gun he'd dropped a moment before he did. I gripped the barrel with my left hand and he jumped on top of me, reaching for my wrist. A gunshot froze the scene, and Deke's body went limp.

"I'd release that gun if I were you." Griffin didn't even sound perturbed. "Now Quint, that wasn't a very smart thing to do, was it? But then you weren't smart enough to keep your nose out of this affair. Why should I expect any other kind of behavior out of you? This is a minor inconvenience for me, but I have about all the information from you that I need." He cleared his throat. "Let me reiterate. Let go of the gun or you're going to die this very instant."

I wondered if Deke was big enough to make an effective shield. Then I realized that an essential part of my anatomy—my head—was a clear shot for Griffin. I let go of the gun and, with considerable effort, shoved Deke's body away so he lay between Griffin and me. I got to my feet slowly. No more than four feet separated me from Griffin. I hadn't figured him for the type to carry a gun. I was wrong.

I looked from Griffin to Deke, then back again. "You missed," I said.

Griffin shrugged like he had just missed the bus. "Perhaps that is simply my way of rewarding incompetence. My employees either function correctly or they are eliminated. Deke here reacted without considering the consequences. Not a good trait for a man in his profession." He cleared his throat and changed the subject. "Your usefulness has come to an end. It's time to start thinking that last great thought, but then you're probably wondering about your girlfriend's fate. No time for philosophical musings when the little woman is in jeopardy."

He began to laugh softly and shook his head like he knew a terrific joke only he was privy to. Then one of his chuckles was punctuated with a surprised cry and he lurched back a step. I glanced at the ground and saw Deke's big hand wrapped around Griffin's ankle. The shelter of the trees seemed miles away, but I didn't stop to think about that as I lit out for them. I heard two gunshots and assumed he'd finished off Deke.

It was almost dark now and I hoped that would give me an advantage. I heard another gunshot and the sound of something hitting a tree very near me. I found the car and the road and ran parallel to it through the woods and toward the highway we'd turned off from, using it to find my way out of here. If I made it to an open road, Griffin might hesitate to blow me away in front of witnesses.

I had figured about a mile and could probably manage that if I didn't break a leg tripping over a branch or a protruding root, but Griffin looked like he was in pretty good shape himself. I tried not to think about what was behind me or that at any moment I might be in his gunsight. I just ran and tried not to trip.

I heard the traffic before I came crashing out of the woods. With only a second's hesitation, I half ran, half slid down the hill toward the two-lane road. Near the bottom of the hill I heard another gunshot, lost my footing, and tumbled, head first, into a ditch.

Griffin was almost on top of me by the time I picked myself up. I glanced at him and at the big semi bearing down the road. I had no idea whether or not I could make it across the road in front of that truck, but I knew I couldn't afford to stay here. The truck horn blared as I ran into its path, and it didn't miss me by much. Griffin, as it turned out, wasn't so lucky.

The semi covered a lot of ground while braking to an emergency stop, and as I ran up to the cab, I intentionally avoided looking for anything it might have left in its wake. When I got there, the trucker, a young guy, had removed his cowboy hat and was running a hand through dark, curly hair, shaking his head. He stood next to the cab, not sure where to look and probably not sure he wanted to find what had to be there.

"Oh my God," he said. "I couldn't stop. You saw, didn't you?" He had a slight drawl.

"Don't worry," I said. "It wasn't your fault." I climbed into the cab to use his CB while he stepped off the road to throw up.

A row of cars were lining up in both directions as I got on the emergency channel. I raised the police in less than a minute and told them to contact O'Henry. "Tell him that an attempt is going to be made on Elaine Kluszewski's life. He has to keep her away from her apartment. You got that?" I released the button on the CB. The cop repeated the message. Then I depressed the button again. "And we've got a fatality here involving a truck and a jaywalker. Hold on." I stuck my head out the window of the cab and yelled into the group of gapers. "Can anyone tell me where we are?" I related the majority opinion to the cop and replaced the CB in the unit.

Then I leaned back and watched as a few snowflakes drifted onto the huge windshield. I was reminded of the way Elaine's hair had looked that night with the snowflakes lighting in it. Outside, the curious were finding out that getting a good look isn't all it's cracked up to be. Inside, I was just sitting there, trying not to imagine the worst.

21

The scene had taken on the dreamlike quality that sometimes accompanies a morbid accident. The truck's trailer blocked both lanes of the highway with the cab partially in a ditch. Traffic was lining up, but no one was honking his horn or showing any signs of impatience. A few people offered to help or asked if the police had been called, but most sat quietly in their cars, engines stilled, prepared to wait it out. It was a strange, expectant silence. No one knew exactly what had happened, only what it looked like.

At this point, there was nothing for me to do but wait along with everyone else. There was enough of Frank Griffin on the grill of the cab to confirm the fact that he wasn't going to crawl into the brush and escape when the crowd dispersed.

The truck driver waited beside me, looking pale in the eerie glow of the car headlights. Finally he said, "That was you who ran out in front of him, wasn't it?"

I nodded. "He was chasing me with a gun. If he hadn't gotten in your way, I'd probably be dead now."

He shook his head like he didn't completely understand but it didn't matter anyway. "God, what a mess," he said. "Who was he?"

A squad car pulled up before I could think of an appropriate response. The two officers took a quick look around, then walked over to me and the truck driver. One was very young. Could have been right out of the academy. The other was middle-aged and a little heavy. He looked pretty grim but not as shaken by the scene as the younger one.

"Which one of you did I talk to on the CB?" I asked. The voice had sounded older, but never assume anything.

"Me." I was right. "We relayed your message to Sergeant O'Henry. Now, are you going to tell me what's going on here?"

"That"—I gestured in the general direction of the truck—"was a guy named Frank Griffin. He had just killed another man and was in the process of trying to kill me."

"You mean there's another body around here?" The younger cop hadn't spoken yet and was watching his elder partner like he was Plato.

"Uh huh," I said and gestured toward the wooded area. "About a mile down that road." The cop looked at the road, then back at me. "He's just as dead as Griffin, but he looks a whole lot better," I added.

Another squad car joined the first, and one of the new cops at the scene began setting up flares. The other approached our group. "Which one of you is McCauley?"

"I am."

"O'Henry said he's on his way."

"Is that all?"

"Yeah."

"Christ," I muttered.

The middle-aged cop said to me, "You want to show me this other body now?"

Deke was right where I'd left him, along with the car, and he appeared to have two more bullet holes in his back. The cop began probing me for details. I guess I couldn't blame him, but I wanted to be out on the highway when O'Henry arrived.

He was looking in the trunk of the car. "So this is where they stashed you?"

"Listen," I said. "Do you think we could get back? I'm anxious to hear about my friend. I want to know if she's all right."

He shrugged. "Why didn't you say so? C'mon."

When we returned to the highway, O'Henry had arrived. I recognized his stocky, slouched figure before I saw his face.

I rushed up to him. "Is Elaine all right?"

He held his hands up in a familiar gesture of appeasement. "Calm down. I sent some of my best men over there. They'll call as soon as they know anything."

I ran an impatient hand through my hair. "O'Henry—"

"Relax, McCauley," he interrupted me. "She'll be okay. Trust me." Didn't this guy ever sound anything but calm and collected? "How are *you*?" he asked.

"I'm fine."

"Coulda fooled me," he said. "Don't tell me they coaxed you into the trunk with a Snickers bar."

"No," I said, "it was an inflatable Dolly Parton with a come hither look on her rubber face."

"That I'd believe," he said. "Why is it, McCauley, whenever I run into you, you're in the company of a corpse?"

"Two corpses," I corrected him.

"Even better. Who's the other one?"

"One of Griffin's little helpers," I told him. "In fact, he's the one who finished off Bonkowsky."

O'Henry nodded. "Were you right? Was it Griffin who killed Hauser?"

"Sure looks that way."

"He confessed?"

"It was more like he was reciting his resumé."

One of the uniformed cops yelled to O'Henry, "Call for you, Sarge." I followed him to his car and listened to his end of the conversation.

"Uh huh," he said. Then "Okay." Then, "That's good." That was when he winked at me and gave the thumbs-up sign.

After he hung up, he removed a new pack of gum from

197

his pocket and unwrapped it as he spoke. "Apparently there was someone waiting for Elaine in the garage. They found a guy lurking around. He was carrying. I doubt we'll ever get a confession out of him though, unless we can link him to Griffin." He pondered that for a moment.

"O'Henry," I said. "Go on."

"Well, before they found the guy, they did a check on Elaine's car and were able to ID her by her license. She was about four blocks away from the apartment."

"Oh, thank God," I said. "So she never got back to the building."

"I didn't say that." O'Henry was milking his audience again. "She did go into the garage, but she wasn't able to park. There was a Honda in her space." He raised his eyebrows. "Sound familiar?"

I gazed up at the stars and silently thanked whoever was in charge of doling out parking spaces and tickets to sold-out ball games that, for once, I had gotten a good one.

"So," he said, "now we know that the good guys are alive and the bad guys are dead. What were you starting to tell me about Griffin?"

"Well, according to Griffin, who, as I see it had no good reason to lie to me—I think he figured his admission would be that last thing these mortal ears would hear—Griffin killed"—I clicked them off with my fingers—"in this order: Melinda Reichart, Ray Keller, the detective, Art Judson, and Deke what's-his-name. Motives were rejection, blackmail, blackmail, and incompetence plus bad aim." Finished counting, I shoved my hands into my pockets. "We didn't get to Hauser. But if Hauser knew about Melinda, he'd definitely have made Griffin's hit list."

"You didn't *get* to Hauser?" I knew he wouldn't let that line slide.

"No. Griffin wasn't exactly letting me lead the conversation."

"Yeah, but couldn't you have brought his name up or something? It would've been so neat." He crammed the gum into his mouth.

I'd been thinking the same thing, but it irked me to hear O'Henry say it. "I'd love to hand this to you gift wrapped, but Christmas was a month ago. Do some work yourself if you're not satisfied. As far as I'm concerned, Griffin killed Hauser. But at this point I admit I could be convinced he was responsible for every unsolved murder since 1960. I really get offended when someone tries to kill me."

O'Henry studied me for a minute. "You finished?"

"Yeah," I said, noticing that it was cold and I was without a jacket.

"You better get your head looked at. I'll give you a lift."

It felt good to get into a car through the door instead of the trunk. The heat felt good too.

"I'm sorry," O'Henry said, and it was a moment before I realized that he had apologized. I looked at him as he continued. "You did real good. It's just that, well"—he shrugged—"it woulda been nice if . . ."

"I know." I didn't let him finish the sentence and I didn't want him to try again so I changed the subject. "I don't need to go to the hospital. Just drop me at the apartment."

"The only way you're getting to the apartment is if you walk from the hospital. Don't be stupid. You've probably got a concussion."

He was right.

The doctor at the emergency room was at least ten years younger than I and cocky as hell. He said I'd been sapped by a pro and offered his congratulations. Even though it was a simple concussion, he told me I might be experiencing its effects for a while and I should spend the night at the hospital under observation. I told him I didn't have any insurance. He said that a guy in my line of work without insurance really should have his head examined. I thanked him for the advice. He gave me two aspirin, and we parted.

I walked into the apartment and straight into Elaine's arms. I kissed her on the mouth and buried my face in her hair and was starting on her neck when she pulled back slightly and said, "Ah, Quint?"

I looked up and over her shoulder at the stranger sitting on the couch.

"Quint, this is Paula Wainwright," Elaine said, "Diana Hauser's stepmother."

22

THE WOMAN SMILED and extended her hand to me. She was attractive in a tanned and fragile way, with simply styled, shoulder-length brown hair. When we shook hands, mine engulfed hers and I was a little surprised to find her grip as firm as it was. One other thing I noted right off the bat—there was no trace of the smile in her eyes.

"I understand this is a bad time to be here." She straightened a pleat in her skirt and pulled at the cuff of her tweed jacket. "Should I come back tomorrow?" From the way she delivered that line, I had the feeling she didn't expect me to tell her I'd call her when I rolled out of bed in the morning.

"No," I said quickly. In spite of the strong desire I had to fall, fully clothed, into bed, there was no way this woman was going to leave before I knew why she was here in the first place. "Wait here. I'm going to change and I'll be right with you."

As I walked into the bedroom, my mind was so flooded with ideas and questions that my brain overloaded and I had to sit on the bed to get my equilibrium back.

"Are you okay?" Elaine was sitting next to me.

"Mostly." I put my arm around her shoulders and pulled her toward me. "Where did that woman come from?"

"She called about an hour and a half ago. Right after you phoned from the hospital. Are you going to be all right?"

"It's only a flesh wound."

"I'm serious. Give me a straight answer."

"I'm okay. Just got my brains scrambled a little. Back to the woman on the couch."

"Well, she said she wanted to meet you at your office." Elaine giggled a little. "I told her you'd probably be coming home first."

"Thanks." I kissed her hair and her cheek and pushed her back on the bed.

"Quint," she whispered, "we've got company."

I hauled her back up and shook my head. Thoughts were difficult to hold onto.

"She hasn't told me anything yet," Elaine said, then lowered her voice to a whisper. "I don't know how she does it, but she makes me feel like an intruder in my own home. I invite her in, offer her a drink, which she refuses, and she sits there flipping through magazines like she's in the waiting room at the dentist's office."

"Small talk failed you?" I whispered.

"Small talk! This woman wouldn't respond to a cattle prod. She sees I'm drinking out of a *U of I* coffee mug and she asks me if I went there. I said, 'No, I never went to college.' She smiles sympathetically and picks up a copy of *Chicago* magazine and I don't hear from her again."

She held my gaze for a moment before adding, "I'd appreciate it if you'd hurry up."

"I'll be out in a minute."

I changed into jeans and a flannel shirt and splashed cold water on my face. Then I took a good look at myself in the mirror and decided that right now I didn't look a whole lot better than Frank Griffin. I forced a smile, which turned into a wince. The blow to my head must have injured my smile muscles.

Grim-faced, I marched into the living room, where both women looked at me expectantly. I sat down in the over-stuffed chair and immediately found myself fighting the urge to fall asleep. I pushed forward and placed my elbows on my knees.

"What can I do for you, Mrs. Wainwright?"

"You may call me Paula," she said, and I hoped she didn't expect me to thank her for that. "Tell me. What happened today? Has Preston's murderer been identified?"

I glanced at Elaine and she shrugged as if to say "We had to talk about something."

Then I said, "We think we know who he is, er, was."

"He confessed?" She sounded relieved. Or was it disappointed?

"Well." I looked at Paula, then Elaine, then at the wall. "Not exactly." I cleared my throat. "I believe the police are proceeding on the assumption that he killed Preston. After all, he killed everyone else."

"Everyone else?"

I buried my face in my hands and just wanted to sleep. Maybe this could wait until tomorrow.

"Here, Quint."

I looked up at Elaine. She was holding a glass of ice water. I took it and resisted the impulse to splash it on my face. I drank some, and the fuzziness in my head dissipated a little. Then I explained what had happened that day. Elaine added the eyewitness commentary when I got to the part where Griffin sent his thug after her.

Paula nodded and listened. When I finished she turned to Elaine. "I'd like that drink now. Scotch. Neat."

Elaine rolled her eyes and went into the kitchen.

"So," she said, "this Frank Griffin died before confessing to Preston's murder."

I was getting real tired of people pointing that out. "Yes, that's true, but the police are working on it. They're trying to find a channeler who's tuned in to Frank Griffin. Confessions from beyond the grave hold up pretty well in court."

Paula studied me in a detached manner, like she was examining a lab rat. "I apologize if I seemed to accuse you of not doing your job. I suppose you were lucky to get out of that situation alive." Paula accepted the drink from Elaine and took a couple of sips.

She continued, "It's been more than five years since I've seen or spoken to Diana. I think the distancing has made me more objective. I also believe that my schooling has made me understand her better so I can almost sympathize with her, in spite of everything.

Before I could kick my brain into gear, Elaine jumped in. "What kind of schooling?"

She smiled at Elaine. "I'm a dissertation away from my PhD in psychology."

Elaine smiled back and murmured, "That's a long way away."

If looks could have killed, Elaine would have been reduced to a puddle of protoplasm on the couch cushion.

I finally remembered how to talk. "What is it that you understand about Diana now that you didn't before?"

"I can understand her animosity toward me better. She was extremely jealous of me. Probably still is. She perceives me as the woman who stole her lover—her father." Paula looked away for a moment, then said, "Not a lover in the physical sense, of course. But the crush little girls frequently have on their fathers, well, Diana never outgrew hers." She turned back to me. "And I suppose I can understand that. Diana's mother died when she was twelve. Robert's all she's had since then."

What she was telling me you didn't need an almost PhD to figure out. I had the feeling that Paula hadn't gone out of her way to make friends with her husband's daughter. "Has she always had it in for you?" I asked.

Paula nodded. "Oh, she was subtle about it. Diana is a very bright young woman. She did little things that made clear her disapproval, like showing up at our wedding wearing a black strapless dress on the arm of a man older than her father."

I smiled and nodded. "That sounds like Diana."

"It goes deeper than the father-figure complex. Diana is a dangerously disturbed young woman."

"Okay," I said, "I'll buy the fact that Diana has a lot of unresolved feelings about her father. That's pretty obvious. And maybe she does go to extraordinary lengths to be noticed, but don't you think you're pushing the limits of your schooling, not to mention the limits of slander, when you brand her a psycho?"

Paula smiled and I knew that I'd said exactly what she wanted me to say. I was getting real good at playing straight man. I decided to continue the role and retrieved a line she had dropped earlier in the conversation.

"You said you sympathized with her in spite of what she did. What was that?"

"She tried to kill me." That line was followed by a dramatic pause.

I lopped it off after about five seconds. "And how, pray tell, did she do that?"

Without looking away from me, Paula reached into her purse and withdrew three white envelopes that spoke louder than any completed dissertation could have.

"These started three months after Robert and I were married," she said.

I felt that familiar chill I was beginning to associate with Diana Hauser, and the fuzziness in my head vanished. I picked the letters up off the table where Paula had placed them. All three were addressed to her at a Pasadena address. No return. The type wasn't the same as the type on Preston's letters—more even and better defined. I removed the contents from the first. It was a news clipping announcing the wedding of Paula Dixon and Robert Wainwright. The bride's face had been disfigured with a red fountain pen and blotches of the same red erupted from her mouth and chest.

Elaine peered at it over my shoulder. "Oh, God," she said. "What did you do?"

Paula sighed. "Nothing at first. That was probably a mistake. But, you see, I suspected it was Diana and, well, she *is* Robert's daughter. I didn't want him to have to choose between the two of us."

I opened the second letter. "That came about three weeks after the first," she explained.

It was a black-and-white candid of Paula with a bulls-eye drawn on her chest.

"Hey," I said, "I had one taken of me in the same pose."

Paula nodded like she wasn't at all surprised.

The third one was an altogether new approach. It was another candid of Paula, only this time she wasn't alone. She was seated at an outdoor café with a man approximately her age. She was smiling and leaning toward the man to hear what he was saying.

"It's not as bad as it looks," Paula said. "He's just a friend."

I looked at her to see if her expression would reveal a clue as to the truth of that line. Her eyes neither gave her away nor invited me to question her statement. I let it pass.

"Let me guess," I said. "This is when you shared these letters with Robert."

Paula nodded. "He was very upset that I hadn't come to him sooner and admitted that it might be Diana, but he also didn't want it to go any further. He's very sensitive about keeping family problems within the family."

"Any more letters?"

"No."

"You said she tried to kill you."

Paula nodded. "It happened about a week after the last

letter." She explained about their infrequent luncheon dates and how Diana had, for the first time, taken the initiative. "I don't believe it was coincidence that the restaurant she chose was the one where I'd had my picture taken two weeks earlier."

Paula went on to describe these luncheons as stressful and how they usually produced a monstrous headache. "Not infrequently I would have to take something for those headaches with coffee and dessert."

"In front of Diana?"

"Usually," she nodded. "That most recent lunch was no different." She drank from her glass of scotch. "As I was driving home I began to feel nauseous. By the time I got home, I knew it was more than my lunch disagreeing with me. I was violently ill and having trouble breathing. I was lucky to make it home. Fortunately, Robert was there to take me to the hospital. The doctors examined my medication and found several aspirin mixed in with my prescription pills." She paused, then said, "I am extremely allergic to aspirin."

"Did Diana know that?" I asked.

"Oh, yes. She knew."

"The pills couldn't have looked the same? Didn't you notice a difference when you took them?"

She shrugged. "They were very similar in size and shape. I've been taking these pills for years. I don't examine each one before I put it in my mouth."

"Did Diana have the opportunity to put them in with your prescription pills?"

Paula nodded. "I was called away to the phone at the restaurant and I left my purse at the table."

"Was it a legitimate phone call?"

She shook her head. "There was no one on the line. I didn't think much of it at the time.

"I told Robert my suspicions and that was all he needed.

There are some things even Robert can't forgive his daughter for. He was outraged. But, again, he didn't want to drag the family name through the mud. He didn't want the exposure something like this would have caused. So he disowned Diana—wrote her out of his will, washed his hands of her. Everything."

"But he tells people he disowned her because she posed in the nude," I said.

Paula shrugged. "It's a convenient lie. She needed cash. That was a quick way to get it."

"Then Preston came along," I said, nodding to myself. "He likes them young and needy." I considered her story. "Preston died several days ago. Why wait this long to come forward with this information? Even if you didn't know about the letters, the means of death had to be disturbingly familiar."

"It was, but I didn't know about his death until yesterday."

"Yesterday? Don't you watch the news?"

"It's the dissertation. I don't have time for much besides that."

"Did Robert know?"

"Yes." She hesitated. "Again, it's the family name he's intent on protecting. Having a murderess for a daughter doesn't do much for the reputation of a law firm, even a highly reputable one."

"Whose clients are the rich and sensitive," I added.

"That can't be ignored."

"Robert sounds like a schmuck," I said before I could check myself. Then I waved my hands in front of me in denial of what I'd just said. "I'm sorry. It's the concussion."

"In ways he is a schmuck," Paula said, doing her best to imitate my pronunciation, "but in ways everyone is." She looked from me to Elaine, then back again.

I studied Paula and tried to read beneath the polish and

poise. The fact was that among the three of them—Robert, Diana, and Paula—Paula was the only one who had emerged a winner, even if she had almost died in the process. I wondered just how far she'd be willing to go just to make her marriage work. Maybe she figured getting her stomach pumped wasn't too high a price to pay to get Diana out of her life. Maybe she'd even enjoy the metaphor.

"Were you aware that your reaction to aspirin would be so severe?" I asked Paula.

"Oh, yes," she responded quickly, as if anticipating the question. "When I was in college, the infirmary accidently gave me aspirin. I was in a coma for two days. The doctors told me if Robert hadn't come home early that day after Diana and I had lunch, well, I probably would have died." She smiled and crossed her arms. "That would have been a rather high price for me to pay just to make a statement against my stepdaughter, don't you think?"

I nodded, conceding the point. "Do you think that Diana really intended to kill you? I mean, I went to school with a guy who was allergic to aspirin and he just wheezed a lot and used it as an excuse to get out of PE. What I mean is, most people with aspirin allergies don't slip into comas. Did Diana know how severe your reaction would be?"

She sighed. "I've considered that possibility. And I really don't know. However, whether she meant to or not, it almost killed me."

The way I figured it, intent would make all the difference in a courtroom. Even so, if someone came close to killing me, whether she meant to or not, and I'd had five or so years to stew about it, I probably wouldn't care whether it had been a prank gone bad or the real thing. Taking it one step further, anyone who engineers five doses of cyanide doesn't figure on the recipient recovering.

"You know, of course, about the similarities between your accident and Preston's death."

"Yes, I do."

"Will you tell this to the police?"

"No, I won't." She set her drink down and began to put the pictures back in her purse.

I hadn't expected her to say that. "Why the hell not?"

"Because I don't want to screw up my marriage. This is family business. That's the way Robert sees it. Still, what happened to me five years ago and what happened to Preston a few days ago is too similar to ignore altogether. Someone needed to know."

"So, you're telling me this just to get it off your chest, but I can't really do anything with it."

"You're a reasonably intelligent man. I imagine you know what has to be done." She stood up and looked at Elaine. "May I have my coat please." Elaine removed the fur from the closet and threw it on the couch.

I stood up. I wasn't consciously trying to intimidate her, but I couldn't help but notice that I was almost a foot taller. Whatever works.

"I have to be going," she said.

"Oh, I see. You've done what you came for. You spill your guts and clear your conscience. Doesn't take much does it? Sort of like making your confession to the local bartender instead of a priest. He's happy to absolve you and you don't have to worry about it going any higher."

"That's enough, Mr. McCauley." She put her coat on and slung her purse over her shoulder.

"No. It's not nearly enough. You want to be helpful and give me just enough rope to hang Diana, but only if your hands don't get dirty in the process. Tell me, there's a little more involved here than desire for justice. Maybe it'd be a very nice feeling for you to have Diana out of your life for once and for all. No more worrying about Robert going soft and welcoming her back into the fold."

She reacted to that statement with a slight narrowing of

the eyes and a fraction of a step backward.

I jumped on it. "Maybe he's gone soft already. He hears about Diana's husband and starts to rethink how he treated her all these years. Maybe he's been reading some of your psych books and understands he's got a lot to do with the way she is. Maybe he didn't realize he'd been snowed by a pro until he woke up under the drift."

Paula and I faced each other less than a foot apart, seriously invading each other's space. It was a glaredown, and possible that neither of us would back off. Without moving her gaze, she reached for something on the table. I thought maybe she needed a quick transfusion of scotch. I was wrong. She grabbed the glass of water I'd considered dowsing myself with earlier and did it for me.

Elaine jumped to her feet. I wasn't sure if she was trying to keep me from hitting Paula or if she was going to do it herself. Whatever the intention, she changed her mind and the three of us stood there for one incredibly long moment.

Paula spoke first, and it was as if the last few minutes had never happened. "Will I have any trouble getting a cab out front?"

"No," I said, wiping my face with a shirtsleeve.

She left and Elaine and I didn't say anything for a few minutes.

Then Elaine broke the silence. "Wow," she said.

"Ditto."

"This sure changes things, doesn't it?" she said. "If it's true, that is."

"If it's true," I echoed.

"What do you think?"

"I think..." I leaned back and closed my eyes without finishing the sentence. Much later I said, "Who was that woman?"

"You okay?" Elaine was leaning over me.

"Yeah," I lied.

"Let's go to bed," Elaine said as she tried to pull me out of the chair.

I didn't resist and I didn't assist. I just said, "Not tonight, Elaine. I have a concussion."

23

IF IRNA WAS peevish during our previous meetings, her disposition as I walked into her office this afternoon could only be described as deadly. She glared her greeting and I smiled and told her it was nice to see her.

"I have an appointment with Mrs. Hunnicutt."

"Yes, I know." Irna inserted a sheet of letterhead into her typewriter. "She said to tell you she'd be about ten minutes late. You can wait here if you like."

Spending ten minutes in a room with a woman who would rather eat live baby eels than say something civil to me was not my idea of nirvana. But I figured I could live with almost anything for ten minutes. The chair was hard and my head still hurt, but aside from that I was feeling pretty good about being alive. I'd slept until noon and Elaine had pancakes waiting for me when I finally got up—pancakes and a message from Grace Hunnicutt.

When Grace swept into the room, I was a little relieved to see that I wasn't the only one Irna glared at. The hostile secretary didn't seem to faze Grace in the least, and she cheerfully ushered me into her office.

"It's so good to see you alive and well, Quint," she said as she took her place behind her brother's desk.

"I do appreciate your coming here. Now, please tell me what happened yesterday. I got a brief account from the police, but I'm dying of curiosity. Can you imagine? Frank Griffin. Though I can't say it surprises me."

I described the events of the previous afternoon and

when I came to the part where Griffin hadn't told me he'd murdered Hauser because we hadn't gotten around to discussing it, I waited for Grace to make the comment I'd found that statement usually elicited.

Instead, she said, "Interesting." She fiddled with a pen on her desk, considering what I'd just said. Finally she said, "Then perhaps Griffin didn't kill Preston."

I appreciated that last statement more than Grace would ever know and debated whether I should tell her Paula Wainwright's story, finally opting not to talk to anyone about it until I'd had a chance to hear Diana's side of it.

"Well," I said, "that's a theory, but I'm afraid that the police are so pleased with themselves for wrapping this up that it's going to take a lot for them to reopen the case."

Grace nodded. "But Quint, if Frank Griffin did not kill my brother, his murderer is still at large. Justice has not been done."

"Yeah," I said, absently rubbing the back of my head and thinking that, while I liked this woman, I didn't want her directing my investigation, "but I'm going to let the cops work on this for a while anyway."

"Of course," Grace said, seeming to take the cue. "Let me change the subject for a moment here," she said. "I really did have a reason for you to come here this afternoon, and it wasn't just to hear the gossip. I'd like to offer you your old job back. Hauser's needs a competent head of security."

I hadn't expected that so I didn't know what to say. I thanked her and asked her if I could have some time to think about it.

"Of course. Take a few days. Whether you decide to come back or not, I'm going to have to replace that Fred Morison. The man's scared of his own shadow and dumb as a post to boot."

So that explained Irna's less than cordial greeting.

On my way out of the office I wished her a pleasant day and had to bite my tongue to keep from asking her how Fred was doing.

I took my time leaving the store, chatting with a few of the employees, and found out that there was some dissension in the ranks. People were concerned about the store's stability. Preston Hauser had been only a figurehead, but he'd been an impressive one. Several of the employees and managers I spoke to felt that his death wouldn't affect the bottom line as much as Griffin's. Griffin may have been a murderer and greedy bastard, but he knew how to manage a store. More than one person voiced their concern about Grace's ability to do the same.

I was a little surprised when someone told me that Pam was working. I found her in the women's jewelry department. She looked tired and pale, but she smiled when she saw me.

"What are you doing here?" I asked.

"I might ask the same thing of you," she said.

"Yeah, but I thought of it first."

She pushed an earring display aside so she could rest her elbows on the counter. "It helps to stay busy. I took yesterday off and spent most of the day remembering and crying. I don't think there are any tears left. But plenty of memories."

"It'll get easier to live with them."

"So they say."

"It will. You'll be walking along someday, maybe watching the penguins at Lincoln Park and something about one of them—maybe the way it looks like it was born to wear a tux—one of them will remind you of Art. You'll smile to yourself, and then you'll realize you just had a memory that didn't hurt. They'll get more frequent after that."

She smiled and touched my hand. "Thanks, Quint." After a few seconds she said, "What brings you to Hauser's?"

I made a show of looking around, to be sure we were out of everyone's earshot, then I leaned toward Pam. "This is top secret, you understand. For your ears only. I was just offered my old job back."

"That's great! You're taking it, aren't you?"

"I'm considering it."

"Mrs. Hunnicutt really needs you. There's rumors about a mass exodus of upper management. A lot of people felt it was pretty presumptuous of her to decide she could run the store without having any experience at it. That hasn't set well."

I shrugged. "She grew up in the business. I think she cared about it more than Preston did."

"Maybe, but there's a big difference between knowing about it and doing it."

"I suppose so."

"Anyway, that's great news about that job offer. Boy," she shook her head, "things sure didn't work out for Irna and Fred. First Hauser dies before he sells Griffin the store, then Griffin dies before Fred gets his stuff moved into your old office."

I thought my hearing had failed me. "Pam, did you just tell me that Hauser was selling Griffin the store?"

"I guess it was pretty hush hush. It slipped out one night when Art and I were talking. He made me swear not to tell anyone." She shrugged. "I guess it doesn't make any difference now."

"Did Grace know?"

"I doubt it. She's the last person they'd tell. In fact, she's probably the reason it was a secret. From what I hear, she threw a fit when Hauser was thinking about selling the store a year or so ago."

I shook my head. "No wonder I'm not head of security anymore. The shoplifters probably knew more than I did."

"Don't feel bad. You weren't one of Griffin's chosen

few. I'd consider myself lucky for that, if I were you."

I had a lot to think about already, yet I was headed someplace where I'd probably be hit with a whole lot more to think about—Diana Hauser's. All this on top of a concussion. I hadn't called ahead because I wanted to make sure she wasn't prepared for me.

Luckily, she was home. But she looked like she wouldn't be for long. She was wearing a shocking blue evening dress that set off her eyes like nobody's business.

"Why Quint, what a nice surprise." Without asking, she made me a scotch on the rocks and took up the cocktail she'd been drinking. She clicked my glass with hers. "Here's to Frank Griffin. He never did approve of me. I'm so glad I outlasted him."

I drank and studied her. As usual, I didn't know how to take this woman.

She cocked her head and furrowed her brows. "You're not still upset about that little incident with the rat, are you? I really didn't mean anything by it."

I shook my head. "Diana, why is it whenever I come near you I feel like I've fallen into the rabbit hole?"

She smiled and sat on the couch, patting the cushion next to hers. I took my place on the piano bench.

"I'm not here to discuss rats," I said and abruptly changed the subject. "You'll never guess who I had a visit from yesterday."

"Who?"

"Your wicked stepmother."

She shifted her eyes away from mine and paled slightly. "What did that bitch want? As if I didn't know."

"She had an interesting story to tell."

"I can't wait to hear." She crossed one leg over the other and began swinging it.

I told her what Paula had said and when I'd finished she

set her drink down and lit a cigarette. "That woman has a very active imagination."

"Are you saying her story is a lie?"

She nodded.

"All of it?"

"All of it," she said through a stream of smoke.

We stared at each other and when it became clear that she wasn't going to break down and confess, I cleared my throat and said, "You know what we're going to do?"

"What?"

"We're going to be honest with each other, and I mean totally honest. We're going to pretend I have a portable lie detector in my pocket that reads your voice. It's very sensitive and can pick up the smallest of lies, even the white ones. And do you know what I'm going to do if it goes off? I'm going to march down to the police station and tell Sergeant O'Henry—you know, the one you hit it off with so well—I'm going to tell O'Henry Paula's story." I winked at her. "I think it'll make his day, don't you?"

"Bastard" was all she said.

"I'm glad we understand each other. Now, back to Paula's story. Did I tell it right?"

She looked at me for one long, hard moment, then something in her relented. It wasn't anything visible—no sighs or lowered eyelids—but it was there.

She said, "I guess that's right. It was a while ago so I don't remember everything, but, yes, that version sounds about right." She took a drag off the cigarette and exhaled slowly. "You know, I didn't intend to kill her."

"No? Then what *was* your intention?"

She smiled, savoring a thought. "I wanted to see her lose her lunch all over those three-hundred-dollar shoes paid for with my family's money."

"If you had intended to kill her, what would you have done different? Used cyanide?"

Diana flicked an ash off her cigarette and smiled, recognizing the challenge of the game she thought we were playing. "No. Not cyanide. I can't stand the smell of almonds."

"Diana, I'm getting a reading awfully close to outright lie on my little machine here. It's only going to take one time. Then I'm out of here and on my way to tell my story to someone else."

She took another swallow of her drink, her eyes still fixed on mine.

"Let me repeat the question," I said. "Would you have used cyanide?"

"Maybe."

"Now we're getting somewhere." I clapped my hands.

Her jaw tightened as did the grip on her glass. "I didn't kill Preston."

I nodded. Not in agreement or denial of what she'd said. Just nodded. "Let's say, just to see how it fits, that you did kill Preston." I paused and she waited. "Is that how you would have done it? Cyanide in his vitamins?"

She appeared to give that some serious thought. Then she nodded slowly and said, "Yes. I think that's precisely how I would have done it. With one difference."

"What's that?"

"I'd have been there to watch." She looked down at her drink and spun the ice cubes around. Then, smiling, she looked back to me.

Before either of us could make a move, there was a knock at the door. Diana snuffed out her cigarette. "That'll be my date. He's a little early." She waved the smoke out of the air and leaned back into the couch, waiting for the second knock. When it finally came, she got up, took a moment to smooth her dress, and walked to the door as if five days was a respectable amount of time to spend in mourning.

Flinging the door open, she spoke to the newcomer but kept her eyes on me as she delivered the line. "I'm famished. I won't be kept waiting for a table tonight."

"You'll be lucky if you eat tonight," came the reply.

She turned to the figure in the doorway. "What are you talking—" Her smile froze in midsentence. "Sergeant O'Henry. Wh-what are you doing here?"

"I'm placing you under arrest for the murder of Preston Hauser." He motioned two uniformed men into the apartment.

As soon as Diana was capable of forming a sentence, she turned to me, blue eyes blazing, "You," she said, clenching her fists. "You'll have hell to pay."

For a second I believed her. Then I remembered that I had no reason to pay hell anything. But I didn't know exactly where I fit into this scene being played out before me, so I kept my mouth shut. One of the uniforms began to read Diana her rights. She told him to shut up after he read the line about the court-appointed attorney. Nonetheless, he continued, unperturbed. The whole time, she never took her eyes off me. By the time they escorted her out of the apartment and down the hallway toward the elevator, I felt like I'd had a hole drilled right through me by a blue icicle.

O'Henry and I were alone now, and his expression bore none of its usual bemusement. "Do you want to tell me what in the hell is going on? Every time I show up here, you're sitting on that damned piano bench. Is there some kind of duet going on here that I should know about?"

"Nope," I said. "Just fishing."

"What's your bait?"

I shrugged. "I was playing out a hunch. It fizzled. What about you? Have I earned the right to know why you've arrested Diana?"

O'Henry thought about that for a moment and then

decided. Whatever acid test he'd put me to earlier I'd passed. For some reason, which I was sure neither of us understood, he trusted me. "We followed up an interesting anonymous tip. It seems that about five years ago, Diana Hauser pulled a stunt on her father's new wife that was very similar to the one that killed Preston."

"Is that so," I said. "And what might that have been?"

O'Henry told me the story I expected to hear, only this time there didn't seem to be any doubt that Diana meant to make her father a widower.

"Have you been able to verify that?" I asked when he finished.

"Yep. We called Robert Wainwright, Diana's father. He hemmed and hawed and threatened us with one of the amendments, but finally he broke down and admitted that Diana had tried to kill his wife. Seems he wasn't anxious to let the press get hold of that story."

"So," I said, after allowing a few seconds so it would appear that I was giving this fact considerable thought. "You think that's enough to arrest her on?"

"Nope. Just enough to get a search warrant for the Wayne address. The four capsules of cyanide we found stashed in her bedroom were enough to arrest her on." He shrugged. "And for whatever it's worth, seems she also offed the horse. We found a hypo with traces of the drug that killed the animal." Shaking his head, he muttered, "Why the horse?" as if there were some benevolent spirit that answered questions muttered by law-enforcement officers.

We stepped out into the hallway. O'Henry closed the door behind him and tested the knob to be sure it locked. We walked the short distance from Diana's apartment to the elevator and watched the illuminated numbers rise. I don't know what O'Henry was thinking—probably how nice it was to have a suspect who wasn't flattened under

221

the wheels of a semi and who might even confess. As for me, I was feeling like I'd been born yesterday afternoon and had learned everything I knew about the art of detection and the female of the species from watching reruns of Andy Griffith.

The elevator announced its arrival with a binging sound as the doors slid open. A distinguished-looking man with silver hair and a cashmere coat stepped out and nodded a greeting. I held the "door open" button and we watched the man walk down the hall. He stopped in front of Diana's door and knocked. O'Henry and I exchanged glances and boarded the elevator.

24

I was TIRED, but sleep refused to come. Every time I felt myself drifting off, my subconscious tripped into overdrive and assaulted me with half-thoughts and perceptions. The authorities were convinced that Diana Hauser had killed Preston, but my mind wouldn't let it rest. My usual insomnia remedy—silently reciting lyrics to old Beach Boys songs—wasn't working. At three-twenty I gave up and, leaving Elaine's warmth, put on jeans and a flannel shirt and retreated into the living room.

Coffee may not be the best thing to drink in the middle of a sleepless night, but it won hands down over my other choices of milk, fruit juice, or beer. Besides, right now I needed to think. While the coffee brewed, I made myself a peanut butter and mayonnaise sandwich. Brain food.

I couldn't stop thinking about Diana Hauser and the way she'd said "I'd have been there to watch." I believed her. Yet, I couldn't completely convince myself that she hadn't killed Preston either. She was erratic and neurotic and her behavior difficult to predict. Still, killing Preston would have been her final insult to him and I was sure she wouldn't want to miss it.

"Is that coffee I smell?" Elaine padded out of the bedroom wearing her ratty blue robe and argyle socks. Her eyes were squinted against the sudden presence of light and her face was screwed up like she smelled something bad. She plopped herself on the couch, rubbing her eyes and yawning. "Is there enough for me?"

"Sure," I said, taking down another mug. "But why do you want to be awake?"

"It's not so much that I want to be awake. I want to be where the action is. So to speak."

"Ah, yes," I said, handing her the mug. I sat next to her on the couch, sipped the coffee, and nodded. "The action. Well, you found it. Do you want half of my sandwich?"

"No," she said, then added, "Well, maybe just a bite." I gave her half and she took it. After her first bite, she peeled it apart and peered inside. "What is this?" she asked. I told her. She nodded and pressed the two pieces of bread together again. "It's good."

We ate in silence and afterward shared an ashtray and my cigarettes.

Finally Elaine said, "It's not over, is it?"

"I don't think so."

"I thought it was. We were going to celebrate tonight."

It was several seconds before my brain began to process that last statement. "We were?"

"Uh huh. I got tickets to my favorite play. The Stonegate Theater is putting it on." She pushed an envelope across the coffee table with her stockinged foot. I opened it and looked inside.

"*Death of a Salesman*?"

I must have sounded a bit incredulous because she said, "What's wrong? Don't you like it?"

"I like it. It's a great play. Maybe even brilliant, but isn't it a little depressing to be your favorite?"

"Oh, I'm sorry," she said, color rising in her face and anger rising in her voice. "I meant to say it's my third favorite play. Right after *The Sound of Music* and *Oklahoma*."

"I'm sorry." I put my arm around her. "I'm not thinking about what I'm saying. I'm too preoccupied with trying to convince myself that what appears to have happened is what actually happened."

224

"So, speak to me. If you don't think Diana did it, then who did?" I didn't answer. "That is why we're up at this hour, isn't it?"

I sighed. "I'm not sure who did it."

"Okay," she said. "Let's start with this. Why don't you think Diana did it?"

"A lot of little things."

"Like?"

"For example," I said, "if I had just told you that your sister-in-law had been cut off from the family fortune, a sizable one by the way, what would your reaction be?"

"I'd want to know why," Elaine smiled. "I'd want the dirt."

I nodded. "That would be a pretty normal reaction, wouldn't you say?"

"Sure," Elaine said. "Everyone loves gossip, especially when it's about someone you know."

"When I told Grace that Diana had been cut off from her family's fortune, she didn't ask why. That bothers me. It tells me either she already knew, even though she said she didn't, or she figured it was none of her business. But it definitely *was* her business. Anything to do with the store and the Hauser name is her business."

"What else?" Elaine prompted.

"If you'd killed someone with cyanide capsules, would you leave the spares lying around your bedroom?"

"Maybe. If I didn't know how to get rid of them." She made a face, admitting that wasn't the greatest reason. "I'm just playing Devil's advocate here. I'm not very practiced at it."

"That's good. Keep it up. Things are coming back to me. Little things. But they don't add up."

"Maybe the concussion cleared your head," Elaine suggested.

"Like who tipped the police off about the incident with Paula Wainwright?"

225

Elaine shrugged. "Paula?" Then shook her head. "That doesn't make sense. Why didn't she just go to them first?"

"Unless she figured I wasn't going to do anything with the information. At the time she left, I sure didn't give her any indication that I would. And," I said, continuing on a slightly different track, "how did Paula know that Preston died? She never told us that."

"Probably ran across an item while doing research at the library," Elaine said dryly and added, "So, what you're saying is that you think someone other than Diana killed Preston, and you're thinking that whoever tipped off the cops might be that person." She paused. "Do you think someone else killed the horse too?"

"Maybe. Something about that bothers me too. It's one thing to drop poison into a bottle and sit back and wait for someone to take it. It's another thing to walk up to a living, breathing animal and jab a needle into it." My mind wandered back to the night in the alley. "Up close and personal." I heard the heat switch off and in the absence of the usual hum, it seemed like the room was breathing. "Maybe she could've poisoned Preston, but I don't think Mrs. Hauser has what it takes to touch whatever she's killing while she's killing it."

"Maybe she had someone do it for her."

I shrugged. "Maybe," I said, unconvinced.

She leaned toward me. "Maybe what you need to do is talk to Grace. Do you think that she might have killed her brother?"

"Who knows," I shrugged. "I used to think I was a pretty good judge of people, but lately I haven't exactly been batting a thousand in character analysis."

Elaine slid her arm around my neck and rested her chin on my shoulder. "But that's the beauty of the sport. To be considered really good, you only have to connect a third of the time."

We talked a little longer and eventually Elaine fell asleep, curled up on the couch with her head on my lap. I considered and rejected theories and ideas and eventually came up with a game plan. Then I must have dozed off because all of a sudden it was seven o'clock and time to get started.

25

I MADE A phone call to the Hauser estate and was told some information that didn't surprise me. I decided to share it with O'Henry. I dropped by the station and he listened to my suspicions with guarded interest. I finished at the police station at ten o'clock and left for Hauser's Department Store. O'Henry thought I was going on another fishing expedition and I guess he was right. But it wouldn't be the first time.

When I got there, Grace wasn't in her office, but Irna was. Perfect. She asked me if I had an appointment.

"No, but I think I'll wait."

I was a little surprised when Irna didn't argue, and I sat down. Neither of us spoke for a while. Irna was devoting all her attentions to a letter she was proofreading, and I was debating how to get Irna to like me.

"Weird isn't it?" I said. She looked at me, waiting. "I mean, isn't this just like last week. Me sitting here in your office waiting for a Hauser." I shook my head. "It's like I'm having one of those déjà vu experiences. You know, that I've-traveled-here-before feeling people used to get once or twice a day in the seventies."

No response.

"You know," I said, "yesterday when I was here, Grace offered me my old job back."

Irna's eyes narrowed and she pulled a stack of papers over in front of her and began shuffling through them. Finally she said, "No one's ever given poor Fred a chance.

That man's had the cards stacked against him."

"I might not take the job," I said.

She stopped shuffling and turned to me, wary but interested.

I cleared my throat. "I would, however, require one small favor in return. It's really very small."

She looked at me and held my gaze. "What is it you want, Mr. McCauley?"

I smiled at her and reached into my pocket, withdrawing an envelope.

Grace arrived a few minutes later, briefcase in hand, looking a little strained. But then, the way I figured it, she had every reason to look strained. She made a visible effort to smile and pull herself together when she saw me.

"Why Quint," she said, "I hope you have good news for me regarding what we discussed yesterday."

She glanced at Irna, who was once again shuffling papers, and doing a fine job of it too.

I followed Grace into her office and asked her how she liked running the store.

Her smile was grim. "I like it fine, but I'd like it a lot better if I weren't surrounded by a management team that is counting the seconds until I fall flat on my face." She sighed and sat down at the massive desk, looking very tired. "I believe management needs a major overhaul. I'm hoping you'll be able to help me out in that area."

I noticed as I took my seat across the desk from her that two of the pictures had been removed. There was no horse and no woman, just the one of Preston in his football jersey.

Nodding at the picture, I said, "Preston must have been quite the athlete in his time."

Grace laughed. "Hardly. That's what he liked to tell people. Preston's place on the football team was much the same as it was at this store—all image. He was a powerful figure, little else." She allowed herself a glance at the photograph. "I don't think he made it off the bench more than two or three times." She was silent a moment before turning to me. "Tell me, Quint, were you surprised at Diana's arrest?"

"Only a little." We talked for a few minutes about her sister-in-law and Grace's concerns that Diana's arrest would have a bad effect on the store and its sales.

"You never know," I said. "People might like to shop at a store with a reputation."

Grace smiled. "Let's hope so."

I took a deep breath and started down the uncomfortable path which I'd come here to walk. "One thing bothers me about the way this was all tied up."

"What's that?"

"The horse. I don't see how Diana could have killed the horse."

Grace shrugged and her smile stiffened a little. "Why not?"

"Well, I learned something interesting today," I said and continued before Grace could respond. "Diana was terrified of horses."

Grace folded her hands in front of her on the blotter in a gesture similar to her late brother's. "Where did you hear that?"

"From Scheherazade's trainer."

"How would he know such a thing?"

"Well," I said, "I don't know this guy, but he seems to know a lot about Diana."

"I'm sure he did, but I don't know how a trainer would be aware of something that I wasn't. I've spent a lot of time with Diana in Wayne. I think what the trainer interpreted as fear was something more like disinterest."

"She hated horses, didn't she?"

"As I said, I think she was simply not interested in them. Diana had, or rather has, a way of completely divorcing herself from people and things that are not, in some way, beneficial to her." Grace was losing a little of her charm now.

"According to Preston she hated them."

Grace removed a pen from her middle drawer and slammed the drawer shut. "What difference does it make?" she snapped. "How can Diana's disposition toward horses make any difference at all?"

"I'm getting to that." I held my hands up in a gesture that made me realize that O'Henry was rubbing off on me. "It's not unusual to hate something you fear, is it? So, for me anyway, it doesn't take a giant leap in credibility to go from the fact that Diana hated horses to the fact that she's scared to death of them. Just suppose for a minute that it is true. If *you* were terrified of horses, would you walk up to one and jab a needle in it? I mean, there's no telling how a horse is going to react. Also, if she was scared of horses, or even if she just didn't like them, she probably didn't know much about them. How would she know where to inject it?"

I waited.

Grace studied me for several moments. When she finally spoke, her voice was cold and brittle. "What are you saying, Quint. Are you saying that you don't think Diana killed Scheherazade?"

"I don't think it's very likely."

"Then perhaps her trainer friend did it for her."

"I don't think so," I said. "Scheherazade seemed to have the same effect on people that Diana did. You don't kill something like that."

There were several more moments of silence. Finally she said, "Perhaps not. Even so, I think it's quite clear that she did kill Preston."

I leaned forward in my chair. "But if she didn't kill the horse, who did? And why?"

"As I said before, Mr., ah Quint, that was a very valuable horse. Very heavily insured." She shook her head. "I don't know. It will have to be investigated."

"Maybe," I said, "maybe someone wanted to make it look like Diana killed the horse. Diana hurt things that made her jealous. That's no big secret. What if someone was trying to make her look a little crazy, or should I say a little crazier, and guilty as hell."

Grace's eyes narrowed slightly and she glanced at her watch. "Why did you come here today? Was there some reason?" She pressed two fingers against the bridge of her nose. "Of course," she said. "The job. Are you going to take it?"

"Just one second, Grace. There's another thing. You told me the deal to sell Hauser's was off."

"That's correct."

"Not according to what I hear. I hear that Hauser was about to sell the store to Frank Griffin."

"I'm shocked to learn that, Quint," Grace said, recovering a little. "I suppose it may be true, but I certainly wasn't aware of it."

"Grace," I said, "you make it your business to know everything."

As it turned out, Grace didn't have to respond to that statement because the scene was about to take a new twist. Irna walked in with the mail and set it on the desk midway between myself and Grace. "Thank you, Irna. Would you show Mr. McCauley his way out."

I stood up and was searching for a snappy retort when I spotted the envelope protruding from the stack. I could only see a few typed letters, but that was enough. Grace had spotted it too. Irna stood waiting for instructions. I removed the letter from the pile and dropped it on the top.

I don't know how long I stared at that small white envelope with the familiar typing and no return address, but it was plenty of time to notice the postmark. I looked at Grace. Her eyes hadn't left the letter. I picked it up. She finally looked at me, then looked away. She cleared her throat and patted her upper lip with an embroidered handkerchief.

"Thank you, Irna," she said, "I'll call if I need you."

Irna left reluctantly.

Using Grace's letter opener, I slit the envelope and reached inside for its contents. It occurred to me briefly that Willie Loman wasn't the only one here riding on a smile and a shoeshine as I placed the single ticket to *Death of a Salesman* on the desk. Showtime eight o'clock tonight.

We both stared at it. "Interesting," I said. "Grace, would you mail a death threat to a man you planned to kill?"

She studied me before answering. "If I were clever I would."

I shook my head. "You've used a lot of adjectives to describe Diana Hauser. Clever wasn't one of them."

I set the envelope down next to the ticket. "The letter is postmarked Thursday, the same day Preston died. The ticket is simple but effective. Diana liked to see the unsettled reaction Preston had to these little notes of hers. She might have wanted to kill him, but she would have waited to see how distracted this"—I held up the ticket—"made him."

Grace didn't say anything, and her expression didn't change. I continued. "If Diana didn't do it, then whoever planted the pills and the hypo probably did. There aren't too many people who had that opportunity, are there? Not a lot of people who spent a lot of time with Diana in Wayne. It would almost have to be a member of family, wouldn't it?"

Grace pressed the intercom button. "Irna. Have security

escort Mr. McCauley out of the store." She released the button and continued to stare at me. Finally she said, "You have a habit of stepping into dangerous waters."

"Why, Grace? I want to know why."

"I can destroy you."

I laughed, and not entirely at Grace's expense. I wasn't exactly proud of the fact that she'd have a lot of trouble figuring out how to destroy me. I didn't have much in the way of assets. "Grace, you've got to have something before you can worry about losing it."

Grace looked from me to her blotter, then back again. She still didn't speak.

"It was the store, wasn't it? That was the last straw."

She elevated her chin and said, "This store has been in my family for three generations. My grandfather established it. My father made it flourish. My brother was ruining it. Not only was he ruining the store, he was ruining the Hauser name with his flagrant womanizing." She paused and let that sink in. "I could not allow that to happen."

She sat straight up in her chair, looking more like a monarch than a murderer. There was something about the way she held my gaze—firm and proud—that gave me a glimpse of what it must have been like for her.

"It wasn't easy, was it, Grace? Seeing Preston ruin the store when you knew you could make it work. You must have felt cheated. You're older than he is. If you'd been born male, all this would have been yours. It wasn't fair." She didn't say anything and I continued. "You lived with it the same way people learn to live with arthritis. Then the stakes changed. Hauser was going to sell to Griffin and that was too much."

Grace looked at her folded hands briefly, then back to me. "Frank Griffin would have turned this fine old store into another one of the underworld's holdings. That was unthinkable."

234

"So you poisoned Hauser and nullified the deal."

She smiled politely and instead of responding to my statement, said, "Quint, there are some things that justify drastic measures. Don't you agree?" I didn't answer. "Quint. You're a bright, sensitive and, I think, sympathetic man. Anything that I might have done, I did for my family name, not out of greed or for personal gain. I'm not a Frank Griffin."

No, she wasn't a Frank Griffin, but the fact that she was an intelligent, attractive senior citizen and I happened to like her, didn't make her Joan of Arc either. Anyway, who was I to draw the line?

"Maybe not," I said. "But both of you are murderers." I began to pace in front of her desk. "I must have been a real frustration for you. There you were, dropping hints left and right about Diana and probably thinking, 'Damn, I keep beating this guy over the head but nothing sinks in.' So you called in the heavy artillery—Paula Wainwright, but I still wasn't convinced." I stopped pacing. "What can I say? I guess I'm a slow learner."

Grace clenched her jaw and took a deep breath. "You're going to have a difficult time proving my guilt. I will deny everything I've said to you."

"What about the letter?"

We stared at each other. I had nothing to lose so it was easy for me to keep my mouth shut. Finally Grace held up the ticket and the envelope it came in. "I think we should both forget we ever saw this." She opened the center drawer of the desk and removed a book of matches. "I think you'd better leave, Quint. We have no business with each other anymore."

She took a small caliber gun out of the drawer and pointed it at me. I was real tired of people pointing guns at me.

"That's okay," I said. "I think I've got enough on you

already. I probably won't need the ticket and the envelope as evidence. But there's one other thing you should think about." I could tell by the way she clenched her jaw that I had her attention and I thought from the way she was avoiding eye contact and fidgeting that she was almost there. Just one push more. "Denying this conversation won't do you any good. The whole thing has been recorded."

"You're lying," Grace said.

"I'm afraid not."

"Then show me," she said.

I walked around the desk and held my hand out to Grace. "Give me the gun." I really didn't expect her to do that, and she didn't disappoint me. "Think about it, Grace. You kill me and you've got a whole pack of new problems. The police know I'm here. You'd have a rather large body to dispose of. Is it worth it?"

Grace stood motionless, gun still pointed at me. I began to unzip the jacket, hoping I would have an opening before revealing the fact that I wasn't even wired with suspenders let alone a recording device.

"I know why you killed him, Grace, and I know why you tried to pin it on Diana. I believe you thought you were doing the right thing. But where does it stop?"

It seemed like a long time before anything happened. Finally Grace lowered her gaze and the weapon at the same time. She laid the gun on the desk and sank into the big leather chair. I picked up the gun. Grace massaged her forehead with her fingertips. She continued to rub as she spoke.

"I never meant for it to get out of hand. It was so simple. Eliminate Preston and I could get the store back in shape before the Hausers lost their connection with it." Her voice drifted off. "I guess that won't happen now."

I heard raised voices in the outer office a moment be-

236

fore Fred Morison erupted into the room with his gun drawn. Christ! He was just what the scene needed. Irna was right behind him.

"What's going on here?" Fred demanded. He saw the gun in my hand and took it from me. I didn't put up a fight. Morison might very well be the kind to shoot first and ask questions later.

He looked at Grace. "Are you all right, Mrs. Hunnicutt?"

"I'm fine, Fred," she said but didn't tell him to take the gun off me. "Irna, would you get my purse?"

All of a sudden she seemed to age before my eyes. The proud, tall woman shrank in front of me, dwarfed by the leather chair. She took the purse from Irna, removed a small pill box, opened it and took out two capsules. Then Grace leaned across the desk and poured herself a glass of water. There was something about this that was disturbingly familiar. I moved toward her, shouting, "Wait a minute."

Fred, convinced that I was going to throttle Grace, lunged between us, gun pointed at my chest. "*You* wait a minute."

I didn't have time for another move before Grace popped the pills into her mouth and knocked them back with two swallows of water, just as her brother had done. She set the glass down, dabbed her mouth with her handkerchief, and smiled at me.

26

It was Wednesday. Two days after Grace Hunnicutt had finished off the last of the Hauser bloodline—herself. I hadn't expected that. I don't know what I expected when I walked into her office intent on having her confess to her brother's murder, but it wasn't that.

I drank some more Guinness and watched Elaine befriend a small shaggy dog wearing a plaid doggy coat. The dog lay on the carpeted floor of the White Hart, several feet from its owner, who stood at the bar. Patrons were stepping over the little animal, acknowledging its presence with a smile and a backward glance. The dog, oblivious to the fact that he was in the way, accepted the greetings of patrons without any fuss and was now concentrating on Elaine's attentions. Smart dog.

I contemplated the glass of stout as I recalled my brief visit with Diana Hauser earlier in the day. She had stopped by Elaine's to thank me. Elaine had been out shopping. Diana appeared fully recovered from her stint in the slammer, and she was flirting, incredible behavior, I thought, from a woman who'd come damned close to spending so long in prison that flirting wouldn't have done her a whole lot of good by the time she got out. But then, maybe I was expecting too much from Diana Hauser to think she'd seize the opportunity to reevaluate her life. And—maybe I'd have been disappointed if she hadn't asked me to take her to lunch.

"Is this how I get thanked?" I said. "I buy lunch?"

She answered, smiling, "There are those who would think that enough."

I shrugged and removed a can of beer from the refrigerator. We watched each other as I opened the can and took a drink. She nodded, still smiling, and walked to the door, brushing my cheek with a kiss as she passed me. "If you change your mind," she said, "I'll be at the store."

She left before I could tell her that maybe she should try feeling just a little bit guilty about this whole affair, which had cost a lot of lives. If she hadn't sent the letters to Preston, he wouldn't have hired a detective to dig up dirt on Hauser employees. The detective wouldn't have been killed. Griffin's thugs, Art, Griffin—they'd all be alive. I had a hunch Grace saw the letters as a nice lead-in to a murder. Unfortunately, Diana was probably on the elevator by the time I put together what I wanted to say. Must have been the after-effects of that concussion still ...

A familiar voice dragged me back from my reverie. "Doesn't anyone pick up their dogs around here?"

I looked up and saw Elaine laughing at O'Henry, who had come very close to tripping over the little dog, who was watching the stocky man with mild interest. O'Henry sat across from me in the booth and Elaine slid in beside me. He ordered a Guinness and Elaine took a sip of mine.

"I was going to bring your ticket," he said to Elaine, "but I looked at the date and figured it wouldn't do you much good since it was for two nights ago."

"That's okay," Elaine said, sounding a lot more cheerful than the situation called for. "Quint is taking me to see it this weekend."

"We're going to *Death of a Salesman* and follow it up with dinner at a rowdy Greek restaurant. That way we can see how many mood swings we can pull off in one night," I said.

Elaine gave my leg a playful slap, and I grabbed and held onto her hand before she could pull it away. Then she smiled and winked at me and said to O'Henry, "By the way, I asked Quint why he wasn't wired when he went to see Grace. He told me to ask you." She stole another sip from my glass. "So, I'm asking."

O'Henry cast his eyes heavenward and shook his head. "They never remember the times you call it right." Then he nodded toward me and said to Elaine, "I thought he was full of it. Grace Hunnicutt? No way. Not a shred of hard evidence. Just a bunch of suppositions. I wasn't put on this planet to respond to this guy's whims."

Elaine started to give him some grief and I interrupted. "Yeah, but you did get that envelope postmarked for me."

"I was just humoring you."

I tipped my glass to him. He shrugged off the gesture and changed the subject. "Guess who's heir to the department store dynasty?"

"Don't tell me," I said.

"Diana Hauser," O'Henry said.

"I asked you not to tell me."

O'Henry ignored my remark. "I talked to the Hauser family attorney. It's official now, and guess who she wants to hire back as head of security?"

"Don't tell me," I said. "And this time I mean it."

"Her lawyer's going to call and make you an offer." He took a drink, reflecting on his statement. Then he added, "Bet she pays good."

O'Henry looked serious. Elaine looked like she was trying not to laugh.

"Can you imagine," I said, "trying to be head of security where the store's most notorious shoplifter is also its owner?" I shook my head at the concept.

"Well," O'Henry said, "I just thought I'd pass it along." He paused and drank a couple of swallows of the stout.

240

"What are you going to do, anyway? Get another security job?"

I shrugged. "Who knows."

We finished our drinks and left after Elaine said good-bye to the dog and we both said good-bye to O'Henry.

"You're awfully quiet," I said to Elaine as we walked to the car.

She didn't answer for a while, then she said, "I guess I'm just wondering what happens now."

"We go home," I said.

"You know what I mean." She squeezed my hand. "We're about to run into reality. We both have to earn a living."

"That's not always bad," I said, but I knew what she meant.

This past week we'd been thrown together in alien territory, with the rules of day-to-day existence temporarily suspended. Something good had happened between us, but here we were, as Elaine said, running into reality. Neither of us knew if that good thing that had happened would work as well in the real world.

We drove to the condo, each preoccupied by our own thoughts. As I turned off Addison, she said, "Are you going to look for your own place?"

"Not tonight." I sounded more flip than I had intended.

I pulled the car up to Elaine's door, leaned over, and kissed her. There must have been something final about that gesture, because when we finished she said, "You are coming up, aren't you?"

"Sure. Where else would I go?"

"Promise?"

"Promise."

She got out of the car, and I watched her walk into the building. Then I began my nightly ritual, wondering as I drove up and down car-lined side streets what beast one had to slay to appease the parking-space god.

342

NGAIO MARSH